KINGDOM'S REIGN

A BAD BOY BIKER ROMANCE

STEAMY BIKER ROMANCE SERIES

MONIQUE MOREAU

Cover Design by Cover Couture
www.bookcovercouture.com

MEET MONIQUE!

Join Monique's Newsletter (and receive goodies and release information)

https://bit.ly/SteamyReadNewsletter

Join Monique's FB reader's group, she'd love to hear from you

Possessive Alpha Reads

Follow her on TikTok

@moniquemoreauthor

Like her Facebook Page

https://bit.ly/MoniqueMoreaufb

Follow her on Instagram

https://bit.ly/MoniqueMoreauIG

Follow her on Book Bub

http://bit.ly/MoniqueBookBub

Learn all about Monique's books

MoniqueMoreau.com

PROLOGUE

KINGDOM

Kingdom's head throbbed like someone had slammed it with a ten-pound sledgehammer.

Cracking an eye open, light blazed through it like a cruise missile. He shut it with a moan. Nails drilling into his eyeball would have caused less pain. He tried to pull himself up. His eyes snapped open again and found his wrists manacled to a white paint-chipped wrought-iron headboard. Fury wracked his chest, and he jack-knifed up off the bed, only to be yanked backward by the cuffs linked to the iron bars.

Straining against the shackles, he growled, "What in the ever-loving-fuck?!"

Kingdom dropped down to the mattress with an exhausted thud. A metallic odor suffused his nostrils. He glared up and caught the blood stains covering his hands. Choking on his saliva, he cried out, "Chop."

Neon snapshots splashed through Kingdom's mind. Heaving up Chop's sprawled body, his wounded face glued to the floorboards. Touching Chop's temple, tainted with coagulated blood. Chop's favorite Glock lay in his palm. Kingdom's gaze sliced from Chop's temple to his hand. Temple, hand, temple, hand.

A single lucid fact coalesced in his mind: Chop had gone and killed himself.

He'd gone ballistic, swinging at the air and smashing objects across Chop's living room. Abruptly, he stood stock-still amid the chaos, snorting through his nostrils like a bull. The next moment, his head rammed into the wall. On and on he went, bashing his skull, leaving splintering holes in his wake.

It took three brothers to take Kingdom and knock him out. "No wonder my damn head is pounding."

They may not have shared the same blood, but they were more than blood brothers to one another. They'd grown up together, served together, and joined the Demon Squad together.

Fighting against the metal cuffs, he cut up his wrists, his fresh blood trailing over Chop's dried blood. "For fuck's sake, I was his keeper. I failed him," he bellowed out.

Out of breath, he paused and surveyed his surroundings through swollen, itchy eyes that begged to be scratched. Chained up in a bare room, the dents and scrapes in the plaster told him that he was in one of the Squad clubhouse's crash rooms.

Christ. I'm on fucking lockdown.

Pissed to hell and back, he thrashed against the handcuffs and the nylon ropes lashed around his ankles. "Cocksucking motherfuckers! You pussies hogtied me. When I get free, I will kill you, every damn one of you!"

The door banged open and Prez, the Demon Squad's president, entered with a warning rolling off his tongue. "Calm the hell down, or I'll get Cutter to come in and tranquilize you again."

Prez's words rattled through his head as if he'd used a bullhorn in his ear. "Again? What in the hell do you mean *again*?" Kingdom raged.

Prez reached the bed and viciously pressed his elbow down on Kingdom's bruised shoulder to get his attention.

Panting through his mouth, Kingdom gasped, "Son of a fuckin' bitch!"

"Get your shit together, Kingdom. Chopper put you down as executor of his will. We gotta bury him, and we ain't doin' it without you."

Prez took out a key and released Kingdom from his bonds. It was the mention of Chop's funeral that kept him from choking Prez out once his hands were free. Peering closely at the cuffs, he said, "Wait, these better not be the ones Cutter uses on his bitches."

Ignoring him, Prez stated, "You've got five minutes to settle your ass down before you join the rest of the brothers waitin' on you downstairs." Lancing Kingdom with a sardonic look, he continued, "I trust you won't wreck this place like you did Chopper's."

The motherfucker walked out, leaving the door swinging wide open. Kingdom wiped the cuts on the mattress, cursing under his breath, and swung his legs over the bed and onto the ground.

Soundlessly, Loki walked in and stood, glaring down at him, arms folded over his chest. "You'll get no forgiveness from me, you murdering bastard. I'll let you live a while longer to see you suffer, but when I'm ready, I will fucking decimate you."

Kingdom stared up at the ceiling. "Bring it, *my brother*." The last words were tinged with sarcasm. He got that Loki was suffering. He really did, but if Loki was looking to heap more hurt on Kingdom than he'd piled on his damn self, he'd be in for serious disappointment. "You at your worst ain't nothin'."

"Is that right? You crowned yourself the motherfucking King of Pain?" He snorted. "I don't think so. You have to suffer a helluva lot more to deserve that honor."

"Fuck you, Loki. I'm not trying to get off easy, but I missed the signs. Shit, man, we all came back fucked up from Iraq. You were his brother by blood and you didn't see one damn thing, so don't think taking your grief out on me is gonna get you off the hook."

Loki was on top of Kingdom in an instant, his hands wrapped tight around Kingdom's throat. He swallowed against the pressure on his windpipe but did nothing to break the other man's hold.

Loki's voice cracked. "I gave him to you for safekeepin', you good-for-nothing piece of shit. You might as well have pulled the trigger for him."

With two sets of fingers pressing on Kingdom's throat, Loki slammed him down repeatedly. The stripped mattress creaked with each impact. Nose-to-nose, Loki snarled, "Too fuckin' easy. It's too easy to kill you now. I'm your fuckin' shadow till I decide to off you. Till then, I will make every second you breathe a living nightmare."

"Stand down, Loki," came an uncompromising voice. Loki released his death grip on Kingdom. "I won't stand for a brother threatening another brother," Prez pronounced. "If you kill him, then be ready to die. Feel me?"

Loki's face went hard with rage, stretching the skin of his cheek and tugging at the ragged edges of his scar. Voice tight, he seethed, "I get you."

"Good. Now get the fuck outta here."

Kingdom covered his eyes with his forearm as Loki's biker boots stomped down the stairs. He understood Loki's point. Chop was thirteen, Kingdom fourteen when they struck up a friendship. Chop was the youngest in a family headed by a son-of-a-bitch named Crimpton Scott, a serial-killer name if he'd ever heard one. He sure as hell acted like a psychopath. Chop's mom was long gone before they'd met because of that son of a bitch. Before leaving for his first tour, Loki had made him pledge to take his place and protect Chop. He sure as hell had fucked that up.

Raising his arm, Kingdom said, "Thanks. I don't blame him for hating me, but it was gettin' a little too real there for a second."

"Get over yourself," Prez grumbled. "Brothers from the neighboring chapters are downstairs waitin' on you to drink themselves half to death. We gotta represent." Walking toward the door, he halted. Holding the doorknob, he counseled, "Watch your back because Loki's gonna be mad-doggin' you for as long as it takes to get over Chopper's death."

After leaving him alone, Prez's message hung heavy in the air as the door shuddered in its frame. Kingdom let out a strangled cry.

With Chop gone, I'm done.

1

KINGDOM

SIX MONTHS LATER

Kingdom sauntered through the door of Angel's Tattoos on the north side of Poughkeepsie with his brothers, Cutter and Tank, following behind him.

Angel was the best tat man this side of New York State. Kingdom ambled over to the counter as his brothers took their seats along the line of chairs backed against the far wall. A wall was coated with layers of photos and designs of Angel's artistry. Dark demons took residence beside brilliant angels while butterflies lived side by side with serpents. He liked the place. Whatever he wanted done, Angel did it, and he did it right. No mess-ups. No repeats. The man had mad skills.

Approaching the new woman behind the counter, Kingdom stared at a bent head. Waves of mahogany hair cascaded down and hid her face. A white tank top stretched over full tits and slanted down to a slim waist. Leaning over slightly, he caught a hint of nice wide hips. So far, so good. In his past life, he would've definitely kicked it to her.

"Hey," his voice came out to alert her to his presence. He cleared his throat, suddenly full of grit.

Emerging from layers of velvety hair were cobalt eyes. Those stunning baby blues were set against fair skin and partnered with generous lips naturally shaped in a slight pout.

Kingdom's breath stalled. *Fuck. Damn.*

Her lips parted a bit, and she stared at him intently.

He rasped out, "When's Angel free?"

A moment of silence hovered between them. She broke it with a brief shake of her head. After flicking through the appointment book, she looked up, her lips curved upward into a perfect bow.

He sucked in a breath. Fuck, he'd thought she had a tight, hot little body, but damn—her *smile.* Coming straight from Chop's gravesite, where he'd lobbed a volley of curses at the gravestone as he did most days, he was caught off guard by the gorgeous creature in front of him.

"You're lucky," a voice broke through his thoughts. "Angel usually has a full day, but there's an opening in approximately half an hour. Does that work for you?"

"Yeah," he responded gruffly.

"What are you looking to ink?"

"What does it matter?" he shot back. The woman flinched. A twinge of guilt pricked him, but he shrugged it off. Hell, he couldn't bother to add more to his already heavy-as-fuck load.

"I'm simply asking to get an idea of how long it will take him," she replied. "I give prospective customers an estimate of how much it will cost and how many sessions Angel will need."

She bounced back fast; he'd give her that. And she was

talking all classy. Prim and proper. He didn't have many opportunities to be around prim and proper. The easy sensuality of her tone eased the tautness in his neck and shoulders. Even his cock twitched for the first time since his brothers had scraped him off the floor after he had found Chop. He had hoped his crippled libido was a permanent condition. A righteous punishment handed down by a vengeful god.

Her bright cerulean eyes framed by dark lashes scrutinized the tattoo sleeves on his arms. His biceps instinctually flexed under her inspection. Consciously, he released the tension in his muscles, but it was too late—lust had surged into his bloodstream like he'd been hooked up to an IV of Spanish fly.

"You seem to have enough experience with tattoos, but I do usually confer with Angel about what a customer would like done before he meets with them. Would you mind giving me an idea of what you're looking for?"

"The tat is for my brother. Name was Chopper." He coughed into his fist. "It's the anniversary of his death." Where the fuck did that come from? Since when did he share his private business with perfect strangers? Never, that's when. Must be her unusual eyes bewitching him. Ignoring the unease pinging in his chest, Kingdom pulled up a photo of a Harley Chopper on his phone. He held it up for the woman to see. "I want Angel to ink a Chopper for my brother."

As she studied the photos, her forehead furrowed. "Oh...I see. His nickname was Chopper because he rode one."

"No, Chop got his name when he was a Night Stalker. It's old school, but Chop liked to keep it real."

"When he was a what?"

Christ. Kingdom reached deep inside for patience. "Chop was in the 160th Special Ops Aviation Regiment." A tic flickered on his jawline. He didn't like outing himself to a civilian.

He sighed at her blank look and, speaking slowly as if to a child, he clarified, "In the U.S. Army, Night Stalkers fly helicopters. Helos." He elaborated further, "Choppers."

Her eyes lit up with curiosity. Finally, she understood. "What kind of helicopter did he drive?"

"Fly," he corrected her. "You don't drive birds. He flew everything, but his favorites were Blackhawks."

A phone was thrust in his face.

"What about a tat specifically of a Blackhawk?" she asked.

Huh. For the first time since Chop's death, Kingdom drew in a complete breath, a near miracle considering his chest was always tightly cinched by an iron band of shame. But the instant Miss Sex and Class showed him a photograph of Chop's beloved Blackhawk, Kingdom's lungs expanded fully with air, along with something more. More of what, he couldn't begin to imagine, but it loosened the noose around his neck by a notch, like the buckle of a belt.

"You can have his name tatted on one blade," she went on, "his birth date on another, a RIP date on the third one, and..." Her forehead creased as she concentrated. "The date he became a member of your biker gang on the fourth blade."

His lips quirked to one side. "You mean patched."

Sex and Class peeked up from her phone with her cute frown. "Patched?"

"Yeah, patched. Bikers start out as trainees. We call them prospects, and after they prove themselves, they graduate to become full members of the club, also known as brothers. Becoming a member of our MC is called getting patched in. The brother gets a patch on their cut." He pointed to his own patch. "The Demon Squad MC." He explained the acronym, "MC means Motorcycle Club. For the record, we're not a gang."

She gave him a slightly embarrassed one-shoulder shrug. "Oh. Thanks for the explanation."

Pleased with her suggestion, he nodded his approval and indulged himself with a thorough perusal. She was worth looking at, for sure. Some men liked skinny bitches; some men liked thick bitches. Him, he didn't discriminate, but he was willing to admit that she carried the perfect balance. Turns out he had a preference after all. Her. On top of her appearance, she was smart too.

Worst yet, he sensed that he hadn't scratched the surface. He'd wager his bike that a woman like her was more dangerous than the sum of her parts. Damn it all to hell, he was hard now. Apparently the extra oxygen he had breathed in had shot straight to his cock.

To distract himself, he resumed their conversation. "I see why you're up front. You have a knack for tats." He shouldn't have, but he asked anyway, "What's your name, girl?"

"My name is Sage," she huffed. "But FYI, I haven't been a girl for quite some time."

Kingdom grinned. Her gaze jumped to the dimple at the side of his lips. He'd never liked it, but he had to admit it was useful with the women.

"I stand corrected." He let his eyes wander all over her in an unhurried fashion. "You're all woman."

Heat tinged her cheekbones, but she gave him a noncommittal shrug. He spotted the flare of interest in her eyes. It caught fire and smoldered in his belly. Kingdom braced the counter with one hand and leaned toward her ever so slightly. He was pleased when her body gravitated toward him like an animal seeking refuge with one of its own kind.

Evading his blatant come-on, Sage said conversationally, "Most people don't ask for advice. It's a shame to waste Angel's talent with boring tattoos like butterflies or the Grim Reaper."

He pulled away and countered in mock offense, "GR is not boring."

Again, he noticed that when he moved away from her, she instinctively inclined toward him before she briskly hauled herself upright.

"You may have a point," she concurred. "A woman came in the other day with a drawing she made for a tattoo of butterflies in flight. The butterfly at the base of her spine was in a pencil outline. Each subsequent butterfly circling up her spine became more detailed and colored. The last one, just below her neck, burst out in Technicolor. I thought it was a beautiful representation her personal journey of transformation. Her manner of interpreting the idea was touching." Sage scrunched her nose. "I doubt the average woman wants a caterpillar and chrysalis on her back for her entire life."

Kingdom chased her expressions and gestures as she relayed her story. He had stopped listening to specific words, instead tuning into the vibrant thrumming energy between them. A fierce, unexplainable sensation lashed against the sides of his ribs. His fingers snagged the edges of his leather vest and gripped them hard.

There was an affinity between them, no doubt, but he had no template for instant connections. Fascination lured him in, not with cut-offs revealing butt cheeks like the club women, but with her odd mix of softness and intensity. She had an air of innocence mixed with a passion he'd forgotten existed. In his world, innocence died a swift death.

"What about skulls?" he suggested just to keep her luscious lips moving and the smart words flying from her mouth.

Sage's pursed her lips in distaste. "Not a big fan. I tend to like pretty things."

"You don't say. That's 'cause you're a pretty thing." He angled his head, his gaze lingering on her.

She fidgeted under the weight of his perusal. Quickly, her head dipped down at his compliment, embarrassment splashing pink across her cheeks. Other than her blush, she refused to acknowledge his flirtation. Twice now.

Bitches always, and he meant *always*, responded to him. Hell, he didn't put effort into baggin' women, especially civilians. Most times, hangers-on were the worst. They didn't know how to play the game. Got clingy.

He couldn't put words to why this woman affected him. Surprisingly, he didn't mind so much, but it was beneath the Vice President of the Demon Squad to show undue interest in any female, much less one separate from his world.

Brusquely, Kingdom shoved off the counter as Angel turned the corner of the hallway and entered the front of the store. By the look on his face, he was none too pleased to hear Kingdom's last words or see Sage's blush. Kingdom repressed a laugh.

Angel bristled, a growl emanating from the back of his throat.

"Kingdom," he called out curtly.

Kingdom turned fully at Angel's tone, and they locked eyes. Few men dared hold his stare for long. He and Angel were on friendly terms, so the woman must have meant something to him. His heart rate picked up as it occurred to him that she might belong to Angel. He didn't like that thought. Not one bit. And worst, he chafed against the idea that he cared either way.

Kingdom queried in a casual tone, "Got a problem?"

Angel's face revealed nothing, but he stood down. Nothing good came out of antagonizing a member of the Demon Squad. "Nope," Angel replied. He gave Sage a hard look, then held up his hands in a gesture of surrender. "What can I do for you, Kingdom?"

Kingdom stared into Angel's eyes for a half minute more to solidify his dominance. He inclined his head toward Sage and clarified, "I'm talking to your girl here."

Sage interrupted gingerly, "Angel, I can run through with you what he'd like done."

Kingdom cast her quelling look over his shoulder. "I'll handle it."

Angel stiffened at Kingdom's command. Reclining against the counter, Kingdom used his large frame to block Angel's view of Sage. *If she is Angel's woman, he'll barrel into me anytime now.* Angel was a genius with a needle, but the bastard had little self-control.

Angel stood still.

Kingdom clapped him on the shoulder. "Relax. I came in for a tat."

Angel hesitated for a moment before taking Kingdom's lead. Shooting Sage a concerned look, he motioned for Kingdom to walk down the hall to his workroom. "Come on back, *hombre*, you can tell me what you want in the chair."

2

———

SAGE

ingdom. I understand how he got his nickname.

Angel had somewhat of a temper, and he did not cower easily to other men. Today, however, he backed down from Kingdom. The biker was clearly a man to be handled with care.

From the moment she locked eyes on him, she was mesmerized. His magnetism coupled with an air of danger had her hooked. It wasn't simple lust either. She was taken aback by an unbidden image of Kingdom unleashing all his unbridled power on her body. What it would be like to have all that raw strength of his let loose on her, unchecked.

She bit down on her bottom lip and squirmed in her seat. She was feeling hot all over and would've fanned herself but for his friends, sitting forward in their seats, at attention. The shop was small enough that they had overheard every word of the pissing match, the aggression bouncing off the walls of the tight space.

The biker was smokin' hot, as Greta, her receptionist, would put it. It was probably commonplace for him to remark on a woman's attractiveness. His was a mild flirtation, at best.

Not that I don't get compliments. Working in a profession dominated by men, she routinely garnered male attention. Admittedly, she had a pretty face, but a man like Kingdom wouldn't show interest in a woman without a sexy body to go with it. Neither model thin nor curvy, her body type inhabited a no-man's-land. A beast like Kingdom wouldn't settle for anything less than an off-the-charts sex goddess.

Nevertheless, it hadn't stopped her from devouring the sight of him during his little showdown with Angel. Beginning at his dark head, her gaze cascaded over his rolling shoulders as he leaned against the counter, down his broad back to that firm ass encased in worn jeans and ended at his motorcycle boots. He was a man who kept a firm hold on the space around him.

I'd like his firm hold on me, holding me down while he pounds into—Sage refocused in time to see him stand tall, saunter towards the hallway leading to Angel's room and disappear around the corner. Even after he was gone, she kept staring at the spot, the ghost of his hulky frame still hovering beside her. She imagined the composition of those toned, hard muscles underneath his clothes. The uber-male type didn't usually do it for her, but he was a thing of beauty. He'd been right when he'd guessed that she loved things of beauty. She so did. Despite his overbearing masculinity, or perhaps because of it, he was a beaut of a specimen.

"Like what you see?" a voice cut into her musings.

Sage's head snapped up to find two sets of eyes turned on her. The bikers who'd accompanied Kingdom. She shook her head, curtains of hair covering her embarrassment for getting caught staring after Kingdom like a lost puppy. Curse her and her bad luck.

In her professional life, Sage was considered tough, but she took off her mask when she covered for Camilla at the store. Angel's name may be on the awning outside, but, except for the needle, everything went through Camilla's hands.

Working at the shop was a welcome break from her hectic work life. *That's right, work life.* Because she hadn't had any other kind of life since Stanton, her good-for-nothing ex-fiancé left. Or as Camilla called him, *that rat-assed bastard.* It was a bad idea to get on the wrong side of a Cuban American woman. Stanton was lucky that his penis was still attached to the rest of his body after cheating on her only a few weeks before their wedding date.

The taller of Kingdom's friends eased back into his seat and nodded toward the empty hall leading to Angel's room, remarking casually, "He's a pretty boy."

She disagreed but wisely chose to keep her opinion to herself. Feigning nonchalance as if she hadn't been caught in the act of panting after his friend, Sage shrugged.

The biker called her out, "Ain't nothin' to be embarrassed about, baby."

She wanted to cover her head in shame except that, well, the look on his face was lenient. He wasn't judging or mocking her.

"A woman would have to be blind not to notice your friend," she remarked.

"I'll be sure to tell him."

She practically choked on her own saliva. *God, please kill me now.*

His expression turned calculating. "What 'bout me? Ain't I pretty?"

At a loss for words, her gaze flitted about the room nervously before landing on him. She scrutinized him, taking in his tall, brawny physique, harsh features, and grimly set mouth. The scar jagging down the side of his face topped off a whole package of menace. Not one of his features redeemed him to a place of normality. Whereas Kingdom was forceful, there was a touch of refinement to him. His friend, on the other hand, could easily be termed scary. A sane woman would require a heavy dose of bravery to tangle with him.

"I wouldn't exactly call you handsome but"—she paused —"you are appealing in your own right." *Appealing in a disturbing sort of way.*

He guffawed. "Good answer. You'd be lyin' otherwise." He stretched his huge frame to standing and sauntered over to her.

Sage fidgeted with the border of her t-shirt.

He rolled the word over his tongue. "Appealing."

Her nerves amped up a level. She didn't think she could handle it if he made a move on her. She searched for an excuse. "I'm a one-man type of woman. I noticed pretty boy first, so it's a bit late to change allegiances."

He chuckled softly as he leaned over with eyes holding a promise. "Little girl, if I wanted you, you fuckin' a brother couldn't stop me."

Ugh. Who came out with a pick-up phrase like that? A sociopath, that's who. She'd dealt with tough men, some of them who had been incarcerated for years, but, even with her experience, this biker was a different animal altogether. An untamed beast lay not-so-dormant beneath the guise of a human being.

"Tank!" his friend barked sharply from his seat against the wall. "Back the fuck off. You're scarin' her. She's a lady. You wouldn't know what to do with one if you caught a real one in your hands."

The man named Tank twisted his torso in the direction of his friend, who lounged back against his chair. He snorted. "Yeah, I do. Lesson number one, brother—insert dick in pussy."

Sage choked on her saliva and coughed.

"There you go, you crude motherfucker. Back up before your nasty face makes her faint. Shit, she was tryin' to be nice when she didn't call you out as the nasty-lookin' fucker that you are."

Tank turned back to her. Coolly, he demanded, "Your name."

Sage looked at him blankly.

"Babe, your name." This was not a question.

Swallowing down her irritation, Sage replied, "I'm Sage." She reached out her hand. "It's a pleasure to meet you."

"I'm called Tank," he drawled as he took her hand. "Didn't mean to rattle you with my plain speaking."

She lifted an eyebrow. *Pfft. Like hell you didn't.* Hoping to distract him, she suggested, "Why don't you and your friend take a break and go grab something to eat? Angel may be a speed demon, but it may take a while. It's an intricate tat."

Tank continued to study her intently.

Feeling her face heat up, she asked blandly, "Unless, perhaps, you would like a tattoo as well?"

Tank held up both arms to show Sage intricate tattoos starting his knuckles and traveling up his arms until they slipped from view under his sleeves. Another tat played peek-aboo from the collar of his shirt. "Ain't got much room left."

Once again, his friend called out, "Aren't you done yappin' your mouth? Sit the fuck down, already."

There was loud cursing coming from the back. "Idiot's inkin' up his ribs," Tank said with a shrug.

She winced, aware of how much it hurt to tattoo the ribs. There was no flesh to protect the bones. A sigh of relief escaped her lips when Tank turned away from her and joined his friend by the wall.

Her courage made an appearance as she joked, "Maybe your friend needs someone to hold his hand."

Tank bit out a laugh. "You gunnin' for the position?"

Sage huffed a surprised laugh. As if. She may be attracted to Kingdom, but there was no chance in hell she'd hook up with him. Even if he returned her interest, she didn't believe in casual hookups.

No matter how many wicked images of his mouth and tongue ran through her head.

3

SAGE

Tank and his friend took their leave, saying they were coming back when Kingdom's tattoo would be done. Sage was grateful for the break and pulled up the legal memo she was working on.

Hours later, the bikers waltzed back in, giving her chin lifts by way of greeting, and sat by the wall of tattoos. Although Sage attempted to focus on the tablet poised in her lap, it was impossible not to overhear their conversation. The fact that the waiting area was tiny did nothing to impede the biker called Tank from talking loudly. While she wasn't one to eavesdrop, curiosity got the best of her.

The nape of her neck pricked when she felt his eyes on her again. She didn't have to look up to know that he was inspecting her. Working around men, she could spot machismo a mile away. Normally, she was immune to men's chauvinism, but there was always ab exception to the rule.

From the corner of her eye, she saw Tank jab his friend painfully in the ribs.

He grabbed his side and glared at Tank. "What in the fuck was that for?"

Ignoring him, Tank tilted his chin "Cutter, what do ya think?"

"What do I think of *what*?" Cutter's eyes bugged out of his head. "You'd fuckin' tear that bitch apart."

"Not for me, dumbass." Tank gave a laborious sigh. "For Kingdom." Cutter squinted at her while Tank elaborated, "First time since Chopper's death that Kingdom's come up for air. He hasn't touched a bitch; he drinks too much and picks too many fights. Something's gotta give 'cause he's working on my last fuckin' nerve. Maybe she could help."

Sage rolled her eyes. One would think they'd talk a tad lower considering they were talking about her. But no, they were completely oblivious.

Proving her point, Cutter continued, "She ain't one of us—"

"'Us' ain't doin' it for him, but a shake-up could do the trick." Tank titled his chin in her direction. "Somethin' like her."

Sage peeked up furtively to find Cutter nodding slowly as he inspected her as carefully as a forensic expert. *Or a butcher,* she thought snidely. *Another heifer moment for me. Happy, happy, joy, joy.*

"She has potential," Cutter conceded.

Sage rolled her lips inward to prevent herself from screeching and tearing at her hair. They were beyond ridiculous. "I can hear you," she muttered, but not loud enough to be heard over their conversation.

Tank snorted. "He's out of her league, but we could make it happen."

Sage's eyes bulged at his comment. These men thought Kingdom was out of her league? *Ha! Good one.*

"Push him at her," Tank ordered.

"Why fuckin' me? I'm sick of doin' the dirty work."

"You're the one with the charm," Tank countered. "Shit, I don't fuckin' do nice; I'm a fuckin' bulldozer." He sprawled out his legs, leaned back, and crossed his arms, grinning unrepentantly. "It ain't in my blood."

Sage almost burst out laughing. Yup, he'd probably been spawned by a couple of over-sized pit bulls.

"I ain't a fuckin' matchmaker, but you got a point. Kingdom might ease up on us if he had a good fuck. He's pretty enough to bag her, and she is hot in her own way. Though," Tank mused, "she's not his usual."

"'Course you'd throw this shit in my lap 'cause your ass would fuck it up."

"Brother, you've taken too many hits to the head if you think you're smarter than me, but no doubt about it, girls rush to do your biddin'. Alright, enough bitchin'. Go play cupid, my man."

With the scrape of the chair legs on the linoleum floor, Sage groaned inwardly. Cutter was taking that moron's advice. She might as well give up all pretense that she wasn't listening and face him straight on.

Cutter threw a punch at Tank's shoulder and strolled toward Sage. *Let's see how he plays his hand.*

"Hey there. Why don't you show me what you got in there for me," began Cutter with a wink and a gesture toward the book of tattoo samples.

Tank chortled, enjoying the spectacle. "She's a sucker," he mumbled.

"I heard that," she called out. But he knew what she knew —she was a sucker. Helping people was what she did; when covering for Camilla at the shop, she sought to help customers find the perfect tat, a tat that held meaning for them. Sage opened Angel's portfolio to her favorite tats. Biker dude or not, she was in her zone. As her fingers flew over the photos, she commented, "Hmm...you are pretty confident of yourself, but I'm going to expand your horizons, so promise to be a good listener."

"My mama taught me to listen to pretty women, 'specially the teacher-lookin' ones," Cutter teased back.

Tank cracked up, and Sage made sure to throw him a good-sized glare.

As they reviewed different tattoos, Sage relented to Cutter's charm. She revealed to him that yes, she was single. Not a big deal since she didn't intend to be pimped out to a biker, even a man like Kingdom, who pushed all her buttons. There was no danger in divulging her age, which was twenty-nine. What she did not disclose was that she was a criminal defense lawyer. The last bit was easy to hide since she was dressed casually. Her killer attorney attire was sealed off with her wardrobe at home.

Footsteps sounded on the corridor's creaky floor, and Cutter twisted toward the sound. Sage sniffed air charged with Kingdom's high-vibrational energy and drank up the vision of a warrior, his torso bare. *Breathe. Breathe.* Her eyes skated frenetically over his chiseled chest; it was covered with a dusting of fine dark hair that narrowed over a six pack and disappeared into the waistband of his jeans. A heavy brass buckle hung over the worn brown leather just above his crotch. She almost dared to dip her gaze lower. *I won't look. Stay professional.*

Kingdom bared down on Cutter, who glanced at his aggressive stance and asked casually, "How'd it go?"

Sage's attention was caught by the fascinating play of Kingdom's pecs and the sharp cut of his abdomen as he shrugged and gave Cutter his leather vest to hold. As Kingdom raised his arms and stretched the sides of his t-shirt to fit it on his torso, a demon tail wrapped around motorcycle handles caught her attention. The fabric of his shirt swooped down and covered the tattoo before she could get more than a cursory look at it. Sage's gaze chased his exposed flesh to the last centimeter until the worn cotton draped down and fully covered him, leaving her momentarily bereft.

He had the body of an ancient god, one painstakingly chiseled out of marble. Tank called him pretty, but Sage wholeheartedly disagreed. Kingdom exuded the power of a man who held dominion over the world. Nothing about him was "pretty." Stunningly sexy, yes. Pretty, most definitely not.

"Hurt like a motherfucker," Kingdom grumbled as he stuffed his shirt into his jeans. He shrugged on his leather vest. "If I had space left on my arms, I would've inked it there instead."

"You shoulda tatted up your face."

Sage gasped. Cutter flashed her a lopsided grin and mouthed, "Gotcha." She slitted her eyes at him. Sly, shifty-eyed devil.

"Pretty Boy ain't got what it takes to pull it off, huh?"

Kingdom's eyebrows bunched together. "Better not be talkin' about me, son," he warned.

Unconcerned, Cutter laughed at him.

Without thinking, Sage spoke, "As a matter of fact, I am rarely impressed with facial tattoos. Or neck tattoos, for that matter."

Kingdom's attention swung to her. "You've got strong opinions, don't you? Let me get it straight—no face or neck ink. No skulls or Grim Reaper. But"—his eyes skittered over her face—"you like pretty."

Sage admitted ruefully, "I suppose I do have pretty strong opinions."

Golden-brown eyes stared down on her keenly. The swivel stool creaked as Sage shifted her position under his scrutiny. Unabashed, his eyes flickered to her breasts before swinging back up to bolt into hers. Sage was ensnared in the web he wove around her, dragging her focus entirely on him with his own undiluted concentration.

Cutter interrupted their stare-a-thon. "You were cryin' like a little bitch back there. Angel give you a big boo-boo?"

Absently, he responded, "Shut up."

Stumbling out of her Kingdom-induced coma, Sage rummaged around for a comment and finally found praise for Angel. "He is a master."

Kingdom's eyes flared, and he retorted, "I'm master here. No man but me."

A shiver ran through her, leaving behind a sheen of prickly awareness on her skin.

"You finish it or do you have to come back again?" Cutter piped up, gesturing to the wall layered with photos displaying Angel's talent.

Kingdom finally broke his lock-hold stare on Sage and cocked his head toward Cutter, irritation etched on his face. Pulling out his wallet, he handed his credit card to Sage. "I'll be back to finish in three weeks."

Angel walked out, pulling off his disposable gloves. After he was done wrapping one inside of the other and tying them off, he clapped Kingdom on the shoulder. "I don't need to explain to you the aftercare instructions, am I right, *hombre*?"

"Think I can handle it," Kingdom muttered, continuing his battle of glares with Cutter. Giving up, Cutter threw his head back with a knowing laugh. Taking his credit card from Sage, he paused to sign the receipt and then turned to Angel. "You did right by him."

The molten pain in his voice was evident in what she suspected was a rare compliment.

Angel gave him a brief smile of his own. "Appreciate it, *hermano.*"

"After we're done, I'll come back so you can take shots of the tat. It deserves to be up there." Kingdom's gaze flickered up toward the wall.

Angel's face registered shock. Sage may not have understood the back and forth between Kingdom and his friend, but it didn't take much to guess Kingdom's reasons for returning to the shop instead of posting the pics online. She very much doubted he was glued to his social media presence.

"Shit, I've done mad tats for the Squad. Didn't think the day'd come when a brother would go public for the shop."

"Not for the shop. For Chopper. For all the fallen brothers," Kingdom intoned, his gaze dropping to the tat on Angel's fist.

"Yeah," Angel commiserated. A recognizable shadow passed Angel's face at the mention of fallen brothers. *Angel, Kingdom, me.* They held within themselves the shadows left by the ones they'd loved but lost. *To the Grim Reaper,* she grimaced in reflection, *the collector of souls.* Was there any wonder she hated the image as much as she did?

Kingdom gave Angel a chin lift while his eyes coasted over Sage one last time.

Tank stood up, and they left, the little bell attached to the doorknob chiming behind the door.

Once they were alone, Angel glared at Sage. She dropped her gaze to her tablet but heated under Angel's continued stare. She had a sinking feeling that she wouldn't be covering for Camilla in the future.

"*Pardon, hermana*, they're a lot to handle. They didn't bother you, did they?"

"Of course not; they were mostly gentlemen. The one called Tank was a little forward, but for the most part, they're harmless."

"Believe me, there is nothing harmless about them. Thank you, Jesus, they're gone." Angel sighed and silently made the sign of the cross. "They're not men you should be around, Kingdom and his crew. If he got his hooks into someone like you, he'd chew you up and spit you out." Angel shot her a piercing look that told her all she needed to know. There was no way in hell Angel would let Sage hang out to dry.

"Damn." He fake shuddered. "Camilla will cut off *mio cojones.*"

"Seriously, Angel, I'm a grown woman, and it's not plausible that a biker like him would be seriously interested in me. They like their creature comforts like, oh"—she tapped her chin lightly—"a harem of willing women at their disposal. Please. If he comes back, it will be for the tat, which is impressive, by the way. Not," she insisted, "because he's interested in me."

Angel harrumphed and stomped toward the back of the shop. Sage could have sworn she heard him mutter, "He's interested, alright, the *pendejo.*"

4

———

KINGDOM

Once the door of the shop closed behind them and cut off the annoying sound of bells, Kingdom rounded on Cutter.

"What the fuck were you playing at back there? You tryin' to push the tattoo chick on me."

Ambling toward their parked bikes, Cutter shrugged. "Why the fuck not? Did you check out her tits?" The asshole smacked his lips for emphasis.

Kingdom threw Cutter a vicious warning look. His blood was boiling. First off, he was irritated that when he had walked out, Cutter and Sage's heads had been joined like Siamese twins as they studied the tattoo book. Then Sage threw her head back and let out a throaty laugh at some lame-ass joke Cutter had made. The moment Cutter spotted Kingdom, he'd jumped away from her as if he'd stuck a wet finger into a live socket. As if Cutter being close to Sage hadn't grated on Kingdom's nerves enough, him speaking about her as if she was a random bitch was blinding his vision to bloodlust red. The woman was bangin', but she had class. Too much class for Cutter.

The brothers were lawless animals when it came to women. How could he blame them when the female was hot as fuck? Against his will, his imagination conjured up her perky tits. If he had his way, he'd spend days licking and sucking on them. Leave a trail of his marks down, across, and around those two juicy mounds.

Are her nipples light pink or dark? Either way, I'll suck and bite the fuck out of them until I leave them both cherry-ass red.

After they were well loved, he'd fuck her tits, pressing them tightly around his cock and marking her nipples with his come.

His dick jerked in his Levi's, and he smacked the center of his forehead with the base of his closed fist. For fuck's sake, feeling good was never on his agenda.

Kingdom snapped at Cutter, "She ain't my type. I'd fuckin' break her."

Tank noted, "I agree that she looks breakable, but she held her own against me. Made a joke. Sagey-girl ain't stupid either because she feared me."

"Fuck, Kingdom," Cutter chimed in, "you ain't tapped no pussy since Chopper. Trixie's chewing our ears off about how you haven't touched her. Mooning over you. Brother, if I have to keep listening to her yappin' and goin' on, I'm gonna fucking lose my mind."

Kingdom clutched Cutter's shirt. "You"—he emphasized with a twist, tearing a wound into the cotton—"ain't my fuckin' keeper. Stay in your fucking lane."

A flash of concern crossed Cutter's face. Cutter didn't do concern, so that was worrying in itself. Placing his hand over Kingdom's clenched fist, Cutter said in a low tone, "She's hot, and, bro, a different flavor would do you good. A man gets tired of the same shit every day. Vanilla might be tasty," he persisted, "at least till you get back in the game."

Kingdom's gaze seized on Cutter's hand. Releasing his hold on his brother, he grunted, "My game's none of your damn business. Get it straight, motherfucker—you get in my business, and I'll beat your ass out of it."

Cutter swung onto his bike. Straddling the monster, Cutter said, "You're trippin' for nothing. We're tryin' to help you, *King*." Cutter purposely used Chop's nickname to remind him that Chop wouldn't have taken his behavior in stride.

He'd damn well make it his business. That was Chop all the way. He'd beat me to within an inch of my life for my own good.

Kingdom mounted his own Harley and grimaced when the inked skin stung underneath the weave of the dressing. Christ, he hated hearing his nickname come out of anyone's mouth, but it reminded him that his brothers always had his back. They weren't purposely trying to torture him. Leaning over the handlebars, he expelled a harsh breath. They were tough assholes, yeah, but they cared about him. Especially Cutter. That motherfucker was like the fuckin' plague; he couldn't get rid of him even if he tried.

Fuck, I must be in a bad state if they're workin' to get me pussy.

Kingdom cut a sidelong glance at Tank. "Ain't you got somethin' to say?"

Tank grinned back. "Nope. Not in the mood to get my outfit mussed up like Cutter there."

"Real glad I ain't gotta kick your ass too." Releasing the throttle and revving up the motor, Kingdom took the lead.

Tank and Cutter fell in behind him. Through his mirror, he caught Tank's wink to Cutter. He couldn't muster up indignation because an image of Sage's heart-shaped face sidled up beside him like a purring cat rubbing between his legs.

5

KINGDOM

Once again, Kingdom caught himself thinking of the chick in the tat shop. Sage.

He blew out a weary breath over his fingers clenched around the scruff of his jaw. The roller shutter door of the garage attached to his warehouse was raised, allowing a spring breeze to drift through the space. Kingdom wrangled with a tight bolt on the Harley he was restoring. It was a side gig for him, but he'd told his client he'd be done by the end of the week, which meant many extra hours.

He had the flexibility to take time off from helping the brothers run illicit goods, mostly cigarettes. The vice taxes imposed on certain states had created a huge industry worth billions of dollars, especially in New York, although they were cashing in from Connecticut and Rhode Island as well.

The Providence Hellions MC were trying their damnedest to push the Squad out of their hustle. Damn New Englanders.

Worst case scenario, they'd dip into the marijuana pool as they did on occasion when they needed an extra influx of cash. Luckily, the Squad hadn't gone into cartel-type drugs like coke or heroin when they'd cornered the market on smokes.

Three more days in this garage with only me, myself, and I, and I swear to Christ, I'm gonna lose my fucking mind. Pushing his weight deep against the wrench, fear swooped down to the pit of his stomach. Every single fuckin' day was a battle.

But Sage, Sage wasn't part of that. Her name called to another world far from his. The fragrance he had inhaled when he'd leaned in close to her at the shop evoked the sweet grass she was named after, with hints that were woodsy but sweet.

Chop. Fuckin' Chop.

With a vicious throw, the wrench flew out of Kingdom's hand and across the room, scraping off a piece of the brick wall on its journey to the concrete floor. He wasn't surprised that Chop tunneled into his headspace on the regular. When he was alive, they were so close they could read each other's thoughts and signals. Their missions as Night Stalkers had sharpened their connection as razor fine as the point of a stiletto knife. An elite squad like theirs had them traveling in and out of combat zones. Cutter had joined their team for a time. Chop, Kingdom, and Cutter were the three amigos. Thick as thieves. Cutter was their link to the Squad years after they'd finished their tours.

Flying behind enemy lines in a tar-colored sky littered with stars, Kingdom had come to love the darkness. Only once he was back stateside did his nocturnal friends morph into a blackhole which sucked him down every night. After both he and Chop were diagnosed with PTSD, they humorously termed those night missions as "the pit." Chop was the quiet one, but quiet was not synonymous with peaceful. Damn him, but he missed those pit missions with Chop on the windswept crags of the desert.

Once he was back, he strove to forget and forge a new life. Chop hid it from him, likely out of shame, but ... *fuck, I should have known.*

Kingdom roared as he launched himself on the abandoned wrench. He slammed it against the concrete floor until pain reverberated up his nerves to his elbow. Cradling his abused knuckles and tremoring arm, he staggered to the low stool by his bike and sat down heavily. Wiping his brow with a shaky hand, he hung his head.

After Chop's death, his night terrors had returned. Night upon night, they dogged him until he dropped into a mindless, exhausted sleep. They reminded him of a kestrel he had once spotted settled on a tree in the Iraqi hinterland. Small and deceptively calm, it transformed into a ruthless killer in the blink of an eye.

He had tried to do what Chopper did, but with alcohol and pills. The memory from several months before shoved its way to the forefront of his mind. Cutter was the one who had found him unconscious on the shower floor, the showerhead pounding water on his back. He hadn't felt a damn thing when Cutter had slapped him awake. Or when ice water had rained down on him.

Cutter's pissed off screaming had woken him right the hell up, though. "You cocksuckin' motherfucker! I won't let you go, you goddamn piece of shit!"

Arms had wrapped around him. Cutter had grunted in his ear as he'd dragged Kingdom's heavy body out. Just in the nick of time too. Water pooled around his face, threatening to drown him as his cheek was plastered to the tiles.. A moment later, the back of his head had slammed against the tiled wall.

Cutter had let go of his drenched cut and slid down the shower stall.

Cutter had whiplashed him with a backhand. *"King,* get the fuck up!"

Kingdom had struggled to his feet. He slid around several times before he managed to brace himself against the wall, his fingernails clawing the slippery tiles.

"Start running in place! Now!" Cutter's commands had echoed off the bathroom walls.

Kingdom had lifted his knees, his ears ringing and arms burning from holding himself up.

"Get those knees up, man! Count 'em out!"

"One, two, three ..." Kingdom had counted off, his feet slapping against the wet floor in a rhythm that put his brain on pause. An old trick. Cutter had been using a CBT tactic that Kingdom had learned to fake himself out of triggers. It was no wonder Cutter had fit right in with Kingdom and Chop.

"You can't fuckin' pull on me the bullshit Chop pulled on you. Hear me?"

Kingdom had nodded numbly.

"Answer me! So you understand, motherfucker?"

Fuck, why is he shouting so damn loud? Kingdom had bent over, his arms braced on his knees, and retched. Running barefoot on a nasty slippery floor was enough to shake him loose. "I understand," he'd croaked out.

"Don't let this happen again, King. We clear?"

"Yeah," he had rasped.

"Clean this shit up. It's disgusting in here." With that parting shot, Cutter had swiped his foot across Kingdom's ankles and left him in a crumpled, bloody mess on the shower-stall floor.

Dipping his chin to his chest, Kingdom let the wrench slip

from his hand with a clatter. Christ, nothing good came from rehashing the past. He stood up, walked to the row of hooks along the wall by the garage door, and shrugged into his jacket hanging there.

The club. His one refuge. He had to get out of his head if he had a fighting chance to hang onto his sanity.

※※※

KINGDOM TOOK a long ride outside the city to clear his head before stopping by the club. Trees were a dime a dozen in upstate New York, but amid the riot of bright green leaves of the typical spring day, one chestnut-colored trunk caught his eye. It was an exact match for Sage's hair. Enthralled, Kingdom drifted perilously close to the edge of the asphalt road.

"Fucking hell," he cursed as he swerved back onto the road. Cursing his distraction, he pulled over.

Bike thrumming between his legs, Kingdom stared up at the culprit. In an insomnia-induced state, Kingdom stretched out to touch the thick, rough lines of the trunk as if they were the brassy strands of her hair.

He decided then and there that he'd get his hands on her. Just the one time. Twist her hair around his fist and hold on fast while mounting her from behind. When he had her trapped, her pussy muscles spasming around his cock, he'd forget everything but the feel of her. No Chop. No club. Nothing but freedom.

It made no sense, no sense at all, but deep in his gut, he sensed he'd catch that feeling again. With her. *In* her, to be exact. It was only a hunch, but at this point he was desperate for a break. While he wasn't dead, he was barely living.

He straightened his bike and turned it back around toward the city. The Squad's main room had a bar area like a speakeasy's cavern in the old brick building. One among many in the dilapidated neighborhoods of Poughkeepsie. The club bought the abandoned building, threw out the squatters, fixed it up, and made it the club's headquarters. Besides the main room, there was a large meeting room, a series of offices, and half a dozen rooms—occupied or used by the brothers to crash—on the second floor. Some brothers, like Cutter, lived there full-time, but most lived on their own. Kingdom, he loved the club, but he had his warehouse for himself.

Kingdom hit the bar for a shot of whisky. The burn brought him a modicum of comfort. Another shot with a chaser, and then another for good measure, and he was calm enough not to wreck the place.

Kingdom sprawled out on one of the black leather couches haphazardly placed around the open space of the room. His jeans were compressing his hard shaft, and he shifted his ass underneath the crackling leather to find a position to ease his discomfort. He glared at his swelling cock. He hadn't fucked a woman for months. On principle, he didn't mess with good girls, but Cutter was right about Sage.

Smug bastard.

Kingdom shoved his boot at the low table facing the couch. The table toppled over. The crash caused the boys at the bar to glance over their shoulders. Kingdom casually stretched out his legs over the tipped length of the table.

"What?" Kingdom growled. Like synchronized swimmers, they shifted their attention away from him. He crossed his legs at his ankles with a huff. Swirling the whiskey in his glass, he ruminated darkly over the unwelcome change triggered by that sweet thang he'd met a week before. He was doing fine by his damn self, righteously wallowing in misery. His long legs stretched out, Kingdom dropped his head back on the rough leather, tuning out the blaring music, the clinking glasses, and the unfettered laughter.

He was certain the woman had put a spell on him, but he'd get his fill and cut her off.

Yep, that there was a solid plan.

6

KINGDOM

Kingdom's hand paused on the door of Angel's shop just before he stepped inside for his last session with Angel.

He was looking forward to seeing Sage—her sweet face and careful manner beckoned him with the seductiveness of the sunny, rolling hills of Tuscany. Made sense since that's where his people came from. Her softness and wit, but especially the elusive sense of freedom he had found with her, wouldn't quit calling to him.

He was about to set his eyes on her pretty face and perky tits. A grin formed on his face when he recalled those lush tits. He loved real tits. Fake tits did the job when necessary, like with Trixie, but the thought of Sage's plump tits and curvy ass brought his cock to standing.

Speaking of which, it was stretching exponentially in his jeans. Before Chop, when his cock had twitched, he'd grabbed a woman and rode her until he wore her out. Needless to say, he had stamina.

The tinkle of hanging bells announced Kingdom's entrance. He stopped short when he found a dark-haired, golden-skinned woman at the counter. Sexy, but not the woman he came for. Irritation rolled through him that she wasn't where he'd expected her to be.

Kingdom advanced on the linoleum tiles and reached the woman with a friendly smile for her.

"Good afternoon," said the woman who wasn't Sage.

"How are you?" he rumbled. "I've got a one o'clock with Angel."

The woman checked and gave him a wide smile. "Kingdom?"

"Yep, that's me."

"Angel should be ready in a few minutes."

"Alright," Kingdom replied, but instead of taking a seat, he asked, "Where's the chick who worked here a couple of weeks back?"

The woman pursed her lips together. "I'm not sure who you're talking about. I'm the only one who works the front."

She was hedging, but Kingdom would rectify that. He wanted to find Sage, and he always got what he wanted. "I came in for a tat and another woman was working the front." He didn't want to use Sage's name. "She has brown hair and blue eyes." Keep it cool and neutral. "So high..." he finished, raising his hand to the level of his mouth.

"Oh. That was Sage. She was covering for me." Angel's woman placed a hand over her belly by way of an explanation. "Sage doesn't work here. She comes as a favor when I have a doctor appointment."

"Is that right?" He queried lightly, "Where does she work?"

Sharp eagle eyes appraised Kingdom, taking in every

detail. She paused at the VP patch on his leather cut, which proclaimed him as a leader in the most powerful MC in the area. Working in a tat shop, she understood the meaning of his cut and patch.

Shaking her head, she decided, "I don't think it's a good idea..."

Kingdom tamped down his irritation. He got it—really, he did. Civilians were wary of bikers, as they should be. Unfortunately, Sage had caught his attention, and when he wanted something, he sure as hell got it. No one cockblocked him. No. One.

Kingdom made a pretense of relaxing against the counter and checking his cellphone as if he wasn't interested. As if he wasn't as dangerous as he was. "She helped me with a tat that means a whole lot to me. Been strugglin' with the death of a brother, and I wanted to personally thank her for helping me work through my grief." Kingdom cringed. "Christ, I'd rather slit my throat than vocalize my personal shit to a stranger, but truth be told, Sage took care of me."

What he'd said was true. Sage gave him the tat, and the tat had saved his ass; it had become something of a lodestone for him. Kingdom massaged his chest where the tat lay underneath his cut.

The woman's face softened, and she introduced herself. "I'm Camilla. Sage is a close friend of mine. I'm sorry for your loss." She gave him a small smile. "I'm not surprised that she helped you. Sage has a gift when it comes to pairing a tat with a person." Her smile slipped off her lips as she murmured, "Not surprised at all."

Clearly, Sage was as loved as a family member, which meant that Camilla was the gatekeeper. "I'd appreciate it if you told me how to get in touch with her."

Camilla took half a minute to consider his request. "I can't do that, although her law firm is public," she mused to herself.

"A law firm?" *Color me surprised.* He hadn't seen that coming. "A woman working at a tattoo place doesn't normally have her own firm."

Camilla chuckled at his reaction. "Sage is a defense lawyer. She's a solo practitioner, which is a fancy way of saying that she works for herself. Not what you expected from a woman you met at a tattoo shop, huh? She's a gem. Even with her school debts, she takes on clients for free. As she always says, they're normal men and women who just made bad choices."

A rush of possessiveness struck him with the velocity of a bullet flying out of a M134 Minigun, and red haze crowded out his vision, giving him an image of Sage in the Oneida County Jail, walking through a crowd of punks with their forked tongues flickering like a cobra's, mimicking sexual acts. Whistles and heckles punctuated by lascivious taunts and threats. He vowed that when he got ahold of her, he'd skin her round ass for her carelessness.

He hadn't thought much beyond the desire to fuck her, but she suddenly felt more valuable than he had anticipated, and it appealed to him. There was no doubt in his mind that she was batshit crazy, but he also had no doubt that she was a badass on her own terms. If she was a defense lawyer, she knew how to handle herself in the local jails and the federal penitentiary, not just in court. The woman was no joke.

"Damn."

Camilla cocked her head to one side. "I'm feelin' you. You've got swag. Just the thing to shake things up, and it's been a long time. She needs a change. Tell you what I'm going to do —I'll call her when Angel's working on you. If she agrees, I'll give you her info. That's the best I can do."

Angel walked out just as Camilla finished her sentence.

Not wanting Angel to get in his two cents 'cause the man had looked none too pleased when he'd seen Kingdom talking to Sage, he swiftly thanked Camilla and hurried down the corridor to Angel's workroom. He hoped for all their sakes that Sage said yes, because his appetite for pursuit had just been whetted.

✵✵✵

CAMILLA: Call me now

SAGE FROWNED as she looked down at Camilla's text. She dialed and waited for Camilla to pick up. "What's up, Cam?"

"What's up is that a hot biker came looking for you," her best friend began. "Told me that he got a tat for his dead brother because of you."

"Kingdom," she replied. Her voice came out breathy, causing her to cringe inwardly.

"That's his name? Different, but then again, he *is* a biker. I didn't expect it to sound like it came out of *The Lord of the Rings,* but whatever. Girl, he asked for your contact info, and I want to give him your name, number, address, *all of it.*"

Sage rolled her eyes at Camilla's dramatic tone. "He could be a stalker nutcase for all we know."

Camilla snorted. "Yeah, he does look a lot like one of your criminals. Just down your alley."

"You must be kidding."

"Of course I'm kidding. Well, not really, but the point is this—you need him. You live like a nun. I get it because I saw what that fucker Stanton did to you, but he's got himself a fiancée, so what's done is done. The question is, what are you going to do?"

"Do?" Her voice raised an octave higher. "How can you ask me that? What *is* there to do? I mean, I died inside when I found out about his womanizing. But it was more than that. My confidence was hobbled. He stopped showing any interest in having sex with me. He'd actively avoid touching me. That does a number on a woman's self-assurance. At least *this* woman's."

"Oh, sweetie. Why didn't you tell me?"

"I was embarrassed." She sniffed. It was still humiliating to mention it to Camilla two years later.

"I know, but it had to do with him. He had some serious issues that had nothing to do with you."

"He had no problem having sex with other women. But, not with me."

"Stanton was rich as sin and charming as hell, but he was fucked in the head. He came from a blue-blood family, but that father of his had him twisted up in some messed-up shit. All of that had nothing to do with you. Honestly, Sage, I saw the two of you together. He loved you as much as he was capable of loving someone, which turned out not to be much. That was a *him* thing, not a *you* thing. Either way, the time has come to let go of the past and move on. Kingdom can be your future. He has no problem going after what he wants, and he's made it clear that he wants you. He's the opposite of Stanton in every way. There's no reason your paths should have crossed, but they did anyway. It's like fate dropped him smack in the middle of your life. Like a miracle. He's a sign, and a sign is a sign. Trust me, it's a sign. I know one when I see one."

"Miracle or no miracle, sign or no sign, I don't want to get hurt."

"Who's talking about getting hurt? Damn girl, I'm not talking about love here. I'm talking about a man to use and abuse. Fuck him, for God's sake. I hate to use the words 'fuck' and 'God' in the same sentence, but see what you've reduced me to?"

"I've lost my ability to attract a man. Anyway, just because he asked for my number doesn't mean he'll actually seek me out."

"Oh *puu-lease*, he'll come after you. You're the only one who doesn't see how beautiful you are. But the rest of the world does. Especially men. Let me give him your contact info. Come on, girl, give it a chance."

Sage twiddled with the edge of the open legal folder laying on her desk. She supposed that if a guy like him went out of his way to approach her, she'd be open to listening. She certainly wouldn't shut him down. Unless he turned out to be creepy, but her creep radar was pretty fine-tuned, and she hadn't gotten any cringy signals from him. Exhaling a heavy sigh, she agreed, "Fine. Give him my contact information."

"Good, now we're getting somewhere. And why haven't I heard about this biker guy before? You, I can forgive because you're clueless. But Angel is going to suffer for keeping this from me. I mean, like blue balls for a week kind of suffering."

"Oh boy." Sage breathed out. "Don't blame Angel. He's busy and overworked as it is. Plus, his primary concern is the baby and you. I don't think he has energy in him for more."

"*Humph.* Yeah, okay, I'll let him off the hook this one time, but I'm still gonna give him a piece of my mind."

Sage shuddered. "I'm sure you will, Cam. I'm sure you will."

7

KINGDOM

Kingdom was pleasantly surprised when Camilla gave him Sage's contact info, although he frowned when Camilla went into a speech on how Sage didn't need any extra grief. "Fun only," she said. "No heartache, got me?"

Heartache? What the fuck? It was a heads-up to respect Sage. Message received—proceed with caution. If he wasn't a selfish bastard, he'd leave well enough alone, but that was currently out of the question. Although it had started out as pure lust, learning about Sage's fragility had triggered a surge of unexpected tenderness inside his chest and brought out his protective side.

He rubbed his aching tat. It had taken a marathon session of massive proportions, but Angel had finally finished the damned thing. Kingdom decided to bide his time for close to a week before showing up at Sage's door. He wanted to be sure that the element of surprise was on his side.

On his ride across the city to her office, anticipation drummed a steady beat in his chest. He rolled up to a medium-sized house with a well-clipped lawn lined with bushes and blooming flowers. In the center of the lawn stood a statue depicting Justice, blindfolded with scales and sword in her hands.

His brows dipped low when he noticed that there were two entrances to the house. One was a plain door that obviously led to a residential space, while the second had a gold-plated plaque indicating that it was a place of business. Near the street, a wooden sign swung from a post, carved with antique lettering reading *The Law Office of Sage Cameron Esq.* Christ, she was advertising that she was a one-woman show and living next door to her office.

Slowly riding into a parking spot, Kingdom threw down the kickstand and shut off the machine. It took a moment to reel back the unpleasant kick of fear. The woman had no common sense. A compulsion to possess her and hide her away gripped him. Swinging himself off his bike, he stalked up to the entrance.

Beep-beep.

The doorbell announced his arrival, but it turned out the warning was meaningless since the reception room was empty. There was a receptionist desk, but it was unoccupied. Upholstered chairs sat in a semicircle around a coffee table like logs around a campfire, but they were unpopulated as well. Monochromatic paintings on the walls amplified the sense of emptiness.

A vicious cycle of words looped endlessly in Kingdom's mind. *Alone, unprotected, defenseless, alone, unprotected, defenseless.* An image of Sage lying on the carpet, beaten and raped, ratcheted up his anxiety. She could be dead. Fuck, not another death. Kingdom's breath stalled, and his fingers clawed at the base of his throat for relief. Taking in cleansing breaths, he dragged himself off the edge of an anxiety attack.

A voice rang out from the back office, "Just a moment, and I'll be right out. Please take a seat and grab a magazine."

Whoosh. His lungs sputtered like a rusty ignition finally catching, and he sucked in a long breath through flared nostrils. "Grab a magazine. Grab a motherfuckin' magazine," he mimicked her tone of voice. "She'd be dead before she got the chance to finish her sentence." Kingdom slumped into the nearest armchair. He dropped his head in his hands, his elbows cradled on his knees.

❋❋❋

Sage heard the front door open. Greta, her receptionist-slash-paralegal was out, dropping off papers at the Clerk's Office at the District Court. She quickly backed up her laptop, logged out of her computer, and walked out with a jaunt in her step.

"Thank you for waiting—" She stopped midsentence, her breath catching as she took in the vision of Kingdom sitting in a too-small armchair in her waiting room. Her gaze first landed on the way his jeans accentuated the curvature of his thick quad muscles. Then her gaze traveled up his shirt, showcasing his broad shoulders, the shirtsleeves bunching around his large, defined biceps. He sat forward with his elbows braced on his spread knees, and his fingers were steepled as if in contemplation. Bird wings flapped a riot in her chest. Her eyes finally reached his face, which was fixed in a disgruntled scowl.

"Good afternoon ... Mr. King, I believe it is?" She winced.

Dammit, she was so jumpy that she'd already messed up his name. The supreme irony was that his name had been frolicking around in her head for weeks.

Keeping a wide berth from him, she propped herself up on Greta's desk and folded her arms over her chest. She maintained her distance because his moodiness, rather than intimidating her, enticed her. As he checked her out in his own right, the initial scold in his gilded eyes turned into appreciation. She swept her hands over her sharp pencil skirt. *Get a grip, girl. You're being ridiculous. A curse on Camilla and her idiotic "signs."*

Kingdom dripped of steamy, hot sex, putting her hormones on high alert, but she beat them back. Not only did she have notorious bad luck, but she didn't think she was a match for his raw sexuality. She was no PG-13, but she couldn't compare with his off-the-charts XXX charisma. Kingdom left a wave of women in his wake like a litter of murder victims in an indie slasher flick.

"Kingdom. I answer to Kingdom," he commanded with a tone expecting complete obedience.

Shutting down her chatter, she beamed her best professional smile at him. "Very well, Kingdom," she responded smoothly. She stood up and invited him to her office with a wave of her hand. "Come on back. We'll have more privacy in my office."

Was she imagining things, or did that sound suspiciously like a proposition? She wasn't normally rattled, but she was off kilter when it came to this man.

8

KINGDOM

Sage turned her back on him, blatantly expecting him to follow her.

No one turned their back to him, but he'd teach her about respect very soon. Sauntering in, he spotted her scurrying behind a behemoth of a desk mounted with stacks of legal files and papers. If she knew what was good for her, she'd stay behind that desk. Sage was sexy at the tattoo shop, with her curvy, delicious body, but the woman standing before him was off-the-fucking-charts hot.

He hadn't been attracted to a woman in a suit or a uniform for a long time. Her silk blouse clung to her chest, dipping low in the center to show off the crease of her tits. And the skirt? Damn the skirt for being wrapped so tightly around her lush body. To top it off, she wore a pair of fuck-me black patent-leather heels.

Kingdom was moments away from pulling up her prim-

and-proper skirt and grinding her pussy on his swelling cock with both hands on her ass. His hands flickered beside his thighs with the itch to bend her over her monster-ass desk and leave his handprint on her ass.

Behind the Great Wall of all desks, Sage linked her hands together with the ease of a professional. *Holy shit.* Sage thought he was here to hire her for her services despite his conversation with Camilla. Oh, she was going to service him, alright. On her knees and with her plump lips wrapped around his cock. She'd leave a nice ring of red lipstick on his dick as her calling card after he was done fucking that sweet mouth of hers.

Kingdom surveyed her office to glean further details about her. He figured the office was converted from the master bedroom of the house. Easy afternoon light suffused the space and drew his attention to the garnet-colored glints in her hair. The wall directly behind him had fancy inlaid shelves from floor to ceiling, stocked with what he assumed were law books. The whole effect was classy, but also welcoming. There were knickknacks along the shelves, likely souvenirs from trips she had taken. Jealousy slithered over him at a sketch of Sage lounging against a railing looking over a beach, in a halter top sundress. Gripping the sides of the chair, he dragged himself off the edge.

"How may I help you, Kingdom?" she began.

Let's cut through the bullshit, yeah. "I came to show you my tat."

Her mouth parted. "Oh, I ... I assumed you came for legal counsel."

Kingdom was pleased to hear her stammer. "You assumed wrong," he stated blandly. Her butt shifted restlessly in her seat, and he reveled in her obvious discomfort. "I came for you," he clarified, the innuendo humming between them. His gaze slid down to her full breasts. Silk looked good on her. Fuck him, but he caught the outline of white lace underneath. He imagined she wore matching panties. She'd fuckin' rock the virgin look. He didn't have an issue with virgins, but he wanted her first fuck to be hard and rough. Teach her what he liked from the get-go. When his cock surged against its prison of denim, he bit down on his cheek to replace one pain with another.

Sage regarded him with a touch of panic in her eyes. "You came all this way to show me your tat?"

Kingdom rounded the desk and wheeled her around to wrap his hands on the armrests of her chair.

Her fingers fluttered toward the chair he'd vacated with a faint plea, "Um, you can show me from over there."

He smirked, daring her with an arched brow. "You can't see the details from over there."

Without waiting for a response, he dragged up his shirt and exposed his chest. Her eyes fell, heavy-lidded, and those fluttering fingers dropped to her knees. Good to know she appreciated a man with chest hair. Her gaze, like warm fingertips, brushed over the dense ridges of his six pack.

He held himself still for her inspection and watched Sage lick her lips. "Nice."

"The tat or me?" He chuckled.

Caught lusting, Sage snapped to attention and inspected his tattoos, first studying the rider on the demon tat over his heart, then moving down to the helicopter inked across the left side of his ribs. In Germanic script, Chopper's name was inscribed on one blade, while the remaining blades held different dates. The sharp relief of the helicopter was softened with details and subtle shading. Sage languidly lifted a forefinger and lightly traced the tattoo. The skin-to-skin contact sent a shock through Kingdom as if he had been zapped with an electric prod. A shudder threatened to rack his body, but he clenched the muscles of his torso and suppressed it in time.

"I have his life inked on me till the day I join him and my flesh rots under the earth like his."

"It is beautiful. Macabre, but beautiful," she stated in a hushed voice.

Macabre. They were talking about Chop, but her fancy words still managed to turn him on.

"It's an honorable tattoo," she went on. "I'm certain he deserved your undying loyalty."

"He deserved more than my loyalty. He deserved my fucking death," he said bleakly.

"Perhaps he sacrificed himself because you have unfinished business to complete. Perhaps he decided that you were worth dying for."

His breath caught in his throat, about to choke him. What the fuck was it with her" It's like she could see into his soul. It was uncanny. "That's a hell of a thing to say to a man."

She dropped her finger. "It might be the truth. I know the thought gives me a margin of comfort," she confided.

She understands. No one, and he meant no one, *really* understood. Cutter was the closest, but it wasn't the same. The brothers tried, while others spouted lame-ass platitudes like, "Sorry for your loss" or "Chopper's in a better place." People handed out this shit like they handed out candy on Halloween. But those few words coming from Sage gave him relief, while also gently castigating him. Burying himself in self-pity and rage was as good as pissing on Chop's grave. A buzzing like a swarm of bees drowned out his hearing. Through it came a voice, crisp and clear. *You stubborn prick. Stop wasting my time with your moanin' and whinin'. Take life by the balls.*

Chop.

Suspicious, Kingdom loomed over Sage and tilting his head to the side, asked, "What do you know about it?"

Sage pushed her chair forward, forcing him back a step. Harshly, she yanked open a side drawer, and his gaze fell on a pair of metal slates attached to a coiled chain.

Dog tags.

They laid beside a Metal of Honor attached to blue moiré ribbon. Both were swathed in the folds of an American flag. That combo wasn't a good omen in a sister's drawer.

"My brother was an airman. Died in an ambush," she stated plainly.

"Fuck," Kingdom uttered, his voice rough with gravel. He couldn't rip his gaze away from the pristine, shiny tags and medal, resting on the bleeding red and lustrous white stripes of the flag. His hand clasped and twisted the dog tags around his own neck, hanging like a seer's pendulum. Reaching for his tags was a habit he didn't bother to break—it comforted him—but the ones she owned had only cold comfort to give.

Here he thought he was special, but the image of her head bowed over fingers caressing the soft material of the flag lacerated his chest like lashes from a strip of coarse leather. He wasn't surprised that Sage didn't know about Night Stalkers since her brother was a motorhead pilot.

He choked out, "When?"

"A little over a year ago." She let out a heavy sigh as if she alone held the weight of her grief. "Experts postulate that the worst of it is over after a year. You know, I have moments when it's as if the officer is right in front of me, telling me that Jordan's gone. The past is a recurring feature in my present."

She fixed her attention to the fringe of the rug beneath her. "All I have left are these." She coasted over the metal and cloth. "Jordan's remains were returned in a body bag."

Slamming the drawer closed, she lifted glistening eyes up

to him, but no tears fell. "For three months, I wore heavy mascara to keep from crying. I thought that if I ruined my mascara, then I'd failed him, but the honest truth is that I was afraid to cry. If the floodgates swung open, I'd drown in a sea of tears." She swiped the air in a gesture of frustration. "A gravestone, a medal, dog tags, and a flag. Four items." The last two words were so muted Kingdom barely heard them. Her grief gripped his heart like an armored fist, squeezing the breath out of him.

"I've been told that my anger shows a lack of gratitude because he was a true patriot; he died serving his country. He died doing what he loved and believed in, and I don't begrudge him his choice, but it gives me little solace. Selfish of me, I know, but I simply don't have it in me to care," she finished with a small shrug.

Motioning to the drawer, she leaned in close to him and murmured, "I'll tell you a secret. On my worst days, I wear them. As if having them on me somehow keeps a part of Jordan alive. Nonsense, of course. He's gone. There's nothing actually left of him to console me."

Drawing in a bracing breath, Sage lengthened her spine and seemed to wrap herself in an invisible cloak of composure. As a rule, he believed that weakness was useless, but it nearly killed him to witness Sage barricading herself behind a wall. She hadn't lied about the tears. Whereas most women wept in their retelling, she didn't shed a single tear. He'd seen countless crocodile tears from bitches, but Sage remained clear-eyed. She shook her head. "I never talk about him."

"Guess my tat is your flag, but like you, it isn't enough."

Sage smiled tenderly. "It's a beautiful tat," she repeated. "You did right by Chop."

Christ, the way she spoke Chop's name so intimately hobbled him. No one spoke his name, especially his nickname. Kingdom didn't allow either, but her innocent utterance irrevocably bound her to Chop. An uncanny sensation crept up his spine and pricked the nape of his neck. It was as if she'd invoked him by speaking his nickname aloud.

Kingdom blinked and saw a vague outline of Chop standing behind Sage, laying his hand on the crown of her head. With a wry smile tugging at his mouth, Chop looked straight at him. A chin lift, and he was gone. He shook his head but couldn't shake off the vision of Chop anointing her as precious, like a damned priest. She was strong as hell, but she was alone and vulnerable. By putting her in his safe-keeping, it meant by default that she had become Kingdom's.

Breaking into Kingdom's trance, she gestured to her desk and said, "Well, thanks for coming by to show me the tat, but if there's nothing else, I have an enormous amount of work waiting for me."

Does she think she can dismiss me like a child? Hell fucking no.

Stepping into her space, he leaned down and firmly grasped her chin. Tilting her head to make eye contact with him, he spoke in deliberately measured words, "I move when I'm damned well ready."

Dropping his hand, Kingdom planted his feet wide and crossed his arms over his broad chest. "I have an issue to take up with you." Her eyes flared wide in surprise. Pointing to the wall separating her office and home space, he said tightly, "You fucking live next door to your office, where your clients, who are *criminals*, know where you sleep at night. Are you insane, woman?"

"I don't work with criminals," she retorted.

"Keep tellin' yourself that until the day you get attacked or raped." Kingdom's finger pointed at her. "I gotta go, but I'll be back later to deal with you."

"W-what?" she blustered, rising from her chair to challenge him.

He didn't budge, the space between them so tight they shared the same air.

"I'm coming back at nineteen hundred hours. Wear a jacket. Spring in Poughkeepsie at night is still cool and we're riding."

"What are you talking about?" she asked, true alarm raising her voice.

Kingdom placed his fists on his hips, huffed out, and looked up at the ceiling as he reached for patience. Like empathy, he didn't do gentle, but considering Chop's dramatic messaging, Kingdom would *try* to handle her with kid gloves. Rephrasing, he declared, "I'm taking you out tonight."

"If this is you requesting a date, you forgot to end your request with a question mark," she replied.

"There was no fuckin' question mark because I don't ask; I take what I want."

"I don't doubt it," she snipped back, "but let me make my position clear: I do not follow commands like a dog."

"I'm not gonna stand here and argue with you. You have two choices. Either you're ready to go when I come back for you, or I will *hunt* you down, drag you over to your house, strip you, and get you ready to ride with my own damned hands. I suggest the first option 'cause I'm not in a patient mood, and you are nowhere ready to take what I'm ready to dish out."

Sage's mouth gaped. She snapped it shut and opened it again, attempting to speak. Without a backward glance, Kingdom swept out of her office, crossed the reception area, and left.

Once outside, he took in mouthfuls of air. *What happened to kid gloves? Good question.*

9

———

SAGE

Sage gaped at the door quaking in its frame, stunned.

What just happened?

The guy had shown such sympathy when she'd told him about Jordan, but a second later, his sharp tongue shot flames, leaving her trembling with indignation. How dare he boss her around as if she were a simpering idiot? It didn't matter how sexy he was. A chauvinist pig was a chauvinist pig.

She took her seat and flipped open her laptop. Poking at the keyboard, she entered her password and slumped into her chair. As she waited for it to load, she ticked off her objections on manicured nails. One, he was arrogant. Two, he was a stranger. Three, he was sexy but sexy-dangerous, not sexy-sweet. Four, he rattled her.

She had bared her soul to him, and when she was at her most vulnerable, he'd turned from Jekyll to Hyde. He wasn't stable, that much was obvious, and she meant to avoid him at all costs. If he wasn't a mistake waiting to happen, then she didn't know what was.

Her eyes caught the row of books on her library shelf across from her desk, light glinting off the gilded spines. Stanton had given her the vintage leather-bound set of the 2nd American Edition of *Blackstone's Commentaries* when she was admitted to the Bar. Despite the pony show, she didn't have the heart to burn them like the other mementos she'd tossed into the bonfire Camilla had ignited behind the tattoo shop after their final break. Those books were a reminder of her past mistakes.

Now, how to get out of this predicament? She tapped her nails on the smooth wooden surface of her desk. She couldn't text him to cancel since she didn't have his cellphone number. Standing him up wasn't an option because he knew where she lived. He was clearly not the type to simply let it go.

He used the word *hunting.* There was no doubt that he was an avid hunter. If she evaded him like a long-awaited challenge, he'd give chase. Her best chance was to appear dull and uninteresting, the opposite of the biker women who surrounded him on a daily basis. Surely, he'd lose interest quickly.

If that didn't work, she'd make him work for it. Flipping open the legal file she'd been working on before his visit, she flicked through a dozen pages until she found what she'd been working on. That man didn't know how to reel in a woman. Reeling was different from hunting. It took patience and perseverance. Sage chuckled at the idea of Kingdom suffering through a get-to-know-each-other coffee date, or worse still, a dinner-and-movie date. A date, not a hook up. She intended to bore him out of his mind and act hard to get. Guaranteed, the combo would turn him off.

Sage lifted her eyes from the file and expelled a soft sigh.

Earlier, when he'd loomed over her, she had caught the scent of him, loamy earth and raw musk. Her tongue darted out and licked her bottom lip. *Hmmm.* She could practically taste him on her palate. If she dared herself to go for it, to do what her body was willing her to do, she'd run her fingers through his chest hair and down his abs, then loosen that large metal belt buckle to discover the treasure underneath. Get the chance to look at the demon and bike tattoo she hadn't had the where-withal to examine when his bare torso was inches from her face. But, it couldn't be helped. The man was surly, uncouth, and violent.

The trick was to tread carefully, like stepping over the flicking tail of a vigilant tiger. He certainly resembled a savage panther on the prowl. Pity, because when he chose to act civilized, she felt a kinship with him. Kingdom was nothing more than a trap, dangling in front of her eyes the glittering possibility of sex and intimacy. The chances of intimacy were close to none, but sex ... he certainly embodied sexual gratification. She'd love the chance to climb that big, rugged body of his like a tree.

Sage swatted away the temptation. He'd never be worth the pain a man like him would bring to the table. Although it was a judgement based solely on his looks, he didn't seem like a keeper, and she didn't think she'd survive another Stanton repeat. Stanton had schooled her in the ways of untrustworthy men. He may have been rich and helped pave the way for her when she graduated with debt, but discovering that her fiancé had cheated on her only weeks before her wedding date was enough for her to swear off men for two whole years.

What she needed to do was avoid complications and focus her energy on building her practice. She was the sole owner of her law firm, and people depended on her. Plus, she had school loans to pay, and no one else was picking up the tab. A relationship took time and energy, neither of which she had to spare.

The plan, then, was to appease Kingdom. Go on a ride with him. Do whatever he wanted with one non-negotiable caveat.

No sex.

10

KINGDOM

K ingdom sauntered into the Squad clubhouse and walked up to the bar, where Cutter and Puck were posted in their regular seats.

Puck greeted him with a chin lift and said, "Good thing you're here, 'cause we have a situation with the Hellions that Prez wants addressed to-fucking-night."

The edges of Kingdom's mouth sloped down. The Squad made more than a quarter of their income from Rhode Island, but the Provincetown Hellions MC were wanting a larger cut than they deserved for allowing the Squad to work in their backyard.

"Aw, fuck, I've got something at seven that I can't miss."

Puck arched one eyebrow. "What in the hell can you not miss when we have the Hellions breathin' down our necks?"

Cutter gave his signature smirk. "It's the chick, isn't it? The one from the tattoo shop. Kingdom's running after tail."

"Tell me it ain't so." Puck laughed.

Cutter snagged his gaze and canted his head to the side. "Oh, it's true. I can see it in his eyes, and I know for a fact he hit her up earlier today."

"Instead of focusing on me, why don't you focus on the fact that we have a problem with the Hellions that'll only get worse?. We worked our asses off to get the distribution channels set up and secure. They want more than they deserve, the bloodsuckers."

It wasn't worth starting a war, especially since it wasn't their territory. Not with Prez going through his first round of chemo.

Cutter picked up his cellphone and shot off a text. A few seconds later, a notification went off, and he checked it. He stood. "Loki's coming down. Let's see if Prez is free and get this over with now."

"Where's Tank at?" asked Kingdom.

"He's already in with Prez," Cutter replied over his shoulder.

They made their way to Prez's office, and Cutter knocked on the door. He pushed it open slightly and poked his head in. Prez's voice came out, telling them to come in. They stepped inside just as Loki strolled down the hall.

"Thought we'd take care of this now. Kingdom's busy later."

The men took their places. Cutter and Loki sat on the couch, and Kingdom and Puck braced themselves against the wall. Tank was in the chair and gave them a "Yo."

"Kane is becoming a pain is what's going on. Don't know what's gotten up his ass lately. We set up this deal with him and no problems. Suddenly, fifteen percent for sitting on their asses while another club does all the work isn't good enough for the Hellions. I've known Kane for years, and he's not a hothead, but he's not letting it go. It's internal club politics."

"We need to get intel on what's going on inside their club. Cutter, you know any of the biker bitches there?"

"Yeah, a few. I can hit them up. Get them talking."

"You do that," agreed Prez.

"In the meantime, though, it's better to look for other opportunities," advised Loki. "Whatever's happening over there can get worse. From the looks of things, it's not going our way, and we can't afford any interruptions in our income stream. Let's find other avenues that could reap in greater profit with less stress."

"Canada's gonna be increasing their vice tax on cigarettes," noted Kingdom. "They're gonna be hurting soon. We have a few contacts up there. I'll put out feelers."

"Problem with the potential destabilization of the Hellions is that it can lead to unpredictability," commented Loki. "Unpredictability can lead to violence."

"True that," chimed in Cutter, tapping his Zippo lighter on his knee. "Bikers like a good fight when ain't nothing wrong. Get them stressed..."

"Which means we need to be careful. They can cut us off at the knees at any time. Break our contract and shut down our access to our customers in Rhode Island."

"You tell Kane about the chemo, Prez?" asked Puck. Each man stilled. He quickly added, "I know you guys are friendly. Shoot the shit. Go to strip clubs together. Just wondering."

Kingdom cringed internally. Prez had been diagnosed not long before, and it was not a subject the brothers were comfortable bringing up. But Puck was a favorite of Prez's. He was like a son to him, so he had the ability to venture places where other brothers tread carefully.

"No offense taken, son. I have. He's got an old lady who's hurting."

"Then they can see us as weak," stated Tank.

"Yeah, it's a problem. Alright. So the plan is to watch our backs and start looking to widen our distribution avenues while we wait for Cutter to come back with the info we need about the Hellions."

"Info is power," mused Cutter aloud.

"Time is on our side. They have no incentive to hurt us at this point because we're still paying them. Even if they have plans to take over our position inside their state, that takes time. No one ever wants to lose out on easy money, which is the kind we provide them."

"What you say is true, Prez, but we can never be too careful." *Especially now.* An unease settled in Kingdom's chest. For the first time, he didn't like what was happening. Normally, he was gung-ho about getting his fists dirty, if it came down to a fight, but Sage wasn't of their world. He'd never forgive himself if she got hurt as a result of being associated with him. If there was trouble coming, she didn't have to be his old lady to get caught in the crossfire.

11

SAGE

Sage heard the pipes of Kingdom's motorcycle long before he arrived.

She wondered how she missed the loud sounds bursting through the air when he'd stopped by earlier. Really, the motor or pipes or whatever they were called were so noisy, she feared neighbors would complain. The bike's engine shut off, and the silence was followed by the scuffing of boots on the sidewalk leading to her front door.

She swung the door wide open just before he pressed the doorbell. Sage took one glance at him and deflated a little. *He looks good. Too good for words.* Clutching the doorjamb, she sucked in every detail of him.

He'd changed into a clean pair of jeans and a long-sleeved shirt branded with the logo of his motorcycle club. He still wore the vest with various patches. At the tattoo shop, she'd overheard his friends refer to their vests as "cuts." The

Germanic script of his motorcycle club's name was the same one Angel had etched on his tat. *He may look good, but remember that a man like that doesn't stay with one woman.*

His eyes roved over her, and she smoothed her moist palms on her waist-length leather jacket. She'd purposely worn it because it showcased the trimness of her waist, one of the few areas of her body she was satisfied with, and it matched the tightest jeans she owned. Finally, she brushed her hair until it gleamed, and put on traces of makeup. If she was doing this "outing" with him, then damn him, she was going to do it looking sexy.

The amber glow of his eyes darkened. He was pleased, and she imagined he was no easy man to please. His inquisitive gaze moved past her to check out her home, but she shifted to block his view. Her home was sacred, and she was too nervous to risk having him in her personal space. She gave him a tight smile and announced, "I'm ready."

Reaching for her hand, he stroked the base of her thumb and murmured in a low baritone, "Easy."

He took the keys from her hand, waved her to step out of her house, and locked her door behind them. A crease formed between his brows as he canted his head to the side, examining the cheap lock. He returned her keys to her, grasped her by the shoulders as if he expected her to flee, and led her to his bike. Sage circled the motorcycle as he got on, taking her time to check out its sleek lines. Her mouth went dry as she drank in the beautiful luster of the chrome. Her gaze fell to the cylinders, "How fast can it go?"

"The max is around 120."

"You are not breaking the speed limit with me on the back of that monster."

His lips twitched. "Don't worry, babe, I know you're a virgin, so I'll take it *real* slow. Break you in easy."

She felt her cheeks flame, but she managed a coherent response, "How did you know?"

"That this is your first ride? Your cheeks are flushed, but your eyes are scared."

"You've had experience with virgins," she teased.

"Not many," he replied seriously. "Since entering the Squad, I've moved in a world of bikers, biker bitches, and hangers-on."

She slanted her head to the side, her brows furrowing.

"Hangers-on are people who like to hang out with bikers but aren't members of a club. Part of the social scene," he clarified. "And before your panties get twisted up in a knot, 'biker bitch' is a term women who are part of a club use to describe themselves, so keep your judgments to yourself."

She nodded readily enough because her blood was thrumming with excitement. That was, until the motor came to life. The deafening noise had her jumping back, her heart pounding out of her ribcage. Eyeing him carefully, she said, "Not many, you say."

"Babe, I'd never let any-fuckin'-thing happen to you on the back of my bike. We'll start slow, but if you get nervous, tap my thigh three times and I'll slow down."

"Okay." She exhaled. "I appreciate your ... restraint."

"You have no fuckin' idea," he rumbled.

"I may let you go faster the second time." Her eyes darted to his, and she shook her head ruefully. "I mean, if there's ever a second time."

Kingdom corrected her promptly, "You can guarantee there'll be a second time." Handing her a helmet, he motioned behind him in an unvoiced command for her to take her place on his bike. Sage hung back, considering the seat behind Kingdom. There didn't seem to be much room, and she had absolutely no intention of plastering herself against his back.

Spotting a foot peg, she knew to prop her foot on it but wasn't sure how to lift herself up without holding onto him for balance. It had been easy for him to swing on, considering he was over six feet tall.

He watched over her shoulder without offering a word of advice. She bit the inside of her cheek to hold back a sharp retort.

Kingdom grinned, clearly enjoying himself, the jerk. "I ain't got all night."

Sage shot him a quelling look. On the occasions she saw bikers riding past her, breaking speed limits like it was nothing, she felt a yearning to be on the back of one of those bikes and wrap herself tightly against a stranger's back. The way they flew through space gave her an indescribable sense of freedom.

Gingerly, she placed a hand on his shoulder. The hard muscles bunched under her hand, and a jolt of energy zinged up her arm as if she'd had an electric shock. She swung a leg over the seat but let go of her hold too quickly. Slamming down hard on the seat behind him, she grabbed the sides to prevent from tipping them over. Sage narrowed her eyes at him when she caught a slight uptick of his mouth. He'd better not be smirking, or she'd fly off the bike and swoop back into her house before this farce of a date even got a chance to begin.

Before she could do anything, a loud, rumbling noise burst out of the pipes. Sage grabbed his waist with a short yelp. She shimmied around until she found a comfortable position. Wonder suffused her as the intense purr of the bike thrummed between her thighs, distracting her.

"Don't take your feet off the pegs, and watch out for the pipes. They'll burn the skin right off your leg."

Sage loosened her fingers on his taut abdomen.

"Hold on tight," he instructed.

She laced her fingers but didn't hold on any closer.

"Tighter, woman."

Sage took a sharp intake of breath when large hands landed on her hips, glided over her ass and thighs, and dragged her forward. Her breasts were crushed against his back, and her arms wrapped firmly around his torso.

"More," he demanded.

She strengthened her grip.

"Yeah, like that," he replied gruffly. He revved up the motor and sped forward.

12

___

KINGDOM

Kingdom suppressed a groan.

Christ, her tits felt good on his back. He liked his women with large tits. Didn't care if they were real or fake if he had tits and hair to hold onto while he mounted them from behind. Sage satisfied in both categories, and then some. Her slim waist and wide hips made him revise his opinion about his requirements.

When she opened the door and he got a look at her sexy little outfit, fuck if his cock hadn't ballooned in his Levi's. Third time, and his physical response only sharpened in ferocity. He was bad off if he was looking forward to giving a woman a ride.

Back in her office, the order to ride had spontaneously popped out of his mouth. Brothers had different rules about having women on the back of their bikes. Some gave rides to anyone. Some gave rides to none. He might pick up or drop off a woman here and there, but he didn't *ride* with a bitch on his back. Till tonight. With Sage.

But she was no easy conquest and required different tactics. Since becoming a brother of the Squad, it was biker bitches or hangers-on. Other women? He looked, but he didn't taste. But civilian or not, his dick stood up for her. He paused at the first light and inhaled the scent of her. Fucking hell, she smelled like vanilla and malt. The pressure in his eardrums amplified, and he swallowed through the lump in his clenched throat. She shifted her butt, inadvertently rubbing her pussy against him. Desire shot through his bloodstream like salmon swimming against the current to spawning grounds.

"I'll start slow. Follow the way my body moves when I take a turn, and I'll do the rest. Trust me, I won't let anything happen to you."

"Trust you," she muttered into the leather of his cut. "Easier said than done."

Kingdom responded with a husky chuckle. His blood simmered when she smarted off. As an officer of the Squad, Kingdom lived a life of crushing responsibility. Despite her quip, he felt honored by the trust Sage placed in him. Her reliance on him roused a primitive instinct to protect the female at his back. With her supple body pressed against his back and her soft thighs cradling his, his cock ached.

The muscle of his jaw ticked. He was damned close to stopping the bike on the side of the road and draping her over it with the motor running under her tits. He'd kick her legs open and place her hands in a hold behind her back. She'd twist around to toss a dirty stare his way, maybe throw him some shade. He planned to answer her all nice while taking out his cock and prepping it with a stroke or two. After making sure her pussy was primed and weeping for him, he'd plunge inside and teach her the definition of a rough ride.

By the way she was unconsciously rubbing herself behind him, she might give it to him, but he wouldn't take what her body was offering. He was a consummate card shark, and he'd play his hand right. He hadn't met a woman as wound up as Sage, but he'd caught a good whiff of an untamed feline beneath her steel armor. Sage might not realize it, but from the way she was moving against him, she was long overdue for an explosion. When she let loose, he'd be there to take advantage of her feeding frenzy. He'd tame that wildcat, but he'd make sure she was docile to his hand only.

✵✵✵

Sage stifled a squeal as Kingdom curved around a bend. Her nerves were as strained as an elastic band stretched to its limit, but her skin tingled with excitement. He must have thought she was terrified because he slowed down and continued to ride in residential neighborhoods. Focused on calming herself, she molded herself against his back. Once her hands stopped trembling and relaxed their grip on the taut muscles of his belly, he sped up by increments. Finally, they left the city behind until they were steadily riding past field after field. As Kingdom accelerated, her hyper-vigilance was snipped off like raggedy tresses from shears in a hairdresser's hands.

She hadn't felt so alive, so present in her body for so long. She'd practically given up hope after Jordan's death. It had toppled what was left of her resilience after the disastrous breakup with Stanton.

The wind rushed over her face, flinging her locks wildly around her helmet. The vibrations of the bike between her legs rippled up to her breasts, titillating her nipples into hard buds. The cleansing wind, the blurry scenery sweeping past her, the deafening roar of the pipes, and the throbbing pulses of the bike were mindblowing. Her lips spread into a wide grin, and shouts of delight almost burst out of her. For once, there was no past, no future, only the present.

Sage tightened her arms around him and flung her head back. A rush of air caught her throat and whipped against her skin. Her freedom was due to the solid male she clung to like a spider monkey. Sometimes it was okay to let a man take control. *Huh, what a strange thought.*

After what seemed like a fleeting moment in time, they were back on streets that she recognized. She grasped his waist tighter, praying for him to ride past her house so that she could stay suspended in the rumbling metal and rushing air. To her disappointment, Kingdom glided back into the quiet of her neighborhood and parked. Turning off the motor, he gave her time to adjust to the absence of the breathing bike. Despite the stillness, her skin continued to crackle with an adrenaline rush. It was time to let him go, but her arms were unwilling to break their bond. Kingdom blew out a breath. Was he as affected by their ride as she was? *Pfft, please.* Men were unreliable and fickle. It was best to keep that in mind, especially around him.

Unlatching her hands, she fumbled with the buckle of her helmet. *Ugh.* In the end, Kingdom helped her unbuckle it and slip it off her head. Tendrils of hair stuck to her hairline. Her hands fluttered to her hair, attempting to untangle the knots.

Sage stretched her arms above her head and gushed, "That was fantastic. I loved it, loved it, loved it!" She glared at him and reproved in a light tone. "We didn't need to come back so soon."

Sliding off the bike, she felt bereft of the heat of his body.

She fidgeted with the buckle of the helmet, and her eyes flitted back and forth from her front door to his bike. Obviously, she didn't want to encourage him, but she was in an exhilarating mood and didn't want the night to end yet. She didn't want to relinquish being close to his warm, hard body. "Do you"—she cleared her throat—"would you … like to come in for a bit?"

"Nah, I'm good."

"You're leaving? Just like that?"

Kingdom shrugged in an easy manner.

"That is not a real date," she accused.

"Didn't see you inviting me in before we went for a ride," he observed. "I didn't promise you a date. I said we'd ride. The ride is over."

Her gaze cut into him like a surgeon's blade, sharp with hurt. Sage thrust the helmet into his chest, and he grunted at the impact.

Securing it to his bike, he beckoned. "C'mere."

She crossed her arms over her chest. "No."

A dark eyebrow raised into a perfect arc. He waited her out as if she were a petulant child, and heat flashed in her cheeks.

"I am sorry for not inviting you in when you arrived. You've been exceedingly kind to give me a ride and it was … it was magnificent." She cast her eyes down, pressure inexplicably building behind them. "I suppose I wasn't ready for it to end."

"Your first ride can't be too long or rough, and I gotta go."

"Oh."

His pause made her suspicious. It was as if he wanted to get rid of her. The thought took the wind out of her sails. She was about to sniff and rubbed her nose to disguise it. "Of course you do. Well"—she cast a glance towards her house—"I guess this is it."

His lips thinned into a straight line. "I don't remember

saying this was it. Don't fucking pretend you don't know what's up between us."

"I really don't think that's a good idea. I mean, I'm sure it would be ... if we were to..." Her voice dropped as she imagined his bare body towering above her. "...hook up, but I'm not into that."

Affronted, he snapped, "Did I say we'd hook up, woman?"

Red heat stained her cheeks. Sage held the sides of her face to conceal the worst of her humiliation. "I'm sorry. I made an incorrect presumption."

"You presumed fucking correctly," he retorted. "Oh, I'm gonna fuck you, babe."

His response should have been insulting, but she was too relieved to hear that he wanted her. Tugging her against his intractable body, he whispered against her temple, "I'm going to work you over, sweetheart. With this tight little body"—his palm coasted over her breast—"you need taking care of, and I mean to be the man to do it."

His heat suffused her, warding off the coolness of the night, and his heady scent enveloped her like a warm stole. Sage arched her back and pushed into his hand like a cat in want of stroking. His palm smoothed her back in circular motions, moving languidly down to pause at the small of her back, where he pressed his advantage. His hands moved faster, one massaging her breast possessively, while the other brushed between the apex of her legs.

"The only man, feel me? No one gets to this pussy but me," she heard despite the pounding in her eardrums. Her flaming skin and the slickness between her thighs began to overwhelm her. As she twisted to escape his hold, her hand landed and slid down the rack of muscles running down his torso.

Embarrassment and shame teamed up on her. Heart

punching against her ribs, she went on the attack. "You don't have the right to tell me what to do or speak to me like that."

Her gaze fixed on the reflection of her porch light on the wheel of his bike to avoid his piercing gaze. The truth was that his words, explicit and dirty, caught fire inside her, begging her to accept his advances.

Flexing his arms around her to keep her close, Kingdom chuckled. "Tellin' it like I see it. I like the fight in you, though." He tilted his mouth to the top of her ear and licked the sensitive outer edge. "You're wet for me, aren't you?"

"I am not!"

Without loosening his hold, he pulled back from her. "If I reach into your panties, you telling me you won't be wet?"

She began to struggle, but her hands had a mind of their own and went from resisting to questing. Horrified, she tracked the movement as they fanned out over his six pack and caressed down to the ridge of his cock. *Oh god, he's hard. And large.* She squeezed down and felt his shaft jump, but an instant later, she threw her hands up. She tried to step back, to put distance between them, but his hold tightened around her.

"You gonna make me prove it?" he taunted.

She didn't appreciate his smug tone, but she was too aroused to take him to task. Her skin was on fire, wanting more of his touch, and he attended to her silent plea.

Blunt fingertips burned their way down her front and flicked open the buttons of her jeans. Stretching her panties aside, he thrust between moist folds. She squirmed as his fingers filled her. Kingdom growled out, "Fuck, woman, you're creamin' my fingers."

He increased the tempo gently. "Baby, look at me. Let me see your beautiful face." Faster, his fingers went. "That's right. You want more, don't you?" His thrusts penetrated harder.

"I'm not hearing a yes, but I'm feelin' it. Your pussy's locking up."

"Yes, okay? Yes. Now stop talking," she gritted out between clenched teeth.

A car engine started down the block, and Sage froze. "Oh God, neighbors." She groaned and huddled behind Kingdom's broad frame as she furtively scanned the street.

He pressed her deeper into his shoulder, covering the crown of her head with his large hand. "I won't let anyone see you."

He held her securely, his fingers lodged her pussy until the car drove farther down the block and its back lights disappeared. Then, and only then, did he move his hand. His fingers pulled out and rubbed liquid heat around her clit, coaxing her back to him. She thought she heard a choking sound, but then he flicked the tight bead, and her attention jerked back to his magical fingers. His thumb swirled as his fingers sank back into her core. A volt of electricity from his digits swept up her spine and popped in her ears. Her knuckles turned white against his t-shirt, clutching the muscle connecting his shoulders and neck.

Bolstering her up, Kingdom said, "Fuckin' A, I wasn't planning to touch you, but your fat tits crushin' my chest and your cunt suckin' on my fingers is hot as hell. Baby girl, if you like my fingers so damn much, you're gonna love my cock."

❋❋❋

KINGDOM WANTED to lift her up, take her into her house, and fuck her to oblivion, but if he did that, he'd give her a reason to reject him. Sage was worth the long game. The way she had reacted to the ride had chipped at his bruised ego with the ease of a freewheeling mallet. It was perfect—not blasé, greedy, or crowing with triumph, but pure, unspoiled joy. She was already halfway toward a climax. He should pull away, leave her wanting more, but he chose to take his revenge in a different manner.

Plunging his fingers deep inside her heat, she cried out in a riot of need. His free hand gripped her ass to keep her right where he wanted her as he stiffened his fingers and goaded her on with a relentless assault on her G-spot. Her arms wrapped rigidly around him, and Sage heaved out spasms as she came. Her features twisted in a beautiful crescendo as she took her pleasure. His dick could pound nails, it was that hard. A rush swept over him as if a speedball of coke and heroin had bum-rushed his system.

He pulled his fingers out before he lost his self-control and ended up doing more than he intended. The plan was to give her only a taste but leave her wanting more. Hands shaking, he peeled Sage off him with difficulty and forced her up to her feet. Shuddering, she wobbled. His hand shot out to keep her steady as he sucked his fingers into his mouth and slurped her clean off him. Her taste was sweet and musky, light and dark. Most definitely addicting.

Kingdom's eyebrows knitted. He instantly regretted his action. He should've smeared her raw scent on his face from nose to chin. Drown in her smell. Later, for cold comfort, he'd jack off to the fantasy of her straddling his face and smothering him in the scent of her sweet-tasting pussy.

He took in her glowing face and glittering eyes, holding himself back from tangling his fingers in her tousled hair and devouring her mouth.

Even though her lithe body was heaving and shivering

before him, he stood firm in his intention to leave her aching for more. She came, technically. But the stark look on her face told him it had only whet her hunger for more. He'd ejaculate by the time he got inside, but if the tightening of her pussy walls around his fingers was anything to go by, it would be well worth the wait.

His dick might be in agony, but his chest puffed out in boastful pride. "Can't wait to feast on that honey of yours, sweetheart."

Her palms raised, then slammed against his chest. "You bastard, you did this on purpose. You pulled your fingers away, leaving me feeling itchy," she accused.

"You came, right?" he returned with blistering menace. "What the hell are you pissed off about?"

"Just barely," she muttered, landing a few more swats on his chest. Panting, she glared him down like an Amazon warrior ready to do battle.

"Gotta go, but thanks for the taste. It sharpened my appetite. I'm busy for the next couple days, but once I'm free, I'll be stopping by for a taste of that pussy."

He wasn't, of course, but he had to regroup and give her time to wallow in sexual frustration. Wagging a finger between the two of them, he declared, "To avoid any confusion, this is happening." Taking advantage of her shock, he leaned over and placed a smug kiss on her lips.

Sage sputtered, "You can't order me around."

"Newsflash, baby. I did, and I'll do it again. Best get used to it."

Leaving her spitting with rage on the sidewalk, he revved up his bike and rode out.

13

SAGE

Gazing out of the bay window of the café, Sage lifted a cup of steaming cappuccino to her mouth.

She had managed to get away from the office for a block of uninterrupted time to finish the memorandum for Judge Costner and opposing counsel.

Across the street, a disturbingly familiar figure parked his motorcycle. She squinted to make sure, but there was no doubt about it. It was most definitely the same man who had given her a ride and left her only marginally on the side of satisfied.

A full day had passed before she'd gotten over her fury at him for abandoning her, because yes, she'd felt abandoned. If he had the time to get his hand down her pants, then dammit, he had the time to ride out her orgasm. He'd left her hanging on purpose. She was sure of it. That was over three days ago, and she still woke up hot and bothered by dreams reenacting that night.

The cup halted in midair when she noticed two small, feminine hands clasped around Kingdom, rubbing his abdomen. Her vertebrae clicked into place as she stiffened, and her cup clattered against the ceramic plate.

The woman leaned over, laughing as her nimble fingers rippled over the hard ridges of his chest. Irritatingly gorgeous, the young woman plastered herself against Kingdom as if she had a claim on him. She obviously did if her hands were all over him. Gorgeous Girl got off his motorcycle and hovered near him.

"She can't be a day over twenty. Practically a girl." She sniffed under her breath indignantly.

Suddenly, sweat lined the bottom of her thighs and stuck to the wooden seat, gluing her to her spot in this humiliating voyeurism. A streak of jealousy struck her like a sharp smack across her cheek. Sure, she was betraying the sisterhood, but envy was trapped in her throat nonetheless.

Gorgeous Girl flipped her hair and leaned deep into Kingdom, and Sage's fingers curled into themselves. It was like watching a train wreck; she was helpless to stop it but unable to look away. Apparently, she had been willing to look over his serious asshole qualities in the real belief that they had made a connection. In the end, she'd allowed lust to cloud her judgment. Her hand grabbed the cup roughly, and hot liquid spilled over her laptop and skirt.

"Idiot!" she cried out as she grabbed paper napkins from the dispenser on her table, mopping up the mess and dabbing at her clothes.

An older man at the adjacent table smiled at her kindly. "Here." He bent over, catching drips of liquid off the edge of the table. "Let me help."

"Oh, thanks so much. Sometimes I'm clumsy," Sage said.

"Messes happen," he replied as he took the soiled napkins from her and threw them into the trashcan by the door.

Indeed. Messes do happen. She thanked him and turned back to stare viciously out the window just as the girl leaned in to plant a sloppy kiss on Kingdom. It gave her little satisfaction when he turned his head away and the thwarted woman ended up slobbering on his cheek. Her lips turned upward in a small smirk at the woman's disgruntled expression. At least Kingdom hadn't so thoroughly rejected her like that. No, he'd tortured her instead.

Gorgeous Girl wasn't easily put off, however. She smashed her big breasts against him and bent low into his ear. Again, he gave her the shrug off with a curt nod. Despite his brusque reactions, Sage's ears burned as she imagined the girl's insidious whisperings, breathy compliments, and urges for future nights.

Kingdom grabbed the helmet from Gorgeous Girl, leashed it to the back of his bike, and pressed down on the throttle. A brief roar, and he turned his bike out, leaving the woman behind without a backward glance. As he moved forward, Kingdom lifted his head as if he sensed Sage's presence, and their gazes crashed. His expression was inscrutable, except for a faint crease stamped between his brows.

No embarrassment, no guilt, not even a trace of surprise. She hadn't misread Kingdom's interest in her, but she had zero claim on him. She heard the purr of his engine coming in from the open side windows as he waited for her, giving her the choice to acknowledge him or not. A swarming buzz infested her ears. Her attention remained fixed on him. If she had been Medusa, she would have decimated him with her stare. Sage's gaze slid over to Gorgeous Girl, whose head snapped back and forth between Kingdom and Sage, a scowl nailed on her features.

With slow deliberation, Sage brought the empty cup to her mouth, pretending to take a long sip, all the while locked in a stalemate with Kingdom. Cars were piling up behind him and, with the strength of numbers, honked for him to move.

Finally, she dropped her gaze, effectively dismissing him. Her head stayed down, her heart sinking as the sound of the pipes faded away. It was for the best. Kingdom was an illusion, the mirage of an unhinged mind roaming the surface of a blistering desert. When she was ready to consider dating, she'd search for a good, stable man.

Dammit! Sage recalled that Greta, her receptionist, had given Kingdom her number to pass onto one of his brothers, promising that she would take his case. Tank, the big biker with the ugly scar from the tattoo shop, had been picked up on an assault charge and was due for a court appearance. Whatever game he was playing, she couldn't afford to turn down a paying gig. No worries, because if she became Tank's attorney, Kingdom would surely avoid her. Sage yanked open the legal folder with a sharp smack on the table, grimly keeping a death grip on the paperboard.

❋❋❋

Kami was a fucking octopus. She was new to the club and flirting with him nonstop, while he was crawling out of his skin waiting to contact Sage again. Kingdom had finally made his getaway when he caught Sage staring at him through the coffee shop window. Unlucky. She'd witnessed Kami's roaming hands on him. He didn't feel an ounce of guilt, but she would be more wary of him, and it would take more effort to get her underneath him.

Hell, he wasn't surprised when she leaned back in her chair and sipped her coffee without skipping a beat as she proceeded to dis him outright. She had a strong will, and she was confident with a healthy dose of grit. Toss in her pride, and Sage wasn't about to tolerate any kind of bullshit. He hadn't felt this alive since before Chop died.

He had put the decision in her hands to see if she wanted to deal with him then and there or wait for later. Later, it was. Unease settled into his chest because, hand to God, he hated the sadness and loss he saw on her face. Reminded of her brother's death and the ex Camilla had warned him about, the unease turned into a sharp pain.

Kingdom was supposed to meet up with Cutter and Tank at the club, but he kept on riding. Unlike most of the women he'd been with, including Trixie, in her own way, Sage's pride wouldn't allow her to cling. He suspected that she'd make a point of keeping her hands to herself. It made him want to push, bring her to her knees until she couldn't help but reach for him.

Feisty little thing. His hands gripped the handlebars, a grin breaking out on his face as he contemplated their upcoming battle. Make him work for it. Get her flat on her back, legs bent at the knees, thighs wide open like barn doors, ready for his dick. He'd take his cock in hand and rub her clit, swipe his cock along her slit, and dip in and out until she was cursing him out. He wanted her furious, yanking on his shoulders, scoring his chest, shoving up against him to get what she wanted. He'd push in an inch, his girth stretching her pulsing flesh, then make her wait. Tight as she was, he imagined her arching and grinding on his wide cockhead, trying to suck him in. He'd withdraw and watch her get mad all over again. *If you want my cock, get hold of your temper. You move when I say so.*

She'd go still, and he'd feed her another inch. She'd writhe, and he'd pull out. *No, please, I promise!*

He turned off the highway onto a sparsely populated country road and rode on.

Kingdom is in control. Say it, he'd demand, cock slathered with her juices.

After an internal fight, she'd eventually give in and say, *Kingdom is in control.*

He'd reward her with a good, hard thrust of a few inches of his cock. Then he'd stake his claim. *Who's sweet pussy is this, Sage?*

Yours, Kingdom, Yours!

Several inches later, he'd hit bottom. With his fingers biting into her ass, he'd lift her up and slam her on his cock, fucking her until they came together.

Adjusting his cock, he groaned. A good pound of stiff dick battered against his zipper. All he needed was a few strokes of his hand, and he'd blow his load. He'd give her a day or two, but then, he was back on the hunt.

14

SAGE

"Remind me why we're meeting at your apartment instead of my office," Sage grumbled, shuffling the papers in a legal file on the desk in her office.

An impatient sigh came through her cellphone followed by a gravelly voice. "You aren't going to Tank's place. It's a shithole, and the asshole's too lazy to go to your office. Only option left is my apartment."

"Which segues into my next question. Why are you the intermediary between my client and myself? I swear it's worse than going through security at a federal penitentiary."

Sage had dealt with her clients' overprotective parents and frantic spouses, but this level of handholding for a grown man was new to her.

A sharp voice echoed through the phone, "You go to jail?"

"County and federal. I mean, Shawangunk is only a thirty-minute drive from here. You do remember that I'm a defense attorney, no?"

"What the fuck?!" Kingdom bellowed into the phone. "Woman, are you insane to put yourself in danger like that? Your ass would be eaten up by the wolves."

"I've been going there for years, and it's perfectly safe. A guard trails me everywhere I go," Sage answered perfunctorily.

He let out a snort. "Doesn't make it any safer. The guards are some of the worst in the pen. No fucking way you're going inside unprotected again," he pronounced, although it resembled a growl more than human speech.

Sage put on the patient tone she used with her most trying clients. "May we return to the subject at hand and please speak about Tank?"

"No, we may not fuckin' return to the subject," he mimicked. "Not until you acknowledge that you're fuckin' done visiting those hellholes alone."

"Calm down, Kingdom, there's no need to have a panic attack," she commented, stifling a giggle. His protectiveness was so precious. Almost, dare she say, cute.

A chilling voice shuddered into her ear, "I'm not having a panic attack."

"I see I've pricked your male pride." The best course of action was to relent and then damned well do what the hell she wanted. He wasn't the boss of her. "Alright, you know yourself better than me," she said in a soothing tone. "With respect to visits to my incarcerated clients, I'll consider your opinion." *Like hell I will.* She wasn't about to let a man order her around, especially when it came to her clients. Normally, she'd tell him where to stuff his pomposity, but his feathers were ruffled. For some reason unknown to her, this issue was a trigger for him. He was a vet, and little things could trigger unusual behavior. Besides, let's face it, he couldn't be so interested in her if he was having sex with other women. The other night, she'd all but thrown herself at him and he hadn't taken her up on her offer.

Kingdom warned her, "Don't think I'm going to forget. You're going to hand over a copy of your calendar, or else I'll use my own ways of getting it, then I'll be at your doorstep at the crack of fucking dawn or whenever you're going to visit your clients."

Sage sputtered, "You wouldn't dare—"

"Fuck yeah, I would."

"I don't even see why you're getting worked up over this. I'm perfectly fine. On. My. Own. Don't think this knight-in-shining armor act is impressing me because it's not. It's bossy and annoying."

"You're our lawyer. At least, you will be after Church. Church is what we call our business meetings. The brothers will vote you in and put you on retainer. You die, and that will put more work on me. I'm busy enough as is with changes in Squad business and a switch up in partners. I'm not in the mood to look for another lawyer."

His explanation was ridiculous, which convinced her that he was having an episode of recurring trauma from older experiences. Otherwise, his bluster was inexplicable. Choosing flippancy, she replied, "Wow, your concern warms my heart."

He must have realized that he was losing ground. "Don't push back, Sage. It's my final word on the matter, and you're under my protection whether you like it or not."

Sheesh, he was sounding serious about this preposterous plan of his. Preempting him from digging his heels further, she replied, "I appreciate your concern, really I do, particularly since it's for the sake of your precious club." She couldn't resist that last little dig. She was human, after all. "I'll take your offer into consideration. Now, can we revisit our discussion later and get back to Tank since his situation is time-sensitive?"

He muttered a string of curses, which Sage pointedly chose to ignore, but he seemed to be moving in the right direction until he paused and inquired with gravel in his tone, "Wait a minute, don't tell me you make house visits to your clients?"

Sage's patience finally snapped. "Kingdom! We are not doing this right now. I'm serious. I'm really terribly busy, and I absolutely must meet Tank this morning." Sounds of a wrench, chain, or some bike thingy prompted her to repeat, "I'm still unclear why I have to go through you, but whatever. Can we just get this over with?"

"Because he's a jackass, that's why you have to go through me." Kingdom snorted. "You want to see him, then get with the program. His ass won't do jack shit if I am not breathing down his neck. You're not the only one who's got shit to do, but that's Tank for you."

She ground out, "Text me your address, and I'll be out of my office in twenty minutes. I hope that works for you."

"Fucking finally. I'm twenty minutes away from you."

"Fine," she conceded archly.

"Fine," he shot back.

Sage disconnected before the last hold on her sanity snapped.

Gathering her materials and laptop, Sage strode into the reception room and waited by Greta's desk as she listened patiently to a client on the other end of the line. Sage gazed off to the wall facing Greta's desk, where a framed poster of one of Greta's favorite Riot Grrrl bands, Bikini Kill, hung. She went retro like that. The poster, which was edgy yet appropriate enough to hang on her office wall, always put a smile on her face. Greta had recently completed her paralegal degree and was taking on more responsibilities by the day. Although their relationship had started out as strictly professional, a friendship had developed between them.

Greta's style matched her attitude. She had a bohemian edge, mixing tight leather pants with a babydoll dress, or wearing an embroidered jumpsuit with a deep V to show off a leather bustier. She looked like the offspring of a hippie and a punk rocker. Greta didn't take shit, and yet she was a favorite among their mostly male clientele. Well, what man wouldn't mind being insulted by a stunning raven-haired beauty with pink tips matching her nail polish?

Finally winding up the call, Greta disconnected and looked at Sage. "What's up?"

"I have to go to Kingdom's house to meet with Tank. Apparently, the man is incapable of making it to an appointment without a babysitter."

"Sounds about right." Greta had hinted at her past, which included bikers. "Are you alright going alone?"

"Yeah." Sage sighed. "It's just that I'm attracted to Kingdom, but he's so bossy and domineering. It's nerve-racking, and I don't get rattled. He twists me up inside, but he's a biker. That can't be a good thing." She turned red. "I'm sorry, I didn't mean to suggest that I shouldn't be interested in him simply because he's a biker."

"They can live a rough lifestyle. I'm not one to defend them, by any means, but I will say this. Get to know him before you write him off. You may end up being right, but as much as he's a biker, he's also an individual. He may surprise you."

Feeling duly chastised, Sage said, "I'm sorry, I was being totally judgmental."

"Hey, there's nothing wrong with being prudent. Especially after your last relationship." Winking, she went on, "And if you do end up being with him, just know that I will take the opposite tack and vet him thoroughly before I give my stamp of approval. He's probably a grade-A asshole."

Stepping toward the door, Sage replied, "Whew, I think I got whiplash from how fast you changed your tune."

"Just looking out for you, bosslady," she sang out as Sage closed the door behind her.

SAGE

Sage looked around as she drove deeper into the deserted industrial neighborhood of warehouses, some in use, some abandoned.

She doubted whether it could technically be called a neighborhood. Not one person could be seen on the streets. She pulled up to a warehouse that seemed better maintained than the surrounding ones. Hesitating, she peered through her front window when the roller shutter of the loading dock facing her clattered open.

A pair of worn motorcycle boots came into sight.

The shutter exposed Kingdom's body as it rattled up. A surge of heat swept through her as she took in his full glory.

He was the vision of a dark god, with thick biceps crossed over his chest, legs planted apart, and a scowl etched on his face. Ares had nothing on him. Sage swallowed and tried to conceal her reaction to him. Kingdom's lips quirked up in arrogant satisfaction, a clear signal that she was unsuccessful.

His voice came through her open window. "Better pull up closer. I'm known around here. Addicts know better than to fuck with my vehicles."

Sage threw her car door open, reached over to grab her briefcase, and stepped out of the car. Kingdom's gaze trailed down her body, taking in every detail of her suit and leaving her flushed with arousal. Jumping down, he led her up a short flight of concrete stairs, over the landing, and into a garage. There were two refurbished old bikes on specialized platforms, and tools everywhere—hanging from the walls, ranged on shelves, and organized in cabinets. The scent of motor oil, solvents, and grease hit her. It was not an unpleasant smell. There was an almost earthy scent beneath it, not at all like the ultra-clean, sanitized version of her dealership service department. She must have been lost in thought because a warm hand tugged hers. She stumbled forward and bumped against the hard muscles of his broad back.

Kingdom paused for a moment but didn't turn around. Instead, he continued and pushed her forward into the main part of the building. Sage's eyes widened with shock. She had assumed he was like a dude or a bro, or whatever the latest slang was for single men who were players. Either way, she had low expectations of his living arrangements. Instead, her gaze zeroed in on a series of intricate stained-glass windows lining the upper level of the walls, reminding her a bit of rose windows in medieval churches. Strands of light infused the atmosphere with a similar glow, as if there were arches, ribbed vaults, and flying buttresses belying the hushed aura above her.

His warehouse resembled the Soho lofts she'd seen when she was in law school in New York City. Without walls, the massive space exposed his living quarters without shame. She couldn't help but rise on her tiptoes and peer into a far corner where he had a sleeping nest. Rumpled sheets, like twisted modern sculptures, were splayed across the vast expanse of his bed. She had a vision of him sprawled out on the bed naked. *Yikes. Head out of gutter, please.*

Sage twirled around and spotted shelves upon shelves of books and LP records lining one entire wall. Kingdom was a man carved out of the raw material of willpower and determination. She wasn't surprised that he was a man with a wide array of interests.

He had a large-screen TV with a sectional couch, pool table, and other accoutrements of bachelors. Everything was of high quality. Hanging from the ceiling by an industrial chain, car wheels lined with bare light bulbs illuminated the living space below. It had taken time and consideration to create such a home as this. She hadn't expected to find a home in a seemingly abandoned warehouse smack dab in the middle of no man's land.

"Shocking," he drawled. "I don't live in a dirty hole in the wall."

"I misjudged you, and here I thought I was a pretty good judge of character," she teased.

Kingdom shrugged off her apology and motioned for her to sit down on the couch. "Hungry?"

"No, thank you. It's only midmorning, and I do try to eat a healthy breakfast since I either end up skipping lunch altogether or snacking throughout the day." Yes, she was quite aware that she overworked herself to the point that she didn't eat three square meals a day.

A possessive glare drilled into her as if to say that if she was his, he'd make sure to sustain her energy for the fucking she'd get when she was off work. His branding stare tracked her as she wandered through his place, studying the books on his shelves and caressing the spines of his LPs. Sage entered the kitchen area and stopped short. "Wow. Just … wow."

Drifting farther in, her hands glided over the black-marbled countertop of the island facing an impeccable mixture of stainless steel and marble. A masculine kitchen. There were touches of him in the poster of a vintage-looking Harley and band posters that reinforced his punk rock record collection.

"You must be quite a cook to have a kitchen equipped with these top-of-the-line appliances," she presumed.

"Nope, don't cook much. Did it for my Moms." Catching the twinkle in her eye, he snorted. "I'm not a fuckin' mama's boy."

Sage's smile broadened. "Of course not," she quipped. Sage returned her gaze to the kitchen, soaking in each detail. A kitchen like this was made for her. "I'm so, so, so jealous."

"You can cook here anytime," he offered.

Sage blushed faintly at the suggestion simmering beneath his invitation. The assumption that she'd share his space long enough to cook for him. There was a level of intimacy in cooking, if, as the saying went, the way to a man's heart was through his stomach. The same went for a woman. Her brother had been a budding cook before he changed course and went into the military. He'd stop by her dorm and cook a feast for the entire floor in the kitchen at the end of the hall. The girls teased and flirted with him. Even then, Jordan was a sucker for the attention of the gaggle of younger women.

Unlike that dorm kitchen, Kingdom's was clean. Too clean. She itched to try it out, to make it as livable as the rest of his space.

"Have you eaten breakfast?" she asked.

"Nah."

"What do you have in the refrigerator?"

"Odds and ends." Kingdom shrugged. "Why?" He smirked. "Are you going to cook for me?"

"I wouldn't mind. Does she have an apron here?"

"Yeah, the woman had everything here. Aprons. Pots and pans. Special knives." He motioned toward a set of knives nestled at a forty-five-degree angle on a butcher's block.

"Had?"

"Moms passed away from breast cancer four years ago."

His admission stunned her. He had built this beauty of a kitchen for his dying mother.

"Chop was at her bedside, holding her hand when she was in a coma. I had gone to get coffee from the vending machine. When I got back, she was gone. She'd given Chop the privilege of her last breath. In many ways, Chop was the son of her heart." Snorting ruefully, he acknowledged, "There I go again, revealing my darkest moments to you."

Kingdom crossed over to her and wrapped his fingers around her hips. Bending his head low, his lips hovered over hers. She braced for him to take her mouth. Instead, he shook his head slightly and averted his face. Tilting her head, she tried to catch his expression. It was inscrutable.

Brusquely, Kingdom moved her to the side, opened a drawer, and pulled out an apron. He dangled it by his index finger. Sage plucked it off and tied it on efficiently. Opening the refrigerator, she reviewed the contents and pulled out the basics for a vegetable omelet. Glancing over her shoulder, Sage warned, "No complaining. I'm making an omelet with mushrooms and onions."

"I eat mushrooms," he replied in an offended tone. "I was the one that bought them. I'm not a caveman who eats their meat raw after hunting down their prey. Sorry to disappoint."

"Aren't you just full of surprises this morning?" she joked.

He pulled out a mug from a cupboard above him and held it up. "Coffee? It's from earlier this morning but it's still hot."

"Sure. I can never get enough caffeine," Sage assured him with a smile. Sniffing into a carton of milk to make certain it wasn't expired she went over to take her mug of coffee. Kingdom graciously held the piping hot coffee mug with the handle out for her.

"God, that's hot! I can't believe you can hold it with your bare hand."

He held up his ten fingers and showed her the calluses on each tip. "My skin's too tough to hurt."

Sage itched to guide his rough fingertips along her cheek, then down her throat and into the crevice of her breasts. His hands would feel exquisite running over any surface of her body. Goosebumps raised over her skin.

Kingdom stilled. His hands returned to her hips and slowly drew her toward him, but this time it was Sage who backed away. Not four days before, another woman was all over him. She couldn't let him get between the fine chinks in her armor. The man was common property, and she was too possessive to share.

Sage aggressively yanked random drawers open in search of various utensils.

"Before you rip apart my kitchen, why don't you tell me what you're looking for?" Kingdom's query was laced with laughter.

Exasperated, Sage scowled.

With one hand on her cocked hip, she declared, "I'm doing you a favor!"

"Sure about that? Fucking up my kitchen is not doing me any favors."

Sage shot darts of pure menace in his direction. "You're right, of course. I should sit down and leave you to your bowl of Rice Krispies or whatever savages eat first thing in the morning."

Kingdom barked out a short laugh. "Raw meat. Savages eat raw meat, remember? Damn, babe, you're hot when you get riled up." Knowing full well that she itched to use his kitchen, he called her bluff with a shallow shrug. "Not a problem, I'm not gonna force you to cook for me."

Kingdom moved behind her and dipped his mouth close to her ear, his voice a seductive murmur. "I'd appreciate it, though. Ma'am."

Sage bit back a groan. Kingdom using that formal term of respect on her lit up her nerve endings like Christmas lights on steroids. Only with him would talking clean be as much of an aphrodisiac as talking dirty. Loitering close to her, the magnetism he wore with imperious ease melted her resolve like a stick of butter on a hot stove top during a Georgia heatwave. His profane sexuality, his alluring voice, and his obscenely beautiful kitchen was an unholy trinity too strong for her to fight. Fine, she'd cook the stupid omelet. For some ungodly reason, she was eager to do that for him.

Sidestepping him briskly, she gathered up the ingredients to prep. Kingdom tracked her progress, leaning against a counter, his legs stretched out with one ankle crossed over the other. Obscene. She blew out a sigh as she struggled to concentrate. It was really unfair.

As she prepped, Sage plotted to escape before he captured her fully. Without a doubt, he was waiting like a spider along the edge of his web, poised for a swift strike. She clutched the counter, the skin of her nape prickling as if he were about to devour her whole.

She made quick work of the meal and slid a perfect omelet onto a plate. She plopped buttered toast beside the dish, assuming he preferred his toast buttered. He pounced on the meal, and she sat by him, taking pleasure at his robust appreciation of her simple omelet.

He glanced up. "Guess I was hungry."

Sage smiled up at him. "I serve to please."

He swallowed, lowered his fork, and locked eyes on her with the intent of a predator. She was becoming familiar with that particular expression. "You please me. Soon, you'll serve me."

Sage took in a shot of breath. He softened his fierce pronouncement with a smooth, "Babe," and returned to his meal. She surged up off the chair and fled to the living room area. The image of Gorgeous Girl from a few days was superimposed on her vision, and Sage cast around for a safe place to land. Glancing over her shoulder, she saw Kingdom's mouth set in a grim, thin line.

"When did Tank say he was coming?" she asked.

"He didn't. I woke him up and told him to get his ass over here." Kingdom gave a shrug. "Hard to tell when he'll show up. Hope the idiot showers first," he groused.

Her hand fiddled with the topaz amulet on her chain as she digested Kingdom's unsatisfactory response. "Is he even coming?" she murmured softly to herself.

Finding a refurbished Amish Mission chair in one far corner, Sage settled in and scrolled through her emails as Kingdom cleaned up the kitchen. The clinking of dishes being washed, the refrigerator opening and closing, and other sounds spread over her. Her phone clattered to the floor, jolting her awake. Bending over to snatch up her cellphone, her head swiveled right and left as she got her bearings. Whew, he hadn't noticed. She suspected that he'd have some harsh words to impart if he'd caught her napping. Staying up late last night working on top of a morning dealing with

Kingdom and the reel-to-reel film roll of emotions he evoked in her had done her in.

Kingdom walked into the living room area and motioned Sage toward the couch. "Grab your shit and work here until he shows up. I've got work to catch up on." He nodded to the garage. Her shoulders sagged, but she quickly got moving.

On the couch, Sage rummaged through her briefcase with brisk movements. A sigh of frustration whooshed out from her. Kingdom was on her in a second. "What's wrong?"

"My laptop is in my car."

"Hand me your keys," he ordered with an extended hand, palm up. She extracted them from her purse and dropped them in his open hand. There were calluses on his palm and traces of black in the creases of his fingers. Answering her curiosity, he declared, "I custom build bikes."

"Impressive. I had a client who was a sculptor. Fashioned metal structures on a massive scale, and he invited me to his opening. I'd been intrigued by the way he wielded his talent in such a masculine manner."

"It's not a big deal," he dismissed. "Women don't care about bikes, except to ride them. There are females who ride. They have their own MCs." Catching Sage's surprise, he smirked. "Yes, there are female-only MCs. Lesbian-only MCs. MCs for everyone."

"All of it is pretty fascinating."

"I should have known that you would think so. Most females I know are interested in riding on the back of a bike, not hearing about how a bike works, much less how to restore one."

He'd surprised her again. His renovation of his living space, his books and records, and now this creative bent? He was Special Ops, so one would assume he was bright, but discovering such a wide range of interests increased her respect for him exponentially.

"What can I say? You have more hidden talents than I imagined."

Flashing her a grin, he rifled through a diminutive desk near the entrance, then went out. A few minutes later, Sage's laptop was set on the coffee table. Her heart jumped up in her throat, where it settled when he sat down beside her instead of going to the garage.

16

KINGDOM

Kingdom was pleased with himself.

Before leaving to get her laptop, he went through the desk by the entrance and found the putty. With the silicone material in hand, he made impressions of her keys as he walked to get her laptop from her car. You never knew when you'd need access to someone's house, and, let's face it, he wasn't letting her get away anytime soon. He shoved away the less-than-murky sense of protectiveness that gained strength the more he was around her.

She was onto him about using Tank as an excuse to see her. Her suspicions were partially true. He'd ordered Tank to come over, just a couple of hours later than he'd told her. Kingdom made certain to sit close to her.

His mood changed for the better when he caught the flutter of her rapid pulse at the base of her throat. He burned to press his tongue against her pulse, then pursue a lazy path over her collarbone and down to her breast. Her lids dipped low, and her lips parted. His finger would loop around her amulet, tug it toward him, and her body would follow.

Hot puffs of air blew against his cheek. He realized he'd inched toward her, his cheek almost grazing hers. Twisting his head, he took her mouth. Greed blasted through him. He grasped her nape to feast on her properly.

Shoving the coffee table away with his boot, he spread her legs to make way for him. He slid one hand down her torso and gripped her inner thigh. Eyes dazed, she collapsed against the couch. Transformed into a languid nymph, the rich scent of her surrender mixed with his blood. Exhaling a husky breath, she finally admitted the words he'd longed to hear. "I give up."

She had, and victory had never tasted so good.

Stroking her thigh absently, Kingdom's hand twitched to open his jeans and liberate his cock. Fucking hell, it hounded him for freedom. His other hand glided over the sinful curve of her thigh to her waist.

"I'm gonna taste you," he said. Expecting Sage to snap her legs closed, he clenched her thigh. "All you have to do, sweetheart, is sit back, and my tongue will do the work." Salivating, he promised, "I'm gonna lap you up."

Sage's pupils dilated in a sea of twilight blue.

"Give me a nod, Sage, let me know you're good with that." She nodded. "Good, baby. Beautiful," he praised her. "Now gimme a show. Unbutton your shirt for me."

Nimble fingers grazed over each button before flicking it open. His fingertips closed on her waist with more force than he realized. She flinched mildly.

He urged her on, "Keep going."

The silky blouse parted, and he was gifted with a vision of lace. Black lace strained against pale globes that rose and fell in rapid succession. He traced a dark areola with his thumb over the lace. Purring now, Sage arched into his digits, so they pressed hard on her firm nipple. Stripping her of her blouse, he unclasped her bra.

"Fuck me," he groaned when her breasts sprang free. "Plump, firm tits. Perfect," he rasped.

Leaning forward, he latched onto a raspberry nipple and sucked hungrily. Her hands crushed the flexing muscles of his shoulders. He drew in a long draught of her flesh and let it go with a noisy pop. Nuzzling between her tits, he licked swirls around her peaks. He suckled anywhere his mouth landed, leaving a staccato trail of pink marks along her tits. Taking a path down her ribs and belly, his tongue traced the waistband of her skirt. Sliding her zipper down, he boosted her up to slip off her skirt.

"The fuckin' thigh highs," Kingdom gritted out, "are killin' me."

Sage's hands twined into his hair, adding extra stimulation, but soon they twisted and yanked the curls on his head. He caught the lacy top of one stocking between his teeth and tugged. Yanking the elastic band taut, he released it with a snap. A cry escaped Sage's throat, but her breathing quickened, and he chuckled. *She's not opposed to a dose of pain. Good to know.*

Her panties were made of matching lace, and Kingdom sat back on his haunches, entranced by the shadows of her pussy and the wet spot seeping through her panties. Fuckin' beautiful. He'd hit the goddamned jackpot.

He opened his button fly to release the chokehold on his cock. Freed, his cock wept pre-come. He stroked himself as he pushed her panties to the side and dipped his tongue along the seam. Inhaling her musk, he savored the flavors of her juices.

Abruptly, Sage jerked up and shoved his forehead away. What the fuck? The shock on her face hinted that she'd never had her sugary pussy tongue-fucked before. *Nah, not possible.* No hot-blooded male could stop from gorging on a pussy like hers. He swatted her hand away and leaned in to put his tongue back where it belonged, but she tugged on his hair to dislodge him again.

"Whoa, what are you doing?" Sage asked, her brows almost reaching her hairline.

Glaring up at her, he snapped, "Woman, you don't stop a starvin' man in the middle of a pussy feast. The hell is wrong with you? Let go of my hair."

Slackening her grip, she blurted out, "Stanton said real men don't dirty their mouths in a woman's vagina."

Pounding the cushion with his fist, he barked, "I don't know who this Stanton asshole is, but I can say for sure that he's an idiot. A real man tongues and fucks every hole he feels like with everything he's got."

Sage blinked. Once. Twice. "A-are you … sure?"

"Fuck yeah, I'm sure. I said I was gonna taste you. What the fuck did you think I meant?"

Sage ran her hands through her hair.

"Christ, she still doesn't get it," he muttered to himself. Snapping his fingers in front of her face, he said, "Sage, repeat after me: you don't stop a man in the middle of eating pussy." She kept staring at him. "Come on, say it," he coaxed.

She shook her head. "I can't repeat that out loud but"— she flicked her wrist and dropped her head back against the couch—"please proceed. I must have done something really, really good in a past life to deserve this. Maybe I was a martyred saint."

Chuckling, he chided, "Yeah, yeah. Stop yapping and let me get back to it."

To emphasize his point, he ripped her panties clear off her body. Then he went on the attack, sucking cruelly on her clit while thrusting his fingers inside her core. Lifting her butt, Sage ground her pussy into his face. A sign of her untamed nature.

Kingdom kissed, licked, and nipped, curling his tongue inside her until he felt the instant she exploded on his mouth. Her inner muscles clenched on his stiff tongue, and his palate was flooded with her taste. Bucking into him like an unshackled marionette, she cried out, "Oh my God, Oh my God!"

Kingdom bit down, taking her pussy lips and clit inside his mouth, and Sage thrashed into a blinding climax.

Shooting to his feet, Kingdom bellowed out an earsplitting, "FUCK!" Tendons corded along his throat, and veins popped at his temple.

Below him, Sage averted her face as a blast of reality sliced through her, cutting off her orgasm. Hugging her legs, she buried her face in her lap and asked in a tiny voice, "What's happening?"

The sound of a lone rumbling motorcycle answered her question.

"Babe." He reached out for her, but she flinched. He hadn't meant to scare her, but he was so pissed off to be interrupted. His ears had immediately picked up Tank's bike's loud but raspy pipes. "Babe," he tried again, reaching for her slowly this time. "Shhh." She allowed him to touch her knee. "Fuckin' Tank. I'm gonna skin him like a slaughtered hog."

Eyes closed and lips pressed flat, Sage whimpered. Kingdom released the painful grip on his cock and tucked it inside. Cupping her cheek, he caressed her until she calmed down. He draped her over his lap and dropped kisses on her eyes, cheeks, and mouth. It dawned on him that he hadn't kissed her properly. Not yet. He'd been so greedy that he'd gone for her pussy first. Tilting her face up, he delved in for a deep kiss. She clasped the sides of his head, and they drank from each other intensely.

Breaking off their kiss, he brushed her puffy bottom lip with his thumb and apologized, "I'm damn sorry, darlin'. If I could, I'd get rid of him and get my tongue back into your pussy, where it should be, but that motherfucker will stay just to mess with me."

Bringing her to her feet, he swept up her garments and dressed her, one item at a time. Her eyes darted around wildly as she heard Tank cut his engine. Rage pounded in his veins. He could kill his brother with his bare hands. Holding her steady by the arm, he promised, "Gonna make it up to you, Sage. I always deliver."

Sage's eyes widened in panic. She backed away until her knees hit the couch, and she tumbled onto it. "It's better if you don't. I shouldn't have let this happen. It was so inappropriate. I usually never act this unprofessionally." She started when she heard Tank jangling the doorknob.

Ruffling his hair, he swore, "Thank fuck I locked the door."

Sage struggled to her feet and ran toward the bathroom.

Fuckin' cockblocker. He told the fucker to come by in *two* hours. Did the dumbass listen? No, the fucker had pulled this shit on purpose.

"Yeah, coming," he roared. He licked his lips. Dammit, his tongue ached for her. Never, and he wasn't lying when he said *never* had he enjoyed a woman coming on his tongue like that. Like last time, it had been cut off midway, although it was no fault of his own.

"I'm fuckin' comin'. Settle the fuck down."

Great, now he'd lost his temper. Kingdom threw the door open to find Tank lounging against the door with a sly grin on his face. He batted his eyelashes. "Interrupting somethin'?" His gaze dropped to the bulge in Kingdom's jeans. "Guess I am."

"When she's gone, I'm gonna officially kick your ass."

"Ain't nothin' you can do to kill my buzz from knowing I fucked up your game," he said gleefully.

Kingdom kicked the metal door hard enough to echo throughout the cavernous space.

17

SAGE

Tires squealed as Sage tore out of Kingdom's warehouse.

She couldn't get away fast enough. After her car had placed enough road between her and Kingdom, she allowed herself to take in a deep breath. It was official: she'd lost her mind. Hours after he had taken his mouth off her and her body was in a riot.

Slouching in her car seat, she pressed her foot on the accelerator. God, the misery of having to get through her initial consultation with Tank knowing that he knew. Pretending he hadn't interrupted her as she almost fully climaxed from her first cunnilingus ever. Astonishingly, Tank had a heart because he didn't mention what had happened before he arrived, although his eyes said he knew everything.

Distracted by the memory of his tongue, Sage screeched to a stop. Gripping the steering wheel with both hands, her heart practically jumped out of her ribcage. She'd practically run down a pedestrian.

There was a close call when she whisked past Kingdom on her way out. He was on her in the blink of an eye, caging her against the door, his thick arms planted on either side of her head.

"Stay," he ordered in a husky rumble that skittered down her spine. His deep voice held promises that put roots in her belly. She had struggled to push one of his arms out of her way, which was an act of futility considering his colossal strength and the savagery bleeding from his eyes.

"Kingdom, it's been an eventful morning, really it has, but I'm tired. I've got tons of work waiting for me at the office and two more appointments today. I can't afford to spend time away from the office if I'm going to finish the upcoming deadlines I have."

"Eat lunch with me."

Sage thumped her forehead against his chest. "Listen carefully to my words. I do not have the time. I'll grab something on the way back or ask Greta to make a coffee run—I mean lunch run." For all the love of God, she couldn't understand why she was explaining herself to him. With Jordan dead and Stanton long gone, she vowed to never be indebted to a man. Yet once again, here she was, on the verge of heartache.

Kingdom looked at her askance. "You don't eat right. You work too much. If you feel tired now and you don't take a break or eat real food, you'll be like the walking dead."

"You're not my keeper. If you want to take care of someone so badly, why don't you take care of that little girl with the skimpy dress from the other day? Make sure she has a balanced and nutritious meal. Us women have actual work to do."

Kingdom raised an eyebrow, his eyes gleaming with triumph. "Little girl? You're jealous of Kami."

"Certainly not," she retorted hotly. *Lie.* "I don't have a jealous bone in my body." *Double lie.*

"You are." He laughed.

"Stuff it!" Sage lashed out. "I'm attempting to explain that I'm a grown woman who's exceedingly capable of deciding when I eat and what I eat."

"Babe, I could care less about Kami. My mouth was sucking on you not an hour ago." A flinty gleam of determination entered his eyes. "Standing in front of me, steam shooting out of your ears with jealousy *definitely* whets my appetite for more."

She felt streaks of red bloom along her cheeks and throat. Honestly, this humiliation was too much to bear.

"You're a grown woman, yeah?" He prowled closer to her. "Then I'm a grown-ass man and you"—he flicked her beaded nipple—"are on the menu tonight. Feel me?"

"No, I do not *feel you*. What I *feel* is that we should pretend this never happened and go on with our respective lives. You get to play around with an array of women—and just for the record, I am *not* jealous—and I need to get back to my work."

A wicked smile spread over his face.

Sage grabbed his cut with her fists and begged, "Please, Kingdom, I don't have the energy to fight you, and I must go. Before I go—"

"You mean before I allow you to go."

Gah! The man was impossible. Sage ground her teeth. "We are not living in the Middle Ages. Women are no longer chattel."

"Kingdom!" came a shout from the center of the loft. He turned partway and leveled Tank a vicious look. Tank was leaning forward on the sofa, staring at the TV with a remote control in his hand. "Where's the boxing at?"

"Fuck if I care," Kingdom snapped.

Still focused on the TV, he suggested in a careful tone, "Brother, find me the fight. You'll catch up with her later." He tilted his head to the side, signaling to Kingdom to ease off.

Kingdom crowded closer to Sage. "Woman, you want to starve yourself today, have at it. But I'm giving you fair warning that I'm seeing you tonight."

Sage squeezed her eyes to shut out the swoon that almost overcame her. As much as Sage tried locking out the image of his dark head bent between her legs, her pussy relived every single sensation he had elicited.

Kingdom pushed off the wall, and her eyes snapped open. "Expect me at seven."

"I find it hard to believe that these bullying tactics work for you when it comes to dating," she said peevishly.

"I wouldn't know. I don't date."

"Of course you don't," she drawled. Her eyes snapped to his, and she rushed to assure him, "Not that we are going on a date."

Kingdom tapped a finger on her nose. "Tut, tut, tut. Now, why wouldn't we go on a date, Ms. Sage Cameron?"

"Because you don't date."

"I'm not so old that I can't change."

"Leopards never change their spots," she fired back.

Kingdom held the door open for her like a gentleman. "Lucky for you, I'm a dawg."

Sage rolled her eyes as she whisked past him.

"Seven o'clock."

"Bully."

KINGDOM

Thank fuck he'd reined himself in in the nick of time.

After throwing Tank out, he had taken off on a ride that lasted hours. Pausing at the side of a road, he pinched his brows. The ride hadn't done a damned thing to cool off his raging dick, but not to worry, there were other methods to fight his compulsion for Sage.

With lust and terror gnawing at him like a pair of jackals, Kingdom had walked into the clubhouse, stopped by the bar, and snapped his fingers at Trixie.

"Up," he ordered.

Trixie's face slacked with shock.

He hadn't touched her in months. Trixie wanted to be special but knew better than to make demands on him. It had taken a while for the brothers to respect her one-way vow of monogamy toward Kingdom.

While she wasn't an old lady, Trixie had clout in the club; it was her choice, and eventually they accepted her as she was. He wasn't changing, not for Sage, and not for any woman. Swallowing down the lie, he led the way to his crash room with Trixie in his wake.

The combination of sexual frustration and fear had driven him to this point. He was falling for that woman, and he needed to get his equilibrium back. Christ, even Tank had to tell him to back off. That was fucked up, but the best way to create instantaneous distance was to fuck another woman. He'd unload his come into Trixie, regain his sanity, and be back in control.

Easy.

Trixie hadn't finished closing the door, and his cock was already out. He gestured to her, and she knelt with a giggle. He was as hard as a rock. Problem was, it wasn't for the woman crouched before him. He wanted Sage; the taste of her was inked on his tongue like a tattoo. His eyelids were at half-mast as Kingdom envisioned Sage as she was that morning—her eyes sparkling indigo and lips pouty and red from his rough treatment.

His craving for her rode him hard. Fear of his intense attraction to her and the instant bond between them constricted his jugular like a wire noose around his throat. Sage had no idea how close he was to flipping her skirt up, taking a knee, and finishing what they'd started whether Tank was present or not. He'd been close to begging her the same way Trixie was begging him right now.

Dick in fist, Kingdom stroked himself near Trixie's open mouth. Sage's face drifted into his mind, obscuring Trixie. *Motherfucker!* Trixie swatted his hand off, stretched her lips wide, and stuck her tongue out to receive him, but the fantasy of Sage's cherry red lips wrapped around his cock short-circuited his brain. He groaned as he imagined Sage leaving a ring of lipstick around the root because he'd fucked her mouth on a workday. Jerking into Sage's mouth, red lipstick smeared on the length his shaft...

With a harsh rasp, he staggered away from Trixie and thundered, "Fucking fuck!"

Trixie extended her jaws like a gaping fish, causing bile to rise from his gut and flood his mouth.

"Your tits. Get on the bed and squeeze 'em."

Trixie leaned back onto the bed, tweaked her nipples, and squashed her breasts together. His head dropped forward in resignation. The mattress dipped on either side of her thighs as his knees bracketed her legs. Kingdom squeezed his eyes shut, and a deluge of images swept through his mind. Sage, knees to her chest, open and ready to take him. Sage, braced on her hands and knees, her head thrown back. Sage, her arms stretched wide and tied to the posts of his bed. His breath evened out with each picture.

When he opened them, his gaze fell on Trixie. He flipped off her and caught himself before he crashed to the floor. Crouching with one palm stable on the ground, he took a deep breath. He crawled toward his jeans, snagged them, and pulled them on.

"Kingdom?" Trixie asked, sitting up and looking down at him with confusion.

Gruffly, he yanked her off the bed, pushed her shirt at her, and hustled her toward the door. Trixie braced her legs and leaned back against his chest. Sliding his hands under her armpits, he hauled her forward.

Her head whipped over her shoulder. Eyes slitted, she hissed, "You're kidding me, right? You're dissing me for that bitch? Tank told me about the chick from the tattoo shop."

"Don't you dare say her name."

"She means somethin' to you? I've been waitin' on you to come back. You belong here with me!" Twisting around, she grabbed his hand. "Chopper was here the night before he died. I fucked him for you, and *this* is how you pay me back?"

Kingdom jerked his hand away, moved around her, and threw the door open.

"Christ, did you fuck Chop out of loyalty to me? If so, that's on you. I never asked you to do anything for me. Listen carefully, Trixie—I don't have a problem with you fucking another man. Whether you wanted to fuck Chop or not is not my business, but for your sake, I hope you did. Either way, I don't owe you anything, and I'm sure as hell not fucking you. End of discussion."

"Don't you want to know why he was with me?"

"Tread real lightly, Trixie, 'cause you're gonna be in a whole world of pain if you keep running' your mouth. Don't think you can use my grief against me."

"Fuck. You!" she spat out. "You're going to regret this."

Kingdom wrapped his hand around her upper arm, his face contorted in fury. He snarled, "If you wanna do you, then go for it, but don't threaten me. I don't tolerate that shit from no one. You're a fool to think you've got extra leeway because we were fuck buddies in the past."

Trixie twisted in his hold. He released her immediately. Freed, she swiped the spittle from her lips. "I hate you."

Clasping her shirt to her bare chest, she kicked at the door and stormed out of the room. Hands clenched on his hips, he puffed out his cheeks and expelled a pained breath. He felt dirty, and her cloying smell clung to him like a layer of coagulated blood. *Shower and wash her off.*

Stomping into the shower, he lathered up the soap and brought it to his nose. Once he was satisfied that he was clean of Trixie, he dried off.

His fingers paused as he wrapped the towel around his waist. A thought chilled his blood. What if Sage found out? Nah, no way she'd find out. His brothers would die before ratting him out.

19

SAGE

Sage's blurry eyes refocused on the screen of the laptop. She rubbed them, convinced she looked like hell. Pulling open a drawer, she took out a compact mirror, snapped it open, and groaned. Her eyeliner was smudged below her eyelids, and her lip gloss had faded to nothing. Laying out her makeup kit, she began fixing her face.

Her body tingled from the memory of Kingdom's hands and mouth on her. She gave a shudder. God, that was incredible. She had no idea what she'd been missing all those years, but after one taste, and she wanted to explore more with him.

Besides giving her mind-blowing orgasms the likes of which she'd never had—and she didn't consider herself a slouch in the bedroom—he'd chipped away at her concerns. His response about Kami was reassuring, subduing her fear that he was a player and nothing more.

The old round clock stationed on her bookshelf

progressed slowly. Instead of checking constantly, she should give up any pretense and simply stare at the clock's moving hands until they hit seven o'clock. Smacking her lips to evenly spread her newly applied lipstick, she felt a twinge of anxiety. Maybe Kingdom wouldn't show up. Although, the glint in his eyes had looked about as breakable as titanium.

With a huff, she logged off, snapped her laptop shut, and cradled her head in her arms. Images of Kingdom's face, strong and angular, shimmered in her mind's eye. The tint of his eyes, which shifted from gold to copper depending on his mood, stood out boldly against his olive skin. Kingdom come, indeed.

Sage startled awake to find Kingdom in front of her. Sitting up, she threaded her fingers through her hair. "I fell asleep," she said.

Propping himself on the desk, his finger coasted along Sage's jaw and traced the imprint of her laptop's logo on her cheek. Her lids hovered low at his touch, and he brushed a kiss on her lips.

"I should smack your ass for leaving the front door unlocked when you're here alone. Napping, no less. But I'm in a forgiving mood."

"I'm going to ignore any reference to smacking butts, thank you very much," she replied drily. Suddenly, the aroma of food drifted up to her, and she inhaled deeply. "Food. I'm famished."

Sage reached for the paper bags of food, but he caught her hand, his eyes dancing with mirth. "You want it, pay up."

"How much do I owe you, sir?"

"How hungry are you?" Leaning forward, he sucked gently on her lower lip. "You owe me a hell of a lot more than that. It won't be cheap."

The flush on her cheeks deepened. "You must be joking."

"I don't joke about what I want, and I want you." Her fingernails swiped at his face, but he easily deflected them, chuckling. "I'll feed you. You'll need the energy for what I have planned."

"What if I don't agree to your oh-so-gracious proposal?"

"I got my ways, mama," Kingdom declared in a cadence drenched with decadence, Cointreau oozing out of a half-eaten chocolate truffle.

"I'm speechless with gratitude," Sage replied sardonically.

"What can I say? I'm a generous man."

Kingdom took out cartons with red Chinese characters on their sides. Sage's stomach grumbled.

"Woman, did you have lunch?"

"Just give me the food."

"I brought you a nutritious meal for a real woman," he threw back to her the line she'd used earlier that afternoon. "Vegetables, protein"—he lifted a carton of rice—"carbs." He handed her chopsticks. "I assume you use these."

"I'm a believer in traditions. Humans have been eating with chopsticks long before the fork came about."

Tearing open a carton of Kung Pao Chicken, Sage popped a bamboo shoot into her mouth and moaned. The tension in her muscles vanished as bursts of ginger and hot pepper hit her taste buds.

Kingdom's expression turned hungry. "Looking forward to the taste of you again."

Sage choked on a mouthful of rice. "For crying out loud, I'm trying to eat here. Mind your manners."

Despite herself, his self-assurance stimulated a coiling heat in her core as her body prepped itself for him. She pressed her thighs together to put pressure on her throbbing clit. Kingdom caught her shifting in her chair. Dropping his chopsticks into the carton, he swore. "Christ, woman, you're wet for me."

Sage avoided his stare and repeatedly stabbed at her food. He stalled her frantic hand, but it refused to remain still. He'd unbalanced her with the casual way he talked about sex.

"Answer me," Kingdom commanded.

Her pulse quickened, and she felt like her heart was going to jump out of her skin with heat. Like a cornered animal, she snapped, "Fine. Yes. Are you satisfied?"

"Nothing between us is bad or wrong. You're a consenting adult female. I'm an adult male. I intend to kick the fucker who made you feel like sex is dirty."

Squaring her shoulders, she countered, "It may not have been a man. I may be naturally prudish."

Kingdom barked out a laugh. "Yeah, no. Prudish and shame are not the same thing. There's no other explanation why a hot chick like you is ashamed about wantin' a man." Picking up his chopsticks, he resumed his meal. "You're welcome."

"I didn't thank you for anything."

"You will," he said in a cocky tone. "I fuckin' guarantee it." Kingdom toyed with a brass bowl filled to the brim with foreign coins sitting on her desk. He fisted a few coins, then stretched out his hand and let them drop through his fingers.

"Jordan brought those coins back from his travels," she explained. "My brother was an old-school globetrotter, although most of them are from Afghanistan."

Kingdom carefully held the bowl in his palm. Peering at the intricate pattern etched on the sides, he remarked, "The bazaars there are full of metalwork, but"—he inspected it in the light—"this looks like an antique. He must have searched long and hard for this."

She nervously rummaged in the takeout bag for napkins, then forced herself to stop and face him.

Kingdom commented, "He must have been comfortable around them. Afghanis, I mean. The stuff you have around your office tells of quests in narrow alleys in remote villages."

"I don't know exactly what he did. I tried not to pry, and he wasn't forthcoming, but Jordan tended to stray off the beaten path. I can't imagine him missing out on an adventure or the opportunity to make new friends. He was good with people." Sage's shoulders drooped, and she placed her chopsticks deliberately by her side. Her hunger had vanished. As if wielding a broadsword, Kingdom whacked at the glass menagerie of her memories and her resistance to him all in one go. This was not the first, but the second time she'd spoken to him about Jordan, and she never spoke of her brother. For the most part, he was an off-limits topic, even with Camilla. Yet her tongue had loosened around Kingdom like a blabbering drunk. That spoke volumes.

"Let's get back to the many ways I'm going to fuck you."

"Nice change of subject, solider."

Kingdom saluted smartly. "I aim to please, ma'am."

She smiled at him and swallowed around the knot in her throat.

20

SAGE

The meal and the conversation about Jordan had done her in.

Kingdom's hot tongue on her body had already battered at the walls she'd attempted to erect against him, but the gesture of bringing her a meal had toppled what remained. After they finished their meal and cleaned up, Kingdom locked up the office and shoved a helmet into her hands. Twenty-five minutes later, he was fumbling with the lock of his warehouse while working his tongue into her mouth.

She was ready to devour him. Light touches skimmed down the crests of his six pack, then caught the bottom of his shirt and dragged it up his torso. He broke their kiss long enough to yank it off, and her hands landed on his hot, hard flesh. Cupping her ass in his large hands, he growled,

"Enough." Boosting her up in his arms, he rose tall. "Hold onto me."

Sage yelped and wrapped her legs around his waist, linking her ankles against his lower back. He threw his keys on the ground, locked the door, and stalked over to his bedroom area. She was tossed onto the massive bed she'd dreamed about nightly. He was on her in a flash, but she pushed on his chest to dislodge him. He snarled with displeasure.

Shooing him back, she said, "I want to take care of you."

The grimace stayed on his face, but he followed her and stood up. She scrambled off the bed in a hurry and almost toppled over, but Kingdom caught her by the nape in the nick of time. Not missing a beat, she shoved him to sit on the edge of the bed. A mad rush of adrenaline burned through her. He leaned back on his elbows and waited for her next move.

Tilting his head, she licked down the side of his throat, then caught a taut tendon between her teeth and bit down long enough to leave a mark. He flinched slightly, but his breathing accelerated instantaneously. She kissed over his collarbone and rubbed her cheek against his chest hair before reaching his nipple. Growing more confident, she suckled the dark bud in her wet mouth. Kingdom twisted the bedsheet in his fists.

Satisfied, Sage sank to her knees, unzipped his jeans, and freed his cock. Kingdom sucked in a shuddering breath as she closed her lips over his crown. Her hands gripped the root while her tongue licked the prominent vein on the underside of his shaft. She popped off his cock, and it bobbed and tapped against her chin. Glancing , she found his attention riveted to her mouth. No matter how many other women had gone down on him, it was clear that this moment was hers to revel in. His cock twitched with sensitivity when she blew on it, then thickened against the rasp of her tongue.

She leaned back to scrutinize her work, leaving his engorged shaft swinging like a metronome before torturing the tip with light taps of her finger. With jaws clenched, he allowed her the liberty to explore him at her leisure for a bit. Then his hand landed on her head, nudging her forward, and she consumed him whole, sucking hard. He lurched backward and fell on the mattress, panting at the ceiling.

His movement dislodged his penis from her mouth, so she wrapped her hands around the base and gave it a few languid plucks. Pearls of pre-come beaded on the slit of his cock, and she smeared it around his cockhead with her open palm as if it was an ointment. She loved the feel of his lubricated skin shifting over the steel of his shaft. Sage plunged her wet, glistening thumb into her mouth, slurping greedily. Kingdom seized up, almost coming. He shoved her hand away, but she took the offensive with rough strokes.

The sounds of his gasps filled her ears as she swallowed his length to the back of her vibrating throat. With excruciating slowness, she moved up and down. Kingdom hissed with pleasure-pain as she administered her award-punishment. Her panties were soaked, her inner thighs painted with her arousal. Apparently, being in total charge of Kingdom was a high in itself.

"I love the sounds you make. So sexy when I'm going down on you," she praised him.

"Yeah? Well, you're a fucking vison with my cock moving between your swollen lips."

Fisting her hair to position her head back for maximum access, he drove into her mouth. Her lips grazed the rough hair circling the root of his shaft. Through quivering nostrils, she breathed in his musk. The sharp tugs of her hair and the demanding thrusts in her mouth had her spreading her legs and rubbing her clit against the rug. She handled his balls, and her throat fluttered against the swollen tip. His control snapped, and he launched a full-scale invasion of her mouth.

"Suck it harder. Harder," he instructed. Her pussy throbbed at his command. Deep throating her, Kingdom yanked her shirt down to expose her breasts. "Fuck, Christ, I'm coming." His voice, hard and pained at the same time, licked at her skin like flames. His body began jerking irregularly. At the last possible instant, he pulled out and sprayed semen over her breasts.

"*Mine.*"

He could've let her swallow, but he branded her instead. Asserted his ownership. She was too overwhelmed by the intensity of what they'd done to care. Sitting back on her heels, she imagined how she looked to him—hair tousled, eyes hazy, lips abused, and, best of all, come dripping over her tits.

Blowing out a ragged breath, he wiped the sweat snaking down the side of his face. His gaze followed a stream of semen rolling down her left breast and falling over the tip. Her lips quirked up. She did that to him.

"Stay," he commanded as he tugged his shirt off the floor and wiped her off. Dropping the shirt, his hands began massaging her breasts.

Placing her hand over his, she stopped him and said, "You want to return the favor, but this was your gift to me. If you want to make me happy, take me to bed and let me just savor the taste of you on my tongue."

Kingdom groaned, his chin dropping to his chest. She reveled in the unbalance between them; Kingdom had sworn to taste her again, but she got the first taste tonight. And, oh, was he tasty. His earthy musk was intoxicating.

Nothing like Stanton. In more ways than one, she reminded herself.

"I'll allow it. For now. But how long till you're done 'savoring'? There's no way I'm waiting all night."

Sage stretched out like a lazy cat on the bed and tapped the empty space beside her. Blood was still pumping to her well-lubricated pussy, and she had to bite her cheek to not beg him to take her. Checking the digital clock on the nightstand by his bed, she said, "Ten o'clock work for you?"

Kingdom gathered her close and nuzzled the crown of her head. "Twenty-two hundred hours, it is."

She breathed in his aura, relinquishing herself to the warmth spreading through her chest, and promptly fell asleep.

※※※

Kingdom's mouth moved over her pussy. Greedy. He was determined to wrench an uninterrupted, never-ending orgasm out of her with his teeth and tongue. Teeth on clit. Tongue in pussy. Fingers wherever. Only once her pussy was exhausted from coming would he fill her with his cock.

Sage had surprised him. He hadn't expected her to seduce his cock and make it her bitch. She may be asleep, but she had committed to twenty-two hundred hours. Time was up.

Settling between her thighs, he pulled her pussy closer to his mouth. He was usually neutral on tongue-fucking a woman, but goddamn, this one tasted good. Her cunt was already nice and slick, and she wasn't even awake. His chest puffed up. She stirred, her head lolling back and forth as she awakened. Suddenly, her head shot up. *Yup, she's awake now.* She instinctively snapped her thighs shut, but his shoulders kept them wide.

"What the...?"

He caught her eyes, and the question died on her lips. Without dislodging his ravenous mouth from its feast, he appraised her carefully. Then he fastened onto her clit and tugged.

Her mouth dropped open as she puffed out, "Oh, my God ... wow."

Just like that, she succumbed to his ministrations. Arching up, Sage pivoted her hips in a silent plea, and he gave it to her. Inserting two fingers, he crooked them against her walls, seeking her G-spot. Her pelvis jerked up, and she clenched her quivering buttocks. *Hell yeah, there's the magic spot.* Kneading one butt cheek, he probed the crack of her ass. Didn't take him long to breach it, and the ring of muscles clamped down on his finger. Her chest heaved as she strained to escape, but his digit chased her and remained lodged just where he wanted it. She was fucking irresistible. He definitely had plans for her ass at some future point.

Two fingers in her cunt and one reaming her ass had Sage panting fast and hard. She buried her head in the pillow to muffle her moans.

"Sage," he spoke sternly, "move the fuck away from the pillow. I wanna hear you loud and clear."

She tossed it away without a shred of complaint. She was all his now. He curled his fingers onto her sweet spot, and her muscles contracted.

"No break. No shame. Loud, Sage, loud and fucking clear," he commanded. Her strained breathing turned into rhythmic grunts in step with his thrusts. He bared his teeth, swiping at her clit like he had the claws of a cat.

Her spine bowed, her shoulders grinding into the mattress. "Fuck!" she shouted as she came. "Goddammit, damn you, fuck!"

And she was coming, for sure. "Nasty little mouth you got there." Biting down, he plunged his finger deep into her ass and twisted. Thrusting her pussy into his mouth, her thighs clamped around his head, and her arms slapped the mattress with brutal force. Tremors coursed through her as she shrieked out his name.

Blinking up at the ceiling, she laid there panting with a single thought spinning through her head.

This could get addicting.

21

SAGE

Kingdom was sleeping like the dead, one arm splayed out to take the spot where Sage's head had lain.

Her lungs expanded, and she was overcome by the savory musk of him. The sheet covering half his body left his chiseled torso exposed for her to drink in like a fine bottle of rich, full-bodied Bordeaux. She admired the thick hair dividing the two sides of his taut abdomen, leading to the tent of his groin. She itched to unceremoniously drag the sheet from him and suck him off again.

Twisting her head away, she gritted her teeth. Since their first ride, she'd vacillated back and forth on whether to hook up with him or not. Yesterday, she had capitulated. How could she not? She'd never seen anything as erotic as the image of Kingdom's dark head nestled between her thighs.

Truth was, she was a goner the instant he'd touched the

coins and spoke about quests; it was as if he *had known* Jordan. Grief and desire was an unholy cocktail. Jerking her panties up her legs, her gaze cut to the sofa, reliving his mouth working on her.

Tugging her bra from under his head, he groaned and turned on his side with a swipe or two of his hand over where she had slept beside him. The air seized in her lungs, but, thank God, he settled down. Dressed, Sage tiptoed across the floor.

Slipping out the front door, she squinted up as the sun was rising above the crumbling shell of the building across the street, outlining it like a black slab of marble stuck over a recently dug grave. Once in the car, Sage checked the time and called Camilla on her speakerphone.

"Why are you calling me so early? How was last night? After the text you sent me, I'm expecting a juicy story."

"Too juicy...I mean, too good," she faltered and bowed her head. *Awkward.*

Camilla's throaty laugh rang through the car. "You were in bed when you texted me? Then, he couldn't have been that good, heh?"

"Technically, I was in the bathroom when I texted you."

"Sooo, what happened next?" Camilla prompted.

"He went down on me."

Camilla's voice rose above the sound of the coffee grinder. "You mean he sucked your pussy dry. Come on, you can say the words, *chica*," Camilla joked. Her cheeks burned. *Ugh.* Camilla was torturing her on purpose.

"I prefer the term 'oral sex.'"

"Prude," Camilla accused. "You're no fun."

"I fell asleep and woke up in the middle of the night with his mouth on me." The car wheels swerved, and she flinched, her heart rearing up like a startled mare. "It was pretty incredible. *He* was incredible, so I left before he woke up. I'm freaking out, Camilla. God, I don't know what's wrong with me. His penis and mouth have scrambled my brain. I felt things that I didn't want to feel again. I miss sex, but I can't afford to get caught up in him. Falling for a man like him will be trouble, and I'm a bonder. I bond. That's what I do. Getting bonded to a man like him is dangerous. I feel it in my gut. Why test fate?"

"Sage, relax. It was sex, nothing more. You've been burned badly, but you can learn how to keep your emotions separated from sex. You haven't been touched in years, and you can't deny that you have needs—physical needs, which Kingdom can take care of. Keep it casual, and you'll be fine."

"First of all, I've never had casual sex. I was a virgin with Stanton, and I've only had sex coupled with intimacy. Second, that man doesn't want intimacy any more than Stanton did, but we spoke about Jordan. You know what that does to me," Sage finished in a whisper.

The clinking of utensils stopped abruptly. Camilla's grave tone came through the phone, "You talked about Jordan? We've known each other since we roomed together in college, and you don't even talk to me about your brother. Anytime you bring him up to Angel, I have to fuck the misery out of him for days after."

"Now you get it. He catches me off guard and digs places that I don't want anyone to go. Being with him brings up desires I shouldn't look to him to fulfill. A man like him isn't built for commitment any more than Stanton was. At least Kingdom's straightforward about it."

"You're making assumptions. Have you spoken to him about dating or relationships? For all you know, he could've been in a long-term relationship or married. You. Don't. Know. So stop throwing shit at the wall just to see what'll stick."

Sage's throat thickened, and her chest constricted. Her nostrils burned as she sighed. "Okay, fine. You're right. I'm overreacting. But he got what he wanted, so who says he'll contact me again? Right now, I'm on my way home. I'll take a shower, make coffee, and head over to the office."

"Not the office, babe, not the office," Camilla pleaded.

"Yes, the office," Sage said with finality. It was her hideout, but she was alive for two purposes: to stay sane and to work. She wasn't feeling sane, so she was damned well going to work.

❋❋❋

Kingdom woke up slowly with thoughts of Sage dancing in his head. He was proud for not fucking her last night. It had taken a dose of superhuman strength he didn't know he possessed, but he'd proven that she wasn't an easy, one-time fuck.

When he'd tongue-banged her, he'd rubbed his face into her pussy and spread her come over him. Felt good to wake up with her scent permeating his nostrils. Eyes still closed, he smiled and licked his parched lips. He was ready for another hit. Reaching out, he tapped the space beside him several times and came up empty.

Sitting up, he scanned the room.

Empty.

For her sake, she'd better be in the bathroom.

Stumbling out of bed, he wrestled with the bedsheet and threw it viciously aside. He crossed the space, checking the kitchen and bathroom, but he already knew. She was gone. The one and only time he brings a woman home, the one time he acts honorably and doesn't fuck a woman, and this was his payback? No, he wasn't having it.

Pacing back to the bed, he stood above it, clenched fists braced on his hips. Yeah, they both got off, but he was consumed with the drive to bury his dick inside her tight cunt. He remembered the way his fingers felt in her narrow channel, and he knew for a fact it'd be a snug fit. He should be fitting into her right-fucking-now. It was more than just sex. She brought a softness into his life that he hadn't experienced before. She was like a balm to his soul, and he wanted more of her. Her presence. Her laugh. Her little sassy comebacks. Sage was the whole package. He'd never felt that way about a woman before, and, quite honestly, it rattled him a little.

Training his breath to slow down, it dawned on him that maybe she'd left because she thought he didn't want to fuck her. Christ, women were impossible to read. Vexation snapped at his heels.

She'd cheated him, and he was coming for her. He'd teach her two crucial lessons. Lesson one: not only did he want her, but he had the stamina to fuck her all night and into the next day. Lesson two: the woman wasn't allowed to walk out on him.

Chucking on some clothes, he was stalking to his bike when his cellphone rang. He checked the caller ID and answered, "What the hell do you want, Cutter?"

"What the fuck got your panties in a twist?"

"You got something to say, spit it out," he snarled. "I got shit to do."

"Fuck, man, it's too early in the morning to be an asshole."

"Yeah, yeah," Kingdom replied dismissively. He didn't have time for bullshit. He was on a mission to pound Sage into her bed. Or against a wall. Whatever.

"Prez said we gotta go over the inventory one last time before it gets transported out tonight."

"Did I stutter? I told you I've got somethin' to do. We'll meet a little later."

"Don't think it's a good idea to put him off," Cutter counseled.

"Didn't fuckin' ask you. I have to take care of a pain-in-my-ass problem."

On that parting note, Kingdom hung up.

22

———

KINGDOM

Bang, bang, bang.

Kingdom pounded on Sage's door.

Minutes later, it swung open, and she stood in front of him in her nightie. If one could call it that. It might cover her ass, but her legs? Not so much. He stifled a groan and bit down on his bottom lip. *Christ, her legs.* They should be wrapped around his waist while his cock worked her pussy. Lust and fury double-teamed him to constrict his breathing.

Fists balled at his sides, he gave her a censuring look. "Don't you check the peephole before you open the door? And do you always answer the door half naked?"

"Usually," she replied drily. Her hand tried to stall him as he moved past her. "What are you doing here?"

Unsmiling, Kingdom stated, "Woke up this morning." He slammed the door shut and hemmed her in against it. "Alone. Wasn't too happy about that." Crowding closer until his chest brushed against hers, he caught her sweet scent, smoldering beneath the crisp fragrance of her shampoo. Sage's pulse was ricocheting just below her jawline.

Slinking away, she tried to cover her agitation with a dismissive shrug. "I figured I was doing us both a favor."

"How'd you figure that?" he gritted out. Her flippant attitude was making his hands itch to give her a swift smack to the ass. He speared her with a narrow-eyed look that had her quickly switching tacks.

"Why don't you come in and make yourself comfortable," she said. "Would you like a cup of coffee? I made a fresh pot."

Giving her a short nod, he marched straight back to the kitchen like he owned the place. He heard her breathe out, "Okay." Sage disappeared for a few moments as he took a seat at her kitchen table and came back fully clothed. Sure, she decided to get dressed when his only intention was to strip her naked. He scowled, a demonic pit of fury roiling in his gut. A black cat nimbly dropped from a high shelf onto the counter and then the floor. By the way she'd bewitched him, it made sense she'd have an all-black cat. Ambling toward Kingdom, the cat sat, bright green eyes on him, tail twitching lightly. He dropped his hand, and the cat looked left, then right, and slid over the wooden floor to Kingdom.

Sage stopped short in the middle of the kitchen when she saw Kingdom petting the cat's back and scratching its head. "That's Phantom," she said as she prepared him a cup and gingerly placed it in front of him. Kingdom relaxed when he tasted the black, heavy-bodied coffee gliding over his tongue. *She remembered how he took his coffee.* A warmth suffused his chest.

Mug in hand, he leaned back to survey her home. Her kitchen reminded him of a cross between a country store and a cupcake shop, feminine but not so dainty that it made a man cringe. He set his mug down on the wide-planked farmer's table painted white. Her bay window held a collection of colored glass vases, from rich amber to deep cobalt blue. Various dried pods, stems, and other random items like chopsticks, even a screwdriver, protruded from their spouts. Strainers, colanders, cake molds, and baskets hung from a variety of hooks on walls and cabinets. A rack swayed above his head, holding pots, pans, and other kitchen utensils. It was no wonder she liked his kitchen at the warehouse.

He grunted his approval and noticed her breathing even out.

"Have you had breakfast?" she inquired politely.

"No. Woke up. Saw you gone. Came over," Kingdom replied, tersely.

"I made scrambled eggs if you'd like some. I don't have any hash browns or potatoes, but I can toast bread."

"Yeah, I can eat." *Then I can fuck you. That will build up an appetite, so I'll eat your pussy. Eat, fuck, eat.* Sounded like a perfect way to spend his morning. Kingdom angled his head and watched her ass twitch around the kitchen as she prepared a plate for him. A pair of jogging pants hung low on her hips. He caught a glimpse of lace when she bent over to grab something from a cabinet. The nightie might have been replaced by a t-shirt, but she wasn't wearing a bra. Her nipples poked out under the thin cotton. Fuckin' hell, he wanted to drag her pants down and love up on her ass. Collaring his t-shirt, he croaked out, "It's hot in here."

Sage glanced over her shoulder at him with a quizzical expression, then leaned over the sink to open a window. A cool spring breeze rushed inside. Her shirt slid up, showing off inches of creamy flesh and reminding him of how inappropriately she'd been dressed when she answered the door. His mouth went dry. He felt like killing someone, but since that wasn't an option, he'd fuck the hell out of her instead. Seemed like a reasonable trade.

She slid the plate of food, silverware, and a napkin in front of him and sat down facing him. Sage poked at her cell phone as he dug into his food. It was good. He didn't realize how hungry he'd been, but the food dulled the raw edge of his anger.

Once he was done, he sat back into his seat and studied her intently. "You left before I could fuck you."

Her cheeks stained crimson at his blunt words. She restlessly worried a nick on the corner of the table with her fingernail. "You had all night to fuck me."

"Woman, I was tryin' to be honorable. I won't make the same mistake twice." Canting his head to the side, he asked in a gentler voice, "What were you thinking?"

Sage stood up and whisked the empty plate and silverware off the table. Moving toward the sink, she replied, "Excuse me for thinking that when a man has all night but doesn't have actual sex with a woman, that ... oh, I don't know, he might not be interested in her after all."

She faced him but white-knuckled the sides of the porcelain sink behind her.

"I call bullshit." He pointed a finger in accusation. "You're sexy as sin, so don't put this on me."

Confusion, embarrassment, and traces of fear flashed in succession on her face. Kingdom pushed his chair back and approached her slowly. Sage scurried away from him, but he prowled after her until she was backed into the oven. Although her back leaned over the stovetop, her gaze dropped down his chest. Her breath caught as her eyes grew heavy-lidded. Damn, what the hell had happened to her to make her question her own sexiness or run from him when she was obviously turned on? "Talk to me," he ordered, caressing the side of her throat.

She let out a frustrated sigh. "You assume that I'm confident, and objectively speaking, I concede that some men may find me attractive, but my ex-fiancé was a fiasco."

Kingdom stilled his hand. The motherfucker. What was his name? Stanton?

"I mean, it's true that men hit on me regularly, but I dismiss their overtures. In my work, I interact with men all the time. A few are pushy, but most are harmless."

Kingdom stared at her incredulously. Was she for real? He twisted his head to catch her expression. It was neutral. Her situation was whack-ass bullshit, but she wasn't calling it what it was: sexual harassment. The fact that she was blasé about the whole thing made him want to tear something apart.

"I haven't had sex with anyone since my ex. You want sex, but I don't know how to do *just* sex. Perhaps the fact that we didn't have sex last night was a sign that maybe it's best to let sleeping dogs lie, know what I mean?"

Bracing his himself on either side of her, he forced himself to keep his hands off her. Flexing his fingers on the corners of the stainless steel, he felt like putting his fist through something like a window. Maybe the sound of crashing glass and the sting of shards on his skin might relieve his fury. Unfortunately, she was already skittish, and he couldn't afford to frighten her or destroy her kitchen. The urge was strong, though.

Sage gave him a vague smile as if they'd come to some sort of understanding. "I appreciate you coming by to clear the air. It means a lot to me that you were kind enough to come over."

A groan rumbled in his chest. Not for a moment would he allow this nonsense to continue. Time to clear up any misconceptions and take her in hand. She wanted more than sex. For once in his life, he wasn't opposed to the idea. She was already driving him crazy. He didn't want another cock but his to ever be inside her, that much was clear as fuck. Another upside of being exclusive with her was that he'd have the clout to act as possessively as he damned well wanted.

"I'm not kind. You've got it all wrong, Sage. I didn't come by to clear the air. I came here to fuck you, but if you want more than sex, I can give you that. Don't know what that entails, exactly, since I've never been in a relationship, but I'm not opposed to the idea. Never had an interest in it before now, but what the hell, I can roll with it. What I do know is that you owe me one orgasm or three that I would've wrung out of you this morning. I'm here to collect."

Tilting her head back, she remarked, "Whoa, that's quite a promise embedded in that statement of yours. An orgasm or *three*?"

A firm grip on her chin, and he bent down and teased her bottom lip with his tongue. She flinched in surprise and leaned back over the stovetop to put distance between them.

"Don't back away from me," he warned. He was done talking. Time to show her what he wanted from her. Looping her hair around his fist, he used it as leverage to slant her head to the side. Panting, relief swept over her features. She wanted—no—she *needed* him to take the reins. A less experienced lover, a less controlled man, would have gone aggro on her surrender, but Kingdom knew what he was about.

Sealing his mouth over hers, he slid his tongue between her open lips and took his sweet time exploring. A throaty moan escaped her, and she gripped the back of his head as her tongue intertwined with his. They sparred and parried like a pair of fencers—Sage out of deliverance, and Kingdom out of dominance.

Ever so slowly, his fingers traced the tendon of her throat, the bones of her collarbone, then squeezed her full breast, plucking one of her nipples. Sage jolted but immediately rebounded and arched in search of greater pressure. Raking her fingernails down his sides, she tore at the fabric of his shirt. Her hands snaked in front and tugged his shirt from where it was tucked into his jeans until there was a gap. Yanking the shirt off him, her nails scored the bunched and twitching muscles of his chest and back. Pulling hard on his belt, she brought him flush against her. She poured out her hunger in the kiss she gave him, her tongue going deep and rough.

"Fuck, you're sexy when your little claws come out to play," Kingdom moaned. He hadn't expected Sage to come out with guns blazing. He peeled off her shirt and went a little dizzy at the sight of her perky, full tits punctuated by raspberry tips.

Sage's hand coasted down his back and hit a hard object lodged in his waistband at the small of his back. She patted it several times, felt the shape of it, and gripped it. Kingdom swept her hands aside, pulled out his gun, and set it beside the stove.

Her eyes snapped to his, then swerved toward the sound. "A gun? You're packing a gun?" Shaking her head in disbelief, she sputtered, "I was about to have sex with a man who leaves in the morning with a sidearm in his waistband."

"And these." He reached into his pocket and slapped down a string of rubbers next to the gun.

"Oh, shit," she whispered. Her gaze darted from one to the other until she chose. Breathing heavily, she handled his 9mm Glock as he remained braced above her. *Yeah, I'm dangerous like that*, he wanted to tell her. He carried a gun like a second skin, but he could see how Sage might freak out. Her wide eyes fixed on his.

"You're a biker who carries a gun," she stated as if wrapping her head around the fact. At least she wasn't losing her shit. Surprised, definitely. Shocked, perhaps. It was best to get it out of the way. If they were gonna do a relationship thing, then he needed to break her in as an old lady, what bikers called their permanent women.

A laugh rumbled lightly from his chest. Guess there was no stopping him now. "Observant. Always did like smart women."

"This does not bode well for your life expectancy. I'm not sure how I feel about this," she mused aloud, lips pursed.

"Yeah, I get the impression," Kingdom deadpanned. She may be jittery, but he wasn't giving her the leeway to change her mind. "Things are a little tense with a club the Squad partners with. Not tense-tense, but I'm a military man, and I'm at ease with a weapon in my possession. It's the way I roll. Let's place this talk on the back burner, yeah? We have unfinished business, you and me."

"That's easier said than done." She snorted.

"Why don't I make it easy for you," he murmured, guiding his hand slowly against the smooth column of her neck as if she were a skittish mare. Her eyes fluttered closed. Suddenly, she slung her arms around his neck and crashed her lips against his. Not only was she back with him, she was a step ahead of him. Mouth devouring hers, Kingdom snagged the roll of condoms, swept her up, and walked into what was hopefully the direction of her bedroom.

23

SAGE

Letting the condoms drop from his hand, Kingdom put her down.

She stumbled backward, fell on the bed, and gazed up at him from under her lashes. He was willing to do non-casual sex, meaning intimacy. With her. If he was willing to go out on a limb and do something he'd never done before *for her*, then she was going to match him pace for pace. Suddenly, everything clicked into place. Sage was in a place she understood, and she felt good. No, not good. Great. *Fantastic.*

Sage leaned back on her forearms, her eyelids dropping as her gaze hovered over his low-slung jeans. His fingers playfully lingered on his buckle as he unbuckled his belt, then whipped it off with lightning speed, snapping it taut between his hands before throwing it aside.

Sage's mouth parted slightly, and her chest rose and fell

like a newborn babe's first breaths. His jeans dropped and his cock jutted out, vibrating like a tuning fork. Her eyes blew out wide. She hadn't noticed that he went commando yesterday. *Like he's primed for sex anytime and anywhere.*

He toed off his boots and stripped off his jeans slowly, as if giving her time to savor him. Her hands drifted up to stroke him. Yanking off her shirt in one swift move, he cupped her bare breasts, weighing them as they settled in his palms.

"That's it, baby girl," he crooned. "Sexy girl. All the right curves and silky skin. I bet you've got a slick pussy waitin' for me, don't you?"

Oh, did she ever. The calluses of his thumbs smoothed over her nipples, and she preened under his gaze, riveted on her taut peaks. He pinched her plump buds, leaving them a bright shade of pink. Kingdom dragged her sweats down and swore, "Goddamn, you're a sight to behold. White lace panties that show off the patch of curls underneath."

His compliments had the effect of plunging her in cauldron of roiling heat.

He hauled her onto his lap, chuckling at her little yelp. Sage squirmed and rubbed against his solid thighs and hard, throbbing shaft. Capturing a ripe nipple between his teeth, he bit down. She gasped from the pain mixed in with the pleasure. Latched onto the peaked tip, he suckled away while her lace-covered ass ground on his cock. "I'm gonna hold onto that ample ass of yours as I ram inside you, hard and deep," he promised darkly in her ear. He roughly palmed the mound of her pussy before moving the damp crotch aside and fitting a blunt finger inside her snug channel. Juices gushed out, and he added another. More liquid heat ran down her inner thighs.

"*Fuck*, you're grip is tight. Remember the last time I fingerbanged you?"

"How could I forget?" she panted out, clinging to his biceps to keep herself upright. She was already close to losing her mind, thrusting against his hand.

Kingdom laid her down and caged her neck lightly.

"Baby, are you gonna cream on my hand? Your pussy is tightening around my fingers."

She shook her head since she couldn't string together a coherent sentence. He added a third finger and curved all three to hit a sensitive spot against her inner wall. Digging her nails into his arms, she arched her neck beneath the cup of his hand and began riding his fingers. With an abandon she never knew she had, she lifted her hips and met his thrusting fingers, her clit banging against the heel of his palm. Her head blew out like a fuse, and she spasmed around his fingers. After thrusting through her aftershocks, Kingdom pulled out his fingers and greased his dick with her come.

Snagging a rubber from the floor, he tore it open, but she plucked it from his fingers. Barely able to catch her breath, she was determined to take care of him. Her tongue stuck out from the side of her mouth as she rolled the condom down his shaft. Ready, he dragged her by the ass to the edge of the bed, aligned his cock, and slowly sank between her thighs. Once the head breached her entrance, the walls of her vagina cinched around his shaft and suctioned him in. His eyes rolled to the back of his head. For a moment, he teetered to the side but caught himself before he collapsed on top of her.

Whoa, this guy was big. She shimmied a little left and right until she adjusted to his size. His teeth were clenched, and a tic was going manic at the side of his jaw, but he held still until she settled. Bending her legs, he spread her open for a perfect bird's eye view and began pumping in and out. Sage didn't protest, but there was no doubt that Kingdom had filled her to the hilt with his cock.

"You're tight as a fist, baby. Look at your pretty pussy swallowing my cock whole like a good girl," he praised. His dirty talk urged her to tilt her hips up and attempt to grind against his downward strokes.

"Taut. Slick. Hot. *Fuck.* Best pussy a man can have." Kingdom picked up his pace until the slaps of his thrusts mimicked the pace of a piston's relentless drill. Her flesh was sucking at his shaft as he hammered faster into her, knocking the breath out of her. The sounds of plunging into her wet heat, along with her gasps and his groans, wound tension inside her.

"Your clutch is killin' me," he declared between heaving breaths.

Sage clamped down viciously, coaxing him into defeat. A desperate screaming of his name and her pussy contracted, undulating on his shaft. Sage watched gleefully as he lost the fight. His fingers found her clit and quickly hurled her over the edge.

Lightheaded, she gasped for air as he emptied himself into her pulsing core.

"I get 24/7 access to this pussy," he commanded. "Come to think of it, 25/8. I'm tapping this on the regular."

"I'm assuming this goes both ways," she quipped. Sage felt warm and gooey inside. Kingdom not only wanted her but was willing to forgo other women to be only with her. Simply to make her happy. Wow. Just wow.

"Oh, babe, anytime you want, I'm game."

24

SAGE

Sage slunk into the bench across from Camilla at the Poughkeepsie Coffee Roasting Company, threw off the jacket of her suit, and gratefully wrapped her hands around a hot cappuccino.

Yup, the swirly heart of foam was there. She looked up, and Billy, her favorite barista, winked at her. She called out, "Thank you." For a guy with a bun, he was a major attraction for customers, both female and male. Taking a sip, she said, "Thanks for getting me my drink."

Camilla twisted her torso and blatantly checked out Billy. "If only I was single." She shook her head.

"Oh my God, will you stop the pretense. One gorgeous guy under your thumb should be enough. And a baby on the way, if I might remind you," she replied pertly.

Camilla threw her hands up. "With the estrogen pumping

through my system, I could take on ten men and still have a climax or two left over."

Hands over her ears, Sage bluffed, "Nah, nah, nah. I didn't hear anything."

"*Gracias a Dios*, you finally, *finally* broke your dry spell. *Hmph*, I'd have thought it'd loosen you up, but old habits die hard, I guess."

"Speaking of Kingdom." She bent toward Camilla. "Not only did we have incredible sex the morning he came over, but he's willing to be monogamous. He's too sexy. Seriously, it's sick what he can do to me with just one look. And he's too charismatic. It's overpowering." Heat hit her face as she recalled the morning she'd spent in bed with him until he got a call from one of his brothers that took him away. He gave her a searing kiss and one possessive look—explicitly declaring that nothing was over between them—before he walked out of her bedroom, leaving her heart beating out of her chest.

"Wow, you poor woman. My heart goes out to you," Camilla replied.

Ignoring her sarcasm, she went on, "Cam, he packs a gun."

"I'm not surprised. Angel has one for the store. He has a license, took a bunch of classes, and practices at the range on a regular basis. Showed me how to keep it safe. At first, I opposed it, but you know him, protective to a fault. I understand how you feel, but remember, Kingdom's not an amateur or unstable. He's not pretending to be a soldier on the field. He's the real deal, and if he was an Army Ranger, he's a trained expert. For him, carrying a gun is like wearing his cut."

Sage pursed her lips, and a frown cut between her brows.

"I understand it's new for you," Camilla conceded. "But Kingdom takes the word 'protective' to a new level. Didn't you tell me he posted a guard or prospect in front of your office? A gun is a drop in the proverbial bucket."

Sage dipped a biscotti into her cappuccino. "Delicious. Billy gets it right every time," she marveled with a sigh of pleasure. Returning her attention to the conversation, she explained, "It's kind of annoying. I mean, I left childhood behind many years ago, and I left a controlling asshole behind in the not-so-distant past. Stanton whisked me away from a life as a scholarship student without two cents to rub together, and I sold my soul in the process. My law practice is paying my bills and loans. I'm the self-supporting woman I was meant to be, and there's no way I'm going to let myself down again. He certainly treats me like an adult in bed, but then he goes caveman on me. Even if it's not all the time, that can't be right."

"He definitely has the broody, moody vibe goin' on." Camilla placed her hand over Sage's fingers tap-tapping out a woodpecker's drill on her porcelain cup. "If you stop and think about it, you might realize that he has a good reason for what he does. If anyone knows about living the thug life, he's the man. MCs have enemies."

"Whatever. I have a bigger issue that I'm grappling with." She looked up at Camilla and held her gaze. "I'm scared. After Stanton, this could turn into a disaster. I've finally managed to create a drama-free life, and I mean to keep it that way," Sage vowed.

Camilla guffawed. "You call your life drama-free? Your rep is based on taking on the most hopeless criminals."

"I take issue with labeling my *clients* criminals. Every individual is granted the benefit of the doubt regarding a crime of which she or he has been accused of."

Mimicking Sage's lecturing voice, Camilla said, "You defend the rights of people who would otherwise be trampled by the criminal justice system, blah, blah, blah. My point is that you mingle with scary dudes on a regular basis. Don't kid yourself that you're normal or that you live a drama-free life. Nothing could be further from the truth."

Folding her arms over her chest, Sage glared at her and asked, "Are you done?"

"As a matter of fact, I'm not. Now that we're discussing this, you know what type of men you're attracted to, don't you? Bad boys, and especially bad boys full of drama."

"Stanton was clean as they came," Sage replied indignantly.

"You're talking about his exterior, but Stanton was like being in a bad MTV reality show. You were attracted to the darkness within him. Unfortunately, his dark side isn't just dark, it's psycho dark. Hell, after him, an outlaw biker looks like a choir boy."

Sage quickly defended, "Kingdom isn't an outlaw, and he's certainly not a *boy*. I concede that he's bad"—her tone dropped low—"*very* bad, but he's certifiably all man." Catching herself lusting out loud, she waved her hand. "Moving on. Did Kingdom genuinely think I wouldn't catch onto those two bikers? They're as obvious as a couple of slapstick actors like Abbott and Costello, and that shit is not funny."

"Stop complaining. It's a gesture of affection and a guarantee that whatever craziness his club is involved with does not touch you. Sure, it's domineering machismo, but I see you." She poked two fingers toward Sage's eyes and back to hers. "It turns you on. You're just bitter because your ego is bruised."

"Know it all," Sage griped, shooting a glare over the rim of her perfect cup of cappuccino.

"Seriously, though. I know that you're scared, but you deserve to have a man care for you. Don't deny yourself someone you're attracted to who wants to look after you. Can you promise me that you'll give this a chance?"

"Yeah, okay. Jeez, you're so pushy," she teased, sticking out her tongue.

"I prefer the term 'proactive.'"

Sage rolled her eyes and grumbled, "Oh, just drink up."

25

KINGDOM

Kingdom lay back, sated, and sedated.

He cast a look at Sage, who was lying across his chest, catching her breath. He shifted her to pull off the rubber, tied it, and threw it into a small basket for trash on the other side of his night table. Kingdom draped Sage back into place. A new one would be on his dick soon enough. His cock didn't seem to stay limp for long around Sage. She slayed him each and every time. Grasping the cheek of her ass, he jiggled it, and she squirmed her pussy into him.

A month had passed, and things were going surprisingly well between them. This morning was typical. He woke to her warm, pliant body beside his. A kiss, a stroke, or a mere touch and he was on her. Sage caressed his chest, smoothing her fingertips over his dog tags. She did that. Mostly in private, but even in public, she reached for them instinctively, like they were a talisman.

Stretching her arms to her sides, Sage arched and pressed her tits firmly against him. She lifted her leg over his thighs and rubbed her pussy against him. Christ, his cock was halfway hard not five minutes after pulling out of her. He was close to flipping her onto her belly so he could mount her.

Sage did love marking him, though. Either with bites on his chest or bruises on his neck. He took pleasure in examining his body in the mirror afterward, admiring her skill and determination. It was bold of her to show off her ownership of him, but damn, if it wasn't hot. He was never interested in a woman long enough to allow her to get close. Now he couldn't get enough of her possessive little gestures. *Who would've thought I'd bask in her attention?*

Sage spread her thighs wider against him. "I'm curious about something."

"Yeah, sweetheart?"

A wave of warmth flowed through his body when he noticed her glow in response to his term of endearment.

"Why did you join the Demon Squad?"

A smile curved his lips. *She cares.* It made him feel wanted and cared for when she got nosey about his life, wanting to know every detail. She was a curious little kitten, this one. He scratched his cheek and rubbed the scruff on his chin with the back of his knuckles as he considered her question, wondering how much to disclose. Sliding an arm underneath her, he wrapped her in an embrace to give him courage.

"I should back up and start from when we were kids. Chop came to live with my mom and me when I was thirteen. I remember the day I found Chop. How could I forget? It was early in the school year, and I came home. Opened the front closet door and found him. He was crouched low with his back pressed hard against the wall. Latchkey kid that I was, I handled my own shit. But staring down at him, shivering in the closet, I was out of my depth. I shut the closet door, walked over to the phone hanging off the kitchen wall, and dialed up Moms.

"A call to Moms during working hours was like the bat signal in Gotham City. Twenty minutes later, she was the one staring down at Chop, his skinny arms wrapped around skinnier knees, his skinny ass crushing our shoes. Moms was a tough Italian woman, but when she pulled him off the floor and hugged him tight against her, I knew I got myself a new little bro."

"Wow. Not every young kid would rejoice over getting a stranger as a new brother."

"He wasn't a total stranger. I knew him from the neighborhood. But Chop was special. His father was a good-for-nothing loser. Loki, who you've met at the clubhouse, was his older brother. He left Chop behind to sign up. Funny thing is that at the time, I thought I was saving Chop. Turns out, he saved my ass ten times over." Kingdom shrugged and tightened his hold on her. "After I graduated high school, I waited on Chop to finish up. He was a year younger than me. With too much time on my hands, I dabbled in the thug life, but Loki straightened me out real fast."

Sage's eyes flashed with surprise. Kingdom chuckled. "Yeah, I'm not a fan, but Loki was a force to be reckoned with back then. He was home on leave, and I was selling weed on the corner by a park near school. Popular spot. Loki walked up to me and *wham*. Took a swing at me without so much as a warning. After stomping all up on my brand-new Jordans, he made a show of dragging my busted-up face around the neighborhood before bringing me home. Tossed me into the house like I was trash. Then he and my mom double-teamed me with guilt and threats. The day after Chop graduated, I drove us to the nearest recruitment center and signed us up."

Sage brushed her hand up to settle on his collarbone, regarding him in her quiet way. He lifted his gaze upward to the tires swaying gently from the rafters of his warehouse. His body twitched, causing him to shift underneath Sage, but her soothing touch settled him.

After a few minutes of lying with Sage on top of him, her fingers caressing him, he resumed his tale. "Being Special Ops isn't for everyone, and after three tours, Chop wanted out. I'd done a few semesters of college between tours, but I wasn't keen on working behind a desk. I was no longer a civilian, and I didn't have it in me to become one again. A man who isn't a soldier or a civilian can get lost in the sauce."

Kingdom scooted up to the headboard of the bed and boosted Sage along with him. Catching a strand of her hair, he toyed with it absentmindedly. "I got certified as a mechanic. Figured it was better to work with cars and bikes than with people. Took me a while to let go of the shit I carried back with me from Al-Anbar in Iraq. 'Specially Fallujah. Chop struggled too, but his way out of the mess was the Squad. Soon after we got back, he reconnected with Cutter, who we'd known from Iraq. After he decided the club was for him, he brought me around. I liked what I saw, and, Christ, someone had to keep an eye on him. We prospected for a year and patched in four years ago. I haven't looked back since."

Her fingertips grazed over the ridges of his chest, her temple resting against his heart. Tracing a soothing pattern on his skin, she mentioned, "I don't charge fees to veterans."

His heart hiccupped. *Damn, she was motherfucking beautiful inside and out.* Her hand splayed over his chest, and he caught it in his own.

"It's not a big deal," she clarified. "The cases are usually simple—DWIs, vagrancy for homeless vets, and assault and battery, which is another term for barroom brawls. The harder ones, well … they're harder."

A band cinched his ribs, and he had trouble breathing. He wanted to taste her, fuck her, devour her. Fuse a part of her with a part of him. It was humbling to realize what a lucky bastard he was to be bound to a woman like Sage. Closing his eyes, he declared, "People don't care about what happens to vets. Sure, civilians thank us for our service, but they have no clue, no idea of what we went through. Who we killed or who we scarified out there."

A hard glint entered Sage's eyes. "I refuse to pretend that we were not engaged in a war, that soldiers haven't given their time and lives for it. At the very least, I have a responsibility to deal with the repercussions. Whether Jordan came back alive or in a body bag does not change the fact that casualties exist everywhere. I'm not doing anything special. Angel, for example, gave you a discount."

The muscle in his jaw ticked. "Why? I don't want special treatment."

Sage squeezed his thigh. "He didn't want you to know about the discount, but remember, his cousin died in Mosul. Angel stayed behind because he'd met and had fallen in love with Camilla. You should see his back. It's a tableau in memory of his cousin. The background is etched with the insignia of the Navy, and his cousin's face rises out from a battlefield scene like an avenging angel. Honestly, I don't know how Camilla manages to live with it every day."

Burrowing into his frame, Sage asked, "What do you love best about the brotherhood?"

"The code. Civilians assume we're no better than animals, but we live by our own rules. We don't traffic in drugs, people, or arms. My brothers make me who I am. Without a stable base, the average man is bound to crash and burn. Luckily, there ain't nothing average about me."

Kingdom cocked an eyebrow when Sage's head immediately swung down to his dick. "Lucky for me, you mean. I can testify that there is definitely nothing average about you."

His cock swelled under her lascivious gaze. He placed her hand around the root of it. "Go on, play with it. I'm good at multitasking."

"You know, there's no such thing."

"Yeah? Try me."

His hand lingered on top of hers as she stroked him. His mind blanked for a bit, but he regained the strand of his story. "I was a 'meat-eater' for a year, meaning that my mission focused on leadership and training. What can I say? I have a knack for training, so I'm the one in charge of those dumbass prospects. Fuckin' hopeless wrecks."

Exhibiting exceptional restraint, Kingdom pulled her hand off him. Guess he couldn't multitask after all. "Perfect example is Whistle getting caught up by the badges over a bar fight."

Placing a trail of kisses along the hard angle of his jaw, she murmured, "I bet you appreciated the parties."

Glad she could joke about that, he shot her a grin. "Ya mean the easy pussy," he corrected.

Sage slapped him hard on the chest.

"Ow." He clutched his chest. "Nah, pussy was easy even before joining the Squad. Girls can't help but love bad boys like me. Coming off a tour was a free-for-all. Military groupies hunt for uniforms, especially men in elite forces. I burned out on 'easy' a while ago."

"What about the rest? What about the club's other activities?"

Kingdom barked out a laugh. "Nothing stateside compares with the mujahidin in the Sunni Triangle. What I didn't do myself, I witnessed another fucker do. Seen it all, babe. Seen strong men cry like babies and weak men fight till the death. Dirty men act with honor and good men kill for the wrong reasons. I've joked and laughed in the middle of an ambush, in the middle of a goddamn battle. Made me into the man I am, but it fucked with my head."

Kingdom shrugged off his memories. "Whatever. I'm done with the past. Only thing I haven't made peace with is Chop. You know, he took a bullet aimed at my head back in the dust bowl." He blew out a shuddering breath. "After what we'd been through together, I left him to die alone."

Staring past the weight of her gaze, Kingdom confessed, "You should know that Loki blames me. If it weren't for the brotherhood, he'd strangle me with his bare hands. He likes using his hands to make sure a job gets done right. Shedding my blood is the only way to cleanse himself of the guilt that's eating away at him. Problem is, he made an oath to protect and respect the brotherhood. I'm his brother, I'm his family, and he can't commit fratricide. That leaves us locked in a lifelong battle." His gaze flickered down to her. "I admit that before meeting you, I thought I deserved to die because I dropped the ball. I missed the signs that Chop was going down the road of self-harm, but I'm not willing to die by Loki's hand, Sage. Not anymore."

"People miss signs, Kingdom. Even the closest friends and family members."

"It was my job to watch over him. From the time I found him in that closet, it was my job." He balled his hand into a fist and pounded his chest.

Sage hushed him. Her hand inched closer to his heart and massaged it right where it hurt the most.

"Blaming yourself isn't going to help. Even if you and Loki think it was your responsibility, I don't believe for one minute that Chop thought that. He was a man, Kingdom. He was a grown *man*, not the same little kid you found in that closet. He had the soul of a man and the demons of one. Even you, as strong as you are, couldn't save a man from himself. And he'd hate for you to blame yourself for the decision he made as an adult about his own life. You may not agree with it, you may hate it, but you must honor it because it was *his* to make. You must forgive yourself because you couldn't have saved him. Even if you caught the signs, this isn't the type of loss people believe will happen. Give yourself a break if only because it wasn't in your power to save him."

She grabbed the sides of his face and brought him in for a fierce kiss. He allowed it, but when she pushed against his chest to free herself, he couldn't let her go. Squeezing his eyes shut, he buried his face in her neck and splayed his hands to grasp as much of her as he could. Forgiveness, she'd said. Forgive himself and honor Chop's free will. *That's the heart of the matter, isn't it?*

26

KINGDOM

Kingdom and his brothers rolled down a two-lane road under a crisp blue sky scattered with clouds like a flock of white doves.

They were on their way to Canada to meet with associates regarding the transport of cigarettes over the border. Talk was that the Canadians were going to significantly jack up the tax on packs of cigarettes. The Squad already had pathways for shipments in places all the way up to Massachusetts.

Time to connect the dots from Mass to Canada because the Provincetown Hellions MC were putting the pressure on them. While the runs to Canada would be much longer, the Hellions were dirty fighters and, with Chop so recently gone and Prez out of commission, the Squad couldn't afford the ugliness of a war.

It got under Kingdom's skin, though, because they'd spent significant time and energy developing contacts and building relationships with a network of individual small business owners. To have the Hellions usurp their hard work was intolerable.

Kingdom concluded that he hated week-long rides linked to jobs. Used to be, he loved the rush of long rides and quick pussy. But not today. He recalled last night—Sage, positioned doggy style on his bed while he battered her cunt. Bucking into her as her pussy milked him, urging him on. *Kingdom, oh God, harder, harder.*

Nothing, and he meant nothing, beat the sound of her screaming his name and begging him for more. He couldn't wait to be back home licking her sweet pussy. Once his nose and mouth were full of her scent and taste, he'd drag her ass to the edge of the bed and pummel into her in one go until he bottomed out. But more than sex, he simply missed her. All of her. He never had that with a woman before, and it was hard to be away from her.

Jaw clenched under his helmet, he clipped out. "Overnight. Fine. Two nights, not so much."

"What'd you say?" Puck asked, riding alongside him.

"I was sayin' thank fuck I got a break from Loki's ugly ass."

Damn his brothers. They whiled away their time trying to rile him up. As long as Sage was safe, nothing would rattle him. Another reason he was stewing—he didn't trust the prospects to take care of her as well as he did. There wasn't a specific threat, but one could never be too vigilant with the current tensions with the Hellions. *Yeah, yeah, I might be overreacting, but I don't give a rat's ass.* He missed the soft warmth of her sleeping body nestled into his own as they spooned in bed. Once they were done with this job, he'd have his brothers debrief Prez without him. Kingdom planned to ride straight to Sage's place, and God help his woman if she wasn't there. He'd hunt her down and fuck her against the nearest wall.

On the outskirts of Albany, the men turned into a gas station across from a tattered, abandoned Methodist church. Ivy dripped off the gabled roofline, cascading down the trimmed stone encasing broken windows. Despite the ornate bell tower, the once thriving gathering site was now fodder for squatters.

Puck loped a leg over the seat of his Harley. "For fuck's sake, quit texting. Wherever we are," he remarked to the rest of the men, "Kingdom's on his phone. Like a sixteen-year-old with his first crush."

Flicking his fingers one by one, Cutter recited the list, "Parking lots, piss stops, stop lights. Hell, he'll text at a stop sign, for Christ's sake. A stop sign doesn't mean you sit on your bike and let traffic build up on your ass."

Kingdom put down his phone. "Quit hatin' on me 'cause you don't have sweet pussy waiting for you."

"If it's a contest between an easy fuck with pumped-up tits or being pussy-whipped like you, I'll take freedom any fuckin' day."

Kingdom guffawed. "Good thinking, since you don't have a choice. You ain't got what it takes to rein in a real woman. After a month, they drop you or you kick 'em to the curb."

"I was with Stacey for five fuckin' months."

"Stacey lied and said she was pregnant by you. You stayed with her until you found out the baby wasn't yours. That doesn't count," Kingdom countered.

"Let me tell you, five months with her was like getting locked up in solitary. One time I don't wrap up my dick, one fuckin' time, and I could've knocked the bitch up."

"You've got no one to blame but yourself," retorted Puck.

Kingdom stuck the nozzle into the tank of his bike. He spoke seriously. "Someone up there's got your back because Stacey would've been the worst kind of baby mama, but she was dumb enough to drag Prez into her shit." He shook his head. "Bad move on her part."

Puck chimed in, "Prez got her to take a paternity test, and that was the end of that."

"Talking about Stacey," Cutter muttered, "is killin' my fuckin' vibe. Rides are about brothers, money, and strippers."

Tank walked out of the gas station convenience store with his hands full of snacks and drinks. He handed each brother an energy drink.

"Drink up, brothers, we got a ways to go before reaching the border."

Times like these, Kingdom felt Chop's absence acutely. They'd ride side by side, partners in crime. The buzz of riding was gone without Chop. At least Sage had infused peace back into his life and placated the wounded beast he'd become. The words from their last discussion rang in his mind. *Forgive yourself and honor him.* The physical distance from Sage felt like a hundred-pound weight on his chest. His lungs would collapse before long if he didn't breathe the same air as her soon. A nervous twitch in his hand forced him to grip the handlebars tighter as he roared his bike to life.

27

KINGDOM

*B*ack in Poughkeepsie.

Thank fuck.

The deal with the Squad's Canadian counterpart had gone well, and Kingdom rode back like the very devil was snapping at his heels. The brothers gripped the entire ride back, and he was sorely tempted to leave them to their debauchery, but it was his responsibility to watch over them and bring them back in one piece.

With the rising morning sun warming his back, he rode straight to Sage's house. The instant she opened the door, sleepy and warm, he hugged her tightly, breathing in the sweet vanilla scent of her. Backstepping her into the house, he released her only long enough to shed his dusty cut, shirt, and leathers. Then his hands were back on her, tearing at her nightie until she was naked beneath him.

They didn't make it to the bed. He was on the floor with

Sage straddling him. She was downright feral. No foreplay. Nothing except her dripping wet pussy aligned above his erection. Without hesitation, Sage impaled herself on the spear of his cock. She took every inch of him. The position was tough for her, but she took it. Every. Fucking. Inch. Fuckin' glorious.

His hands steadied her as she lifted and slammed back down, angling herself to the left or right, grinding her clit against his groin on each downward sweep.

She fucked him as if possessed, scoring his shoulders and chest with her sharp incisors. She lashed his thighs with her nails. He reached for her, but she brushed his large hands off and slapped them down on the rug. Bending from the waist, her ass rose and fell as she rode him for gold, both moaning and cursing.

"Slide down on my cock, baby. Just like that," he praised.

Licking the curve of his cheekbone, she nipped along his jaw and moved down his throat for a bite. Kingdom twisted his head away, but she latched onto the exposed tendon, clamping down on the sensitive flesh. He exhaled harshly at the sweet pain. He took her attack with twitching muscles, barely leashing the lust thrashing against his ribs. Kingdom lifted her up and spread her knees wider. "Goddamn, you missed me. Should leave more often."

"Don't you dare," she warned. "I'm getting attached to you, you bastard, and I don't like it when you leave me."

That was the first time she's admitted to caring about him. He'd seen it in her actions, but hearing the words made him want to mount her from behind with his teeth locked on her nape. "Mark me, baby. Do me harder," he demanded.

Sage licked the juncture between his neck and shoulder, then chomped down, shaking her head like a puppy with a toy. Damn, she withdrew and there was blood smearing her lower lip. She'd drawn blood. His body shook fiercely. Not aware of her bloody lips, she dipped her head and sucked on his nipple. When she released it, the flesh was circled red.

When the awareness dawned on her of what she'd done, her arousal gushed around his cock and balls. Whimpering, Sage undulated her hips, giving her clit the pressure it needed. Thrashing on his dick, she exploded. It was like watching a tornado power through her. He braced his hands on her hips and hammered into her with unrelenting speed and strength. Another orgasm hit her, and he convulsed under her, hot spurts shooting out and filling her with his come.

Mindless, she collapsed, and he caught her shoulders, easing her down onto his chest. Gently he withdrew, tilted her off him, and laid her gently on the rug. Once on his feet, he picked her up and brought her to her bedroom. On the bed, she sighed and grasped the bed sheets. He lay down beside and snuggled her into his chest. Within seconds she was asleep. Blood trickled from the puncture on his neck and the nicks covering his shoulder and back. He peered over his shoulder and chuckled. The sound roused her. Sage turned to her side, her chin on the back of her hand, watching him.

"Babe, I've never been marked like this. You were demon possessed. No woman's drawn blood like you."

She gingerly touched them. "I better get the first-aid kit and clean these out."

His grin widened. "Lie back down. You're not touching these. I'm going to show off your claw marks the minute I hit the club."

Sage covered her face and groaned. "You will do no such thing. The brothers will massacre me."

He scoffed. "*My* woman did this. They'll burn with envy."

"You're going to strut around the clubhouse shirtless to flaunt the bites and scrapes on your back?" She shook her head ruefully. "I don't understand men." He was tempted but decided not to tease her because they both knew what she was doing; she was branding him. She had stained his skin like a consummate calligrapher. Hot as fuck.

"I'm your woman, then?" she asked, peering closely at him.

What the hell did she think?

"Of course you are. And you know it. You purposely chose fresh, clean skin, free of tats, for your teeth marks. To brand me. Because you own me, and you want everyone to know it. You own me as much as I own you, Sage."

His cock thickened and waved like a flag on a mast, weeping for her attention.

"Again," he growled.

She was on him in an instant, flattening her tongue on the raised flesh of his nipple. He braced himself to see what type of torture she was going to administer next. She grazed her teeth over his nipple, but instead of a strong bite, she pressed her lips and pulsed her jaws gently, urging blood to the tip.

By the time her mouth reached his cock, Sage had left a trail down his belly. A collection of stains, bites, and sucks were imprinted across the canvas of his body. He gazed down with pride. Pure and unadulterated ownership, that's what it was.

"I do own you, don't I?" she said, a Cheshire Cat smile spreading on her lips. Her hands splayed out and glided down his chest to wrap around his cock. "I own every inch of this."

"Yeah, baby, you do," he breathed out like a prayer.

※※※

The following afternoon, Kingdom was dozing in her bed after his appetite for her had slaked a bit. He fucked her, showered, ate, and fucked her again. Then he blacked out. Lounging with his hand behind his head, Sage's authoritative tone filtered down the hall and through the bedroom door left ajar.

He overheard Cutter say, "I gotta talk to Kingdom." What the fuck was his brother doing intruding on his time with Sage? It'd barely been twenty-four hours.

"Don't even think of waking him up, Cutter. Kingdom is recuperating."

He grinned. No one ever bothered to attend to his needs until now, and it felt good.

"Recuperating? Shit, it's not like he's sick. Are you seriously not going to invite me in? Not even for a beer?"

Kingdom suppressed a laugh, knowing Cutter was using his well-honed weapon—his puppy-dog look.

"Emotional blackmail will not work with me. If I invite you in, then you must promise not to wake him up. Otherwise, I will murder you. Premeditated first-degree murder would be the exact term."

"Warning fucking received," Cutter grumbled.

He shifted his head and glanced at the clock; it was past five o'clock. Linking his other hand behind his head, he relaxed to enjoy their sparring outside. If he told her that she didn't have to take care about his sleep, she'd have a smart answer and toss in some crazy-ass statistics about how the lack of sleep could affect his libido or semen count. She knew how to scare the hell out of a man. A man's dick was not a topic to be taken lightly. He heard Sage shush Cutter.

"Cutter, lower the volume of the TV. Didn't I explain in the simplest terms possible that I will kill you if you wake him up? Is something wrong that you're incapable of retaining what I just said?" Sage snapped. *Better save the asshole before she maims him for good.*

Kingdom rolled out of bed, padded to the entrance, and revealed his presence. "She's a spitfire, for sure."

Cutter griped, "Yeah, yeah. Shut your trap, I can't hear the show."

"I told you to keep it down. Look"—she threw her hand in his direction—"now you've woken him up," she accused Cutter. "Go back to the clubhouse if you want peace."

Cutter twisted around and looked at her aghast. "The brothers aren't gonna let me watch my show in peace."

Sage stared at the screen, and her brows knitted. "You're watching *The Real Housewives of New York?*" She broke out in peals of laughter. "Oh my God! A biker shamelessly sucking up the drama of spoiled rich women. Unbelievable."

Catching the spark of mischief in Sage's eyes, Cutter vowed, "If you tell any-fuckin'-one, I will make sure your cat connects with the front wheel of my bike."

"Phantom." Sage inhaled sharply. "Don't you dare threaten Phantom." She covered her ears. "I didn't hear that. To think she curled up in your lap just the other day. Traitor."

"What can I say? I'm a dog. Cats love dogs. Pussies act all uppity, but they love themselves a dirty dawg like me."

Turning on Sage, Kingdom spoke hotly, "You hassle me when I play with Phantom, but you let him get away with threatening her life."

"You're too rough with her."

"Not as rough as I'm going to be with you," he growled and grabbed for her. She stepped back at the last moment. Leaning against the back of her sofa, her gaze dragged down his bare torso, stopping at the open top button of his jeans. Her rapt attention had him shaking his head. Growing hard under her appraisal, he said in a soft voice, "What you do to me."

Strutting past him on the way to the kitchen, Sage's fingers skimmed over his abs. Her touch caused goosebumps to break over his skin. His fist wrapped around her forearm, and with a brisk yank, she flattened against him. Kingdom nuzzled her ear before whispering, "I'm gonna punish you for letting Cutter get one up on me. I own Phantom like I own you."

Grasping the back of her neck in an unyielding hold, his mouth crushed hers. With a twist of her braid around his fist, Sage's lips opened wider, and he slashed his tongue inside like a swashbuckler. Keeping her in place, he broke the hard kiss and threw Cutter a look of admonishment. "You're botherin' my woman."

Unabashed, his brother lifted his beer bottle to his lips and took an unhurried swallow. "Hell no. For fuck's sake, she threatened my life with that evil eye of hers." He took another swig. "I'd be safer fighting insurgents in the dust bowl."

Laughing, Kingdom released his grip on her and batted her bottom. She cried out, "A *soft* touch," and rubbed her butt. Sashaying into the kitchen, she called, "I'm going to invite you and whichever brothers you think can behave themselves here for dinner. Kingdom can barbecue. I'll take care of the rest and bake you guys some incredible cakes."

Cutter's head snapped toward Kingdom, his eyes wide with surprise. "Does she know what she's getting if she invites those roughnecks over here?"

"No fucking idea," he replied, shaking his head ruefully.

"This is a big step," Cutter observed quietly. "I didn't think you could do it, but you might have snagged yourself an old lady. Good on you, son."

28

SAGE

Sage dropped two large paper bags full of Thai food on Greta's desk, then stripped off her suit jacket and dropped it on the seat in the waiting room.

"It's June, and summer has officially arrived. No more jackets," she said, giving the offensive item a narrow-eyed stare.

"You're getting hangry," Greta noted, moving piles of papers and folder files off her desk. "Come on, take out the food so we can chow down."

Greta was right. She hadn't had a proper breakfast, and she was starving. Pulling out cartons and plastic containers, she arranged the food and took a pair of chopsticks between her fingers.

"Go ahead; don't wait for me," Greta urged with a wave of her hands.

Sage dug in and moaned around the first bite. "So good. Being in the car with the food smell was killing me." She jabbed another bite of Drunken Noodles into her mouth. Greta sat down in her seat, whipped a napkin over her short leather skirt and grabbed the carton of rice. Spilling it onto her paper plate, she queried, "So, how are things going with Kingdom?

Sage grinned around her food. Holding up a finger to tell Greta that she needed to chew properly and swallow, she answered, "Good. What am I saying? Great. Really great."

"I'm glad for you, Sage, really I am. I'll admit that I was suspicious of him for a while there because, in my experience, bikers are basically man whores, but I'm glad you found the one guy who can keep it in his pants. Otherwise, I've done my research, and the Squad is a respectable enough club in the MC world. I repeat, MC world, not the civilian world."

"Are you attempting to make a specific point, Greta?"

"You know the point I'm making."

Sage put her chopsticks down carefully on the napkin beside her open container. "Their businesses. The way they make money. Am I okay with it? I would prefer if they made their money in a way that wouldn't jeopardize their freedom. I don't know the details, and I don't want to know. In this area, I've put blinkers on because I want to be with him."

"You must want to be with him badly, then. I understand. I fell in love once, and I was willing to do anything for him. Including returning to my father's club, which would've been a disaster."

"Is that the definition of love, then? Being willing to do things one would not normally do."

Greta snorted. "If you're dealing with a biker, the short answer would be yes. I'd say it's a pretty strong indication that you are in love with him. I don't see you being with someone like Kingdom otherwise."

"I'm not a snob," Sage said in a quiet voice.

"I never thought you were. I'm talking about accepting that Kingdom is in a club that has an illegal side to their business."

Sage picked up her chopsticks and dug in again. They ate in quiet for a while. "I care about him more than I thought possible. At first, I thought I was too fragile to be with a man, but he persisted through the walls I erected. After that hurdle was cleared, I assumed that he had no interest in commitment, but he didn't bat an eyelash when I told him that I didn't do casual hook-ups. He's caring, if a bit too overprotective. And he makes me feel special, like I can do something for him that no one else can. Then there's the sex, which has been a game-changer. I mean, I had no idea what I was missing until he barged into my life."

Greta chuckled. "The sex. What I wouldn't do to find a man who could satisfy me the way I needed."

Sage tilted her head to the side, watching her curiously. Greta had hinted at special needs before but never elaborated. She always made it sound like it was near impossible to find.

"Definitely hold onto someone who knows how to satisfy you," Greta continued, "because that doesn't come along every day. I hope that you don't feel like you're sacrificing a part of yourself to accept the Squad's activities."

Sage pursed her lips and pondered the issue. Did she feel that it was a heavy burden? "My concern is about the safety of him and the club. That's it. Not that what they're doing is right or legal, but they aren't into hardcore stuff. That might have been a deal breaker. You know, if I had married Stanton, he could've given me everything. He came from a family that was the closest to aristocracy as there is in America. A prestigious, old-monied family. His father's a senator. He's one of the youngest prosecutors in the county. Yet underneath the success and material trappings, he was empty inside. He feared intimacy and dealt with it by cheating on me. Hell, I'd choose a man like Kingdom, a man with emotional depth and honor, over a man like Stanton ten times over."

The phone on Greta's desk rang. Sage reached over to pick up the handle, but Greta's hand dropped over hers and stopped her. Shaking her head, she said, "Let's make a rule. When we're having lunch, which only happens once a week, let's have it go to voicemail. In fact, we should lock the door as well."

Sage flashed Greta a brilliant smile. "That sounds like a fine idea."

"Cool."

"That reminds me," began Sage, "I've been thinking about taking on some pro bono clients since you've officially received your Paralegal Degree. I've been thinking about creating a program where we take on work from indigent clients. A core group that really needs help. Any ideas?"

"I have just three words for you—domestic violence survivors. They need help, especially if they fight back against their abusers. The Domestic Violence Survivors Act was signed into law over a year ago, and it can reduce the sentences of survivors who can prove that domestic violence contributed to their criminal acts. I don't know if you've been following the recent case here in Poughkeepsie, but Judge McLoughlin denied the defense's request under the D.V.S.A., and she got nineteen years out of a max of twenty-five. These are the people we need to help," Greta ended vehemently.

"Of course," Sage murmured soberly, "I've been paying attention to it. It was a case with complications."

"Not so many complications that it warranted not giving the defense a chance to discuss the level of abuse the defendant had suffered. Besides helping survivors in general, we should take these kinds of cases because the more that come in front of judges, the less they'll be able to dismiss them so easily."

"Yeah, okay. We need to start slow, but we will focus on this target group."

Greta let out a heavy sigh. "Thank you."

Sage reached for Greta's hand and squeezed it. "Of course."

29

KINGDOM

Loki swiveled on his stool and followed Sage with his eyes as she moved past him to the end of the bar.

Kingdom raised his glass to his lips as he clocked Loki's move, placing the drink on the bar top just as Sage launched herself into his arms. He caught her and held her close, whispering words of desire against her ear as his eyes bared down on Loki.

"There goes one fine piece of ass," Loki commented to Cutter, who sat beside him, a few stools down from Kingdom. Cutter threw Kingdom a look of alarm.

Kingdom held Sage close to him. Although she squirmed against him, rubbing against his crotch and making him hard, Kingdom whispered low, "Hush, I gotta listen to Loki's bullshit."

She stilled at the seriousness of his tone of voice. Tightening his grasp, he ordered, "Don't look at him. Just pretend everything's normal." She followed his lead and allowed him to lift her onto his lap, facing away from Loki.

His gaze cut to Loki for a moment as he overheard Cutter caution, "Turn away, Loki. Don't start trouble."

"Wasted on that fuckin' cocksucker."

"Stop hatin' on him already," Cutter replied, exasperated.

Kingdom's eyes flicked their way again. Loki had crossed his arms over his chest, a mule-like expression stamped on his face. "I didn't vote for him as VP, and I sure as hell don't like him. He didn't take care of Chopper. How's he gonna take care of the brothers or a class act like her?" Loki snarled, loud and clear.

His words hung in the air like a red flag in front of a bull. Everyone's conversation sputtered and shut down. The gauntlet was thrown at his feet. Kingdom swept Sage behind him and into Tank's arms. Glancing back to check on Sage one last time, he rose slowly out of his seat. Cutter shot to his feet and blocked Kingdom's approach.

"Our brother, my brother"—Loki sneered with a violent roll of his shoulders—"dies and you're fuckin' whores. You were oath bound to watch over Chopper, but you fell down on the job."

"Yeah? Easy to blame another man when you abandoned him at the fuckin' ripe old age of twelve. You, the big man fighting for his country, but I didn't see you man up to fight for your brother. You left that to others." Kingdom fisted the cotton of his shirt, stretching the material taut, and spat out, "You want this, then bring it."

Cutter covered Kingdom's front, attempting to hold him back. Loki lunged around him, but Cutter slammed a sharp elbow into his belly, leaving Loki winded. Staggering back, he doubled over. His head snapped up, straining the tendons of his neck, and he let out a wild roar. Three brothers rushed

Loki before he charged at Kingdom and dragged him toward the door. Someone had flung open the clubhouse entrance. They were hauling a howling Loki out the door when Prez stormed out of his office.

Stalking toward the crowd, he bellowed, "What the fuck is going on in my clubhouse?"

Loki snapped his mouth shut but didn't stop his struggle.

Prez got in his face. "We voted in an election. You lost your shit, and the brothers had to drag you out. I took that as a vote of no. Kingdom is VP, and there ain't nothin' you can do about it. Sort your shit out, Loki, before I sort it out for you. You won't like what I do with you, feel me?"

Prez stepped back and signaled to the brothers, "Get him the fuck outta here." They dragged him out by force, but even with him gone, the shut door didn't drown out the sounds of the men scuffling.

Prez swiped a hand over his face and turned to Kingdom. "Leave him be. You're brothers of the Squad. You can't be killin' each other over this shit."

Cutter put in his two cents. "What he did wasn't right, Prez. I can testify from what I've seen. Kingdom was there for Chopper." Kingdom clasped Cutter's shoulder to shut him up, but he shrugged off the hand and finished, "Loki, not so much. But I reckon he's holdin' onto more guilt than you."

Prez gave Cutter a directive. "Watch Kingdom's back because a wounded dog bites out of pain." He gave Kingdom a thoughtful look, then glanced over Kingdom's shoulder at Sage. With a chin lift, he said, "She's gonna be trouble, that one. Claim her already."

Kingdom clipped out, "Respectfully speaking Prez, mind your business."

"Suit yourself," Prez replied with a shrug and headed toward his office.

Kingdom drew a harsh intake of breath. Spotting Sage behind Tank's back, he growled low and seized her arm. Bringing her within the cove of his protection, he caressed her back with a gentleness he didn't know he was capable of. The closeness of her body puffed life back into his lungs.

His fingers were still locked around her upper arm, causing red spots to form in the spaces between his fingers. He lifted his hand off her and massaged the print marks. "It's alright, baby, it's alright."

Embracing him, she hid herself in his wide shoulders and pleaded in a muted tone, "I don't want anything to happen to you."

"Nothing's going to happen. It's club business, that's all," he replied as he stroked her hair. Tilting her chin up, he caught the few tears beading at the corners of her eyes. Rubbing his fingertips dry of Sage's tears, he realized that he was done taking Loki's punishments. Done. There were better things to do with his life than drowning himself in grief. Things like hope, forgiveness, and Sage.

She was right; Chop would've never tolerated him wallowing in self-pity. He would've told Kingdom to fuck off, that it was his decision and he'd done exactly what he'd meant to do. It was a hard pill to swallow, but swallow it, he would because it was the truth. And because he had something to live for again. Someone to protect and look after. Someone who could look after him too. Loki's resentments festered because Kingdom was getting better, and the better he got, the meaner Loki got. His hand wrapped around Sage's nape and pulled her in closer.

His lips flattened in a grim slash of determination. If Loki fucked with him again, brother or not, he was a dead man.

SAGE

Sage tried his cellphone again, and it went to voicemail for the fifth time.

She was ready to scream. Whistle was a certified pain in her butt.

Why, but why, did clients flake out when there was a court deadline?

After Tank's case was dismissed, Sage had taken on other cases for the Squad. Turns out, Tank had put Whistle's behavior to shame. *Deep breaths, deep breaths.* Unclenching her balled fists, she took in a breath and exhaled slowly. The kid—and at nineteen years old, he was an immature kid—was totally unreliable. It'd be a miracle if he made it through a year of prospecting and managed to patch into the club.

Sage tapped her manicured fingers on the Motion to Dismiss sitting on her desk, ready to file minus Whistle's signature. It wouldn't take but a minute, and still, the man-child didn't bother to show up or call her. Sage considered her options. Kingdom was busy, and she didn't want to bother him over something as simple as this.

The phone on her desk rang, and she snatched the receiver immediately.

"Hey Sage, it's Whistle. I'm stuck in the middle of something, but I can run by the clubhouse to sign what you need if you can swing by."

A niggling discomfort blew across her nape. Sage had never gone alone, even for her appointments with Prez to update him on cases. Kingdom was always by her side. But Kingdom wasn't around, so she had to get her butt into gear and do it herself.

"Sure, Whistle. I'll leave now and meet you there."

"I'll leave as soon as I can," he answered and hung up.

Swiping the file off her desk, she gathered her purse and stepped into the reception area. "Greta, I've got to get Whistle's signature. He's a no-show, and I have to file this thing today."

She perked up at the mention of Whistle.

Sage waved the legal folder file in her hand. "I'm going to the clubhouse."

Greta's spine straightened like a flagpole. "Alone?" Swerving in her chair, she planted her knee-high leather gladiator boots akimbo on her desk. Her head shook, causing the long strands of chunky jewelry hanging from her throat to sway from side to side. "Why don't you call up Kingdom and he'll track Whistle down for you?"

She shouldn't blithely dismiss Greta's concern, but if Kingdom's life was the Squad, then she should be comfortable enough to walk in there without hanging on his arm.

"Sheesh, I'll be fine. The brothers know me. I'll get the signature and be out of there in a jiffy. I must get this stamped at the Clerk's Office by the end of the day. A simple motion that should have taken a couple hours is going to take up half my day. I swear, I'm going to give Whistle a piece of my mind."

She was on a mission, and when her mission was on behalf of a client, there was no swaying her from her conviction.

❄❄❄

The Demon Squad headquarters was housed in a large renovated brick building that wrapped itself around the corner of the street. It was the one detached building on a street lined with brick rowhouses that had once been the adobe of middle-class families. The clubhouse was surrounded by an ominous eight-foot chain-link fence. A warning to intruders.

Sage's car raced over potholes and cracks spouting tufts of weeds. She parked alongside a succinct line of bikes, peering out her windshield to see if she recognized the prospect leaning against the fence. Dragging on a blunt, his face was obscured by the blue smoke enveloping him like a delicate veil before merging with the foggy morning. She approached him with a strong desire to wave her hand and cleanse the air of the pungent smoke.

His name escaped her, but Sage graced him with her brightest smile. "Hi there, I'm here to see Whistle. I'm his lawyer, you see."

The prospect's eyes roved appreciatively over her V-neck blouse. She sighed. Predictable. She was beginning to sympathize with Kingdom and his exasperation over some of the prospects.

"Aren't you Kingdom's woman?"

"Yes, but I'm here to see Whistle."

"Whistle isn't in there, but sure, go on in," he replied, waving her toward the door.

Although it was midmorning, the bikers were getting up for the day. Sage recognized Cutter at the bar with a woman hanging off his side. Gunner, behind the bar, slid a concoction of some kind in front of Cutter, who downed it without a thought. Probably to cure his obvious hang-over. Walking over to him with a grin, she slid onto the stool next to him. "Rough night, Cutter?"

Bloodshot eyes focused on her. "Hey, Sage, how ya doing?" he asked with a wide smile. He swiveled on the bar stool and looked around her. "Where's Kingdom?"

"I'm not sure where he is at the moment. I'm here to meet Whistle. He missed his appointment with me this morning, and there's a motion he has to sign as soon as possible."

"Oh, I think he's with Kingdom. Let me give Kingdom a call and have him bring Whistle here for you. Believe me, it'll be faster this way."

Cutter prodded the woman off him and moved away to use his cellphone. Pursing her lips, Sage placed Whistle's file on the bar and demurely folded her hands over it.

"You don't belong here, bitch."

Sage whirled around to find a biker bitch staring her down. Her aggression hit the air, disrupting the space surrounding her. She looked used, sporting her peroxide-white hair, raccoon eyes, and skin-tight clothes.

"You're kidding yourself if you think you can be Kingdom's old lady," she jeered. "You're nothin' special. You sure can't satisfy a man like Kingdom." Her lips curled as she scoured Sage's suit with derision. The bikers fell silent, brazenly eaves-dropping on the confrontation. Sage's eyes narrowed. Who did this woman think she was? Her face was familiar, although they had never been introduced. Her name was Tammy or

Terry. She snapped her fingers. Trixie. Already stressed about the motion, Sage wasn't in the mood to deal with this woman's aggressive posturing.

"Jealous much? What goes on between Kingdom and me is none of your business."

"Same goes for me. What goes on between Kingdom and *me* is none of *your* goddamned business."

Sage reared back as if Trixie had backhanded her. A jolt of shame, eerily familiar after Stanton's betrayals, struck her. The noxious creature of humiliation coiled deep in her belly.

"Wh-what did you say?"

"For an uppity bitch, you're stupid as fuck. You ain't the only bitch Kingdom is fuckin'."

The blood drained out of Sage's face, rushing down to feed the growing monster in her gut.

Stepping up, Trixie cupped her silicone-pumped breasts and thrust them in Sage's face. "See these? Kingdom fucked them and came in my mouth. He tastes good, doesn't he?" She smacked her lips grotesquely. "Love the grunts he makes when he's coming and sprays over my tits. Yum-my."

Sage was paralyzed, incapable of tearing herself away from the vitriol spewing out of Trixie's mouth. Her ears pounded with a rush of incoming blood and then drowned in a roar. Burning fire competed with ice-cold chills across her skin.

God, she was *such* a fool.

Stark breaths racked her frame, playing havoc with her nerves. Of course Kingdom sexed up other women. She'd arrogantly thought she'd learned her lesson with Stanton, but nothing had prepared her for Kingdom's treachery. Her head was inundated with a strange, loud buzzing as if her heart had been pummeled and knocked out of the ring.

Trixie's eyes gleamed with triumph. "Kingdom will always come back to us *bitches* to give it to him good. He loves *biker* pussy, not high-class whores like you. I get why a desperate and bored bitch like you wants to fuck a man with a real dick, but he's been using you for lawyering." With a harsh laugh, Trixie taunted her, "Honey, you ain't got what it takes to keep a man like him."

"Trixie! Back the fuck off," barked Cutter, his tone laced with the threat of murder.

Swooning slightly, Sage forced her broken frame upright and slipped off the stool. It tottered and crashed onto the bare concrete. Cutter's head whipped in Sage's direction. He rushed over, towering over her with arms out as if to pen her in against the bar. He couldn't put his hands on her. Even though Kingdom hadn't made her official, to Cutter she was another man's property.

Taking advantage of that fact, Sage dodged his arms and staggered away from the bar. Her gaze collided with Cutter's. His expression held a fear that might have matched her own. It only made her believe Trixie more. *Why isn't he denying it? If it wasn't true, surely he'd deny it.* Moving away quickly, her eyes swept over the bikers, but her vision became a blur. Before she knew it, her legs buckled underneath her, and Cutter was holding her up.

Glaring at the bikers, he bellowed, "You didn't shut up her fuckin' mouth when you saw I was on the phone with Kingdom? Useless motherfuckers, every one of you!"

Not one of them answered, and one by one, they cast their heads down, dodging eye contact.

He turned on Trixie. "Bitch, have you lost your fuckin' mind? She's Kingdom's old lady, for Christ's sake."

The expression on Trixie's face lost some of its insolence. "She isn't," Trixie hissed. "He hasn't claimed her, not officially. And Kingdom fucked me too. He's with her because of what happened with Chop."

"Bitch, do you have a death wish or what? You better make yourself scarce before he shows up and sees her like this." Cutter hauled Sage up as if she was an exhibition. Tearing herself out of Cutter's vise hold, she stepped back. Her back hit the bar. Caging her in, he took a soothing tone with her. "Calm down, Sage. Look at me, sweetheart, he's comin'. He's coming back for you."

It didn't matter if Kingdom was coming. Trixie had confessed to having sex with Kingdom. Cutter kept talking in a cajoling, gentle voice, but she stopped registering his words.

She pounded on his chest, and he took the blows until she wore herself out. Her arms dropped listlessly to her sides. She concentrated on the planks on the floor, counting the scuffs and marks, murmuring low, "Catch and release. Catch and release. He caught me, but he let me go, just like Stanton. Trixie's right, of course. I don't have what it takes to keep him."

Sage looked up at the brothers, holding their gazes one by one, and said, "You thought I was slumming it, didn't you? But you're wrong. I care..." She swallowed. "Cared for him. I'm not the one in the wrong." She jabbed a finger into Cutter. "Kingdom is. He wronged me. Calling me his woman repeatedly. I showed up for him. I showed up for all of you. I was 'lawyering' for the club, not because I wanted to hang around bikers. I respected you and gave it my all when I represented your cases."

Sage slid under Cutter's arm and sidestepped him. "Don't touch me." Raising her gaze to his, she whispered, "He's all yours. I asked only one thing from him, and he gave it to someone else. A lot of things are worth fighting for, but a cheater isn't one of them."

"This is not good," Cutter blurted out. "Not good. Wait for Kingdom. He'll fix this clusterfuck."

Sage snatched Whistle's file with the toss of her head, her

eyes flickering from side to side like a panicked horse. Her hands mashed the stiff spine of the legal file in her grip. In a monotone, she ordered, "Tell Whistle to contact Greta. She'll get the signature and file the motion."

Sage swallowed the urge to cry bearing down on her, about to rip a gash in her self-control. This experience was not new to her, and she knew that she didn't have much time before shock set in. Already, she had to clamp her jaw down on her chattering teeth. *Chin up, girl.*

Head high, she draped herself in a cloak of a majesty. Nodding once to Cutter, who watched her with his hands stretched out like a supplicant, she pivoted on her heels and ran out, leaving behind the ghost of her presence.

31

SAGE

age peeled out of the parking space.

Fuck, fuck, FUCK!

With trembling hands, she raced through the neighborhood and steered onto a highway ramp. Hitting the accelerator, her gaze fixated on the speedometer as the needle spun farther and farther to the right. Seventy miles... seventy-five... eighty... eighty-five... *Hell yes.*

She began cackling, clearing out the pent-up hysteria jamming her throat. In the wake of her last laugh, tears welled up and coursed down her cheeks. Just as she feared, the flood-gates burst.

It was her own fault. He'd addled her brain with hot sex, and she'd given her trust too easily. So, they'd spent some time together. So, they'd had a few deep conversations. Clearly, it didn't mean anything beyond sex. "Damn him to hell and back," she screamed as she twisted the steering wheel in time to get off at the exit. She'd fallen for his suffering, for his wounded hero act. Believed that he'd let down his walls for her because she was special. *Special! Ha!* God, she was such an idiot.

Focus, Sage.

Her mind clicked into OCD planning mode.

Item one: Get to the office without crashing.

Item two: Reveal miserable story to Greta because she'll have to take over the office when I'm gone.

The option to bury herself in her work wasn't going to cut it, and the very idea of staying was unbearable. Leaving town had helped her with the Stanton debacle. Although, this already felt so much worse.

Item three: Go home, throw clothes into a suitcase.

Item four: Get the hell out of here.

She'd hole up in a hotel or bed and breakfast somewhere far out of reach. Once she was far enough away, she'd figure out her next steps. Offing herself was always an option.

Hold up! Hell no! No man was worth it. Alright then, she would weep her heart out and wallow in righteous self-pity.

The car screeched as she hit the brake hard, sending herself flying forward. Her forehead smashed into the steering wheel. *Fuck, that hurt.* She slammed the door closed and stumbled her way down the graveled path. She made it into the office and crumbled in the nearest chair.

Greta shot to her feet and flew to her. Sinking down on her knees, Greta lifted her face up gently. Horror was written on Greta's face. With what was surely a welt blossoming on her forehead and streaks of black mascara tracking down her cheeks, Sage bet she looked like a crazy woman. Greta enveloped her in an embrace. The comfort was too good to reject, and Sage dropped her head and sobbed on Greta's shoulder.

"Who hit you? Kingdom?" Greta asked, her tone jagged with anger.

"I hit my head on the steering wheel of my car. At least I didn't kill anyone driving over here," she muttered.

"What the hell happened?"

"A biker chick named Trixie told me that she had sex with Kingdom," Sage choked out and buried her face in her hands.

"Shhh. Whatever happened, Sage, you'll survive this. I will do everything I can to help you." Tightening her arms around Sage, she spat out, "Fuck him. I trusted that fucker not to hurt you. Man, I'm usually on point when it comes to bikers, but I should've known it was too good to be true. A biker committing to one woman. *Ack*, ridiculous notion."

Pulling Sage away from her, Greta looked straight into her eyes with concern dotting her tensed brows. "He'll be coming after you. You have to leave."

A hysterical guffaw escaped Sage. "Did you not hear what I said? He had sex with another woman. A woman from his world. He's not coming after me. He cares nothing for me."

"He's a biker. In his mind, he's claimed you, even though he fucked around on you. I know it sounds insane, but he cares. Like that asshole ex of yours, he doesn't think he's done anything wrong."

"Whether he comes or not is irrelevant because I already decided to leave for a while. I can't stay here."

"Good girl." Greta heaved a sigh. "My mother and her old man have a place in Vermont. We're going to pack you up, and I'm gonna call her to let her know when to meet you at the train station. She'll take care of you because you can't be alone right now. You'll drive yourself crazy. I know I would."

Sage shook her head adamantly. "Your mom has no obligation to stay with me." Her hands fluttered down her torso. "Look at me, I'm a wreck. I feel like I'm going to die." She heaved. "He's just a man, but it hurts so badly that it feels like I'm dying. Please, I want to be alone."

"No. Way. You can't go through this alone. Believe me when I say that she has a long history of dealing with a bastard who stepped out on her. You're in for a tough time, and someone must be there to pull you off the edge. I must stay here to keep things running. My mom is the next best person."

Greta got to her feet and pulled Sage up with her. She went into her office and grabbed her laptop and the necessary files, then allowed Greta to drag her out the door. "I'll take Phantom, but let's get you to the train station first."

In her bedroom, Sage hauled out her Samsonite spinner luggage from the back of her closet and threw a random array of clothes in it as Greta phoned her mother and made the necessary arrangements. After purchasing a ticket for Sage, they discussed clients and any pending deadlines Greta should keep an eye on.

"Whistle and his deadline. Make sure you file it," Sage ordered. She laughed at Greta's reassurance that she'd make sure that "cocksucking bastard Whistle," would follow her orders. They hustled into Greta's car. While driving, Greta turned to her and gave her a hard look. "You're not going to dive under a heap of work to avoid what's happened. You need to give yourself the space and time to work through the damage he caused and to heal. There's no way that's going to happen if you work the entire time you're there."

"I promise I won't work non-stop," vowed Sage. "Anyway, I didn't bring enough cases with me for that."

"Good," replied Greta.

At the train station, Greta held her hand as she leaned against a column, willing herself not to succumb to her tears.

"Listen, Sage. My mom will wait for you to show. Do not

disappoint her. She'll take care of you and help you get through this."

Sage nodded mechanically, sniffled, and averted her eyes. Startled, Sage found her face cradled in Greta's warm hands. Raising Sage's chin, Greta held her gaze with knowing eyes. "You're strong, and you will come back even stronger. Do you hear me?"

Trembling from the energy it took not to lose her composure in public, Sage nodded her acquiescence.

The train pulled in. Sage gave Greta a fierce hug and swung her luggage up a series of metal steps. Settled in her seat, she massaged her breastbone with the heel of her palm, repeating Greta's words in an endless loop. It was all she had to keep her sane on her journey north.

32

KINGDOM

H is heart flatlined when he flew into the clubhouse and found that Sage was gone.

Cutter relayed the entire drama in all its ugly glory. He trembled with thundering rage. Cutter was aware of Sage's history with her cheating ex-fiancé. Trixie had hit Sage where it hurt, dragging up old trauma and piling a new one on top of it.

He felt it in his gut: Sage was gone for good. By failing to protect her, or at least keep her from escaping, Cutter had fucked up in a major way. But the onus was on Kingdom because he had failed to claim her in front of the club.

Seething with wrath, Kingdom unleashed his fury on the brothers. "You let Trixie trash talk her, and about something that happened inside this clubhouse, no less. Any shit"—he turned in a semicircle to stare down the men around him—

"that goes down inside this fuckin' club is sacred. You back-stabbed me when you let that bitch open her fuckin' mouth. And then you shit-for-brains motherfuckers let her go before I could implement damage control. If need be, you should've locked her up!"

Hearing the commotion, Prez stepped out of his office. Already briefed on what had gone down, he clamped an iron-strong hand down on Kingdom and shoved him roughly toward his office. One last slap to his back, and Kingdom stumbled into Prez's office. Shutting the door, Prez spread out his legs and folded his arms over the barrel of his chest. Blind and deaf to everything but his pain, Kingdom tossed whatever was in his reach and threw shit around the room, ranting against Trixie and the brothers.

After a while, Prez cut Kingdom off. "They fucked up, yeah, but what *you* do not fuckin' do is punish them. That's for me to do. Have no fear," he declared grimly, "they will be punished."

Kingdom caught the expression on Prez's face and winced.

"Son, she doesn't wear your property patch. If she was your old lady, then they'd have known what to do. Those boys live in two colors. Black and fuckin' white. You throw in gray, and they don't know which way to go. It's a mess, yeah, but you didn't claim her."

Prez held up a hand to stop when Kingdom was poised to interrupt him. "An unattached woman walked into the club unattended by her man. Something was bound to happen."

Kingdom propped his butt against Prez's desk and rubbed the back of his neck. "I'm fucked. Before her, I didn't give any bitch my time except to wet my dick, but the day I got a taste of her, I was a goner. So, being the asshole that I am, I fought it. I hit up Trixie. Having another woman in my bed was like a brush with death; I didn't go through with it. Tossed her out and this is her way of taking revenge."

"Yeah, I got that, son."

Glancing up at his leader, he braced himself for ridicule when he confessed, "I talk and laugh with her, for fuck's sake."

"My boy's done went and fallen in love."

He glowered at Prez. "I was close to lockin' her down when Trixie opened her damn mouth."

"Trixie was gunnin' to be your old lady."

Kingdom scoffed. "That was never going to happen. Told her so on more than one occasion. Always been straight up with her. An old lady is a man's other half, his better half."

"Why'd you wait to make Sage your property?"

Kingdom swallowed down the bile caught in his throat. "Chop didn't live long enough to have an old lady. If he couldn't, then I sure as hell didn't deserve to. My thought on the matter changed when Loki stepped up to her the other day. I saw that the time had come. For her protection and for my peace of mind."

Prez fixed Kingdom with a somber look. "Keep your distance from the brothers you're pissed off with till you find your woman. We put up with your fighting because of Chopper. We aren't gonna do it again because you fucked up with Sage."

"Fair enough." Watching Prez's thoughtful expression, Kingdom licked his dry lips. That look did not bode well for him. Not one bit. *Here comes the lecture.*

"The real question is whatcha gonna do to get her back?" Prez inquired.

"Fuck if I know. I texted and called her, but she didn't respond. Called her co-worker Greta. Turns out she cut out of town. Headed somewhere up north. New England, maybe. Put

Cutter on her trail, but nothing's come up so far. Until I get more intel, there's no way to do recon or contact other clubs to track her down. My only choice is to wait her out. I posted a prospect on her house for surveillance, for what it's worth. That's about as far as I'll go without asking you first. Like you said, she's not under our protection. We might not deal in hard drugs or arms, but fuck, Prez, we've got enemies out there."

"How long will she hide out for, you think?"

"A couple weeks. Three at most. I got Flicker to hack into the court's database. She ain't due for court until next month, and it's a trial. She'll be back to meet with her client before that." Kingdom repeated, "Three weeks."

"Hope you've learned your lesson. I'm not judgin', mind you, since it took me almost losing Stephanie to learn the same lesson." Prez's expression turned bleak. "She was a motherfuckin' bitch to get back. But," breaking into a far-off smile, he said, "even though she's passed on going on three years, she'll be my old lady till my last breath. The woman was worth her weight in gold."

"Sage is hurting bad. Her ex was a cheating son of a bitch. There's a chance she won't let me back in."

"Nah." Prez batted his hand. "The girl worships you."

"The fuck are you talking about?"

"She follows you with puppy dog eyes like you've got the last dick on earth," Prez insisted.

The harsh lines bracketing the corners of his lips quirked up briefly.

"Son, you've got a twisted mind. If you find her or when she comes back, put it to good use and get her flat on her back. While she's gone, I'm warning you, I'm going to keep you real busy so you don't stress the brothers. When she's returned, I'll put you on light duty to get after her ass."

Kingdom choked up, swallowed, then lowered his head in gratitude for his president.

"We good?"

"Yeah," Kingdom rasped out.

Prez's plan made sense, but work wouldn't do him any good. He was crippled without Sage.

33

KINGDOM

Kingdom slapped the door open and stormed toward the woman manning the reception desk.

"Where the fuck is she?" he growled in her face.

Greta leaned back in her swivel chair and swung her legs onto the table, one leather-clad ankle landing gracefully over the other. Inspecting her nails, she drawled out, "I already told you when you called. She's gone." Her gaze flickered up to Kingdom, and she graciously added, "She's in a safe place."

"Safe, my ass. If I don't know where she is, then she isn't safe."

Greta let out a mocking grunt.

"Now, I'm asking again, where the fuck is she?" he ground out, the tic above his jaw working like mad. He pinned Greta with a stare that made grown men cry. Not her, though. *Christ*, he was going to wring her neck.

Without so much as a flinch, she repeated, "Again, my answer is *gone*."

Kingdom deliberately spread his fingertips on the desk and loomed over her. In a grim tone, he threatened, "Do not fuck with me, Greta. You won't like the result."

Greta's eyes turned a cool green. Despite being in a lower position, she stared him down like he wasn't much better than a piece of gum stuck under her shoe. How the fuck did she do that when he was the one with the strength to snap her into pieces? He sensed she'd had dealings with bikers before, but this proved it. She wasn't cowed one bit. In fact, the look of fury on her face would freeze the balls off a hardened biker. Not him, but still.

Her posture ... her eyes ... they teased his memory. Fuck, he didn't have time to dwell on it, but he was going to investigate her. If there was something in her past to exploit, he'd use it to get his woman back.

"I'm not afraid of you, Kingdom. I've dealt with men like you all my life. One thing I learned from those good-for-nothing men was loyalty. Loyalty. Unlike you and your club." Her lip curled up in a snarl. "Few bikers live up to their standards. You have personal first-rate experience with that, don't you, Kingdom? Not living up to standards." Smacking her feet to the ground, she stood her ground and hissed, "You're insane if you think I'm going to let you have access to her again."

Damn, she was a pain in the ass, but her next tirade struck him like a four-by-four steel beam. "I've never seen Sage in less than complete control, and she deals with misogynist bastards every single day. She has nerves of steel, but you"— Greta poked his chest—"you broke her."

Standing nose to nose, he backed off and wiped his face. Voice scratchy, he vowed, "I've got to fix this clusterfuck."

"This clusterfuck is of your own making. Before you go

ballistic on me, I'm going to let you in on a little secret. You aren't doing yourself any favors by harassing me. Sage is extremely protective of the people she loves. Whereas you"—she stared down her upturned nose at him—"you know nothing about love or protection."

Whoosh. That punched the breath out of him. The woman was ruthless, but he had a creeping suspicion that this was but a taste of what he would face with Sage.

"I'm going to play nice and lay it out for you because your brothers either can't or won't. You don't need to thank me afterwards," she assured him, bleeding sarcasm.

Kingdom's eyes glinted with menace at her unrelenting audacity.

"You did what bikers do. Cheat. It's nothing to you. You fuck anything with inflatable tits without a second thought. You *knew* Sage was forbidden fruit, a civilian, when you touched her. You also knew what she went through with Stanton. Cheating was her worst nightmare. It was the worst way to cut her." Greta threw her hands up in the air. "For fuck's sake, stop letting your dick lead you in life."

Kingdom's fingers choked the lacquered edge of the desk. He barely suppressed the urge to lift his head and howl in agony. He didn't technically fuck Trixie, although he wasn't about to go into the details with Greta. Fact was, he did enough to give Trixie the ammunition to hurt Sage. That was on him.

"Someone's got to have her back," Greta finished with a tremble in her voice.

Kingdom lashed out, "I have her fuckin' back!"

"You're such a hypocrite. If another man touches your Sage, you're ready to beat him to death. Meanwhile, you blindly hurt the woman you claim to love. Your arrogance is what toppled you, Kingdom."

"Hitting close to home, much?"

"This isn't about me," she retorted too quickly. Damn straight it was about her. Problem was that she had spoken the truth. He *had* counted on Sage never knowing what happened.

"Your first order of business is to calm the fuck down and leash your inner rabid dog. Going crazy on me isn't going to help," she said.

"Who the hell are you to give me advice?" He looked at her suspiciously. "And since when do you care?"

"Sweetheart, I don't care. If you died today, I'd do my happy dance on your grave. This is about Sage. She fell for you in a bad way, and the least you can do to help her is to admit your mistake. Don't dismiss or underestimate the harm you caused her. Unless she doesn't mean anything to you. But if you do care for her, then man the fuck up."

Greta gave him one last forbidding look and took her seat. Then she had to gall to ignore him and begin typing away on her laptop as if it was normal to get into a vicious argument with a rampaging biker.

Kingdom withdrew in a feigned retreat. He'd leave and Greta would have a good story to recount to Sage about how she'd reamed into him. Fuckin' whatever.

Kingdom shoved off the desk and pounded angry steps out the door when Greta called, "If she's crazy enough to take you back and you ever fuck up again, I will personally take a gun to your head."

Christ*fuck*.

34

KINGDOM

The wagons had circled around Sage like an impenetrable force field, shielding her from him.

Greta had told him off, the truths smarting like ugly welts on his skin. At Angel's shop, he was confronted with a furious Camilla, who cursed him out in Spanish. Angel pleaded the Fifth, his pained expression saying that his hands were tied. Fucking eunuch.

He rolled up to his house and turned off the engine when his adrenaline spike dropped off and the shakes got to him. Taking in gulps of air that cut like a switchblade, he wheezed through his panic attack. Hadn't had one in years. Despite the breakdown of his body, he was eerily alert.

He waited for darkness to break into her home. Her plants were alive, but Phantom was gone. Another bad sign. For one thing, he couldn't use the cat as leverage. Pouring water from a galvanized metal can, Kingdom watered her plants, naming them as Sage had taught him: rosemary, basil, tarragon. He'd make sure to come back and water them in a few days.

Ransacking her closet and drawers, he discovered that Sage had packed enough clothes for at least two weeks. The clues at her house reinforced what he already knew. It was what he didn't know that was driving him insane. What if she had crashed and was laid out on a road somewhere, getting an electric shock to her heart by some EMS fucker? Sage had abandoned her cellphone on her bedside table, leaving the GPS app, which he'd downloaded surreptitiously, inoperable. What if he had driven her to her death? Kingdom blew out a rattling breath, willing himself to fight off the irrational fears crowding out his sanity and dooming him.

Locking up behind him, he broke into the office next door. She hadn't taken any heavy files, which again confirmed his prediction. Images of Sage alone and helpless in a two-bit hotel snapped at his heels like a predator, its jowls crushed his hind legs. The tables were turned, making him the prey.

Flicker was the Squad's resident master hacker and security-system man. The story went that he had downed a whole network. The dude was a ninja, for sure. After half an hour of guessing her bank password, *phantomgirl*—Christ, the woman was naïve as fuck—he and Flicker got into her account. Sage had made one ATM transaction and cashed out her personal checking account. The good thing was that she hadn't touched her business account. Cutter came up empty too, which meant that she was too off the grid. This was bad.

She could be anywhere. Battered. Raped. Stabbed. "Oh God," he groaned. He'd go down like Chop if she was DOA on a metal gurney somewhere.

Beams of moonlight crisscrossed his pacing shadow as he roamed around her office. Collapsing in her seat, he inhaled to catch a whiff of her scent. If he was a good man—scratch that—if he was a *better* man than he was, he'd leave her alone. Eventually, she'd meet another man and turn to him for comfort. *No way in hell.* The thought of Sage wrapped in another man's arms punched him in the gut. He balled his hands, the jagged nails grinding crescent-shaped indentations into his palms. He clenched and released, oblivious to his abused flesh. Now that she was gone, he understood that Sage was his lifeline.

Whether he was good, bad, or better was irrelevant. No way he was going down without a fight. Fortunately, he was a merciless bastard, conniving and relentless. He'd run her to the ground and tie her to his cock if need be, 'cause there would be no replays of the chaos he'd unleashed.

Kingdom stroked the grains of wood on her colossal desk, roaming over her laptop and files. Sage didn't know him as a hunter, but he was a damned good marksman. In Baghdad, whenever his squad had set up an overwatch on a rooftop, he'd casually prop up his M16 baby, thumb resting lightly on the trigger. Biding his time, he scanned the area below until he caught sight of a flicker of movement. Trance-like, he'd press down in a satisfying burst. *Rat-tat-tat-tat.* Done.

Kingdom was venerated for his precision and a patience that rivaled Job, but Sage was the ultimate prize.

35

KINGDOM

"I swear I won't give you a reason to doubt me again." He whispered it like an incantation, praying his oath would take to the air and reach her like a homing pigeon.

Kingdom inhaled the curls of smoke wafted his way. Cutter came out of the woodwork, a guarding presence. Fuck, he was so wrapped up that he hadn't heard the flick of Cutter's Zippo lighter. And that sound was not soft.

"Yo, you're thinkin' too hard, brother. Gimme a heads-up before you go postal on me 'cause I like my life the way it is."

"Your time will come, yeah. Learn your lesson from me, brother."

Cutter gave him a wry smile. Taking a drag from his cigarette, it sparked a neon-red burn from the end of the butt. Blue smoke streamed out of his nostrils. Leaning back against the brick wall of the clubhouse, Cutter's gaze focused on the tidy backyards of the neighboring row houses through the chain-linked fence. Cutter threw the finished tobacco on the ground, and Kingdom crushed it underneath his motorcycle boot. Pulling out a pack, Cutter tapped it against his palm, and a cigarette smoothly slid out. Pressed firmly between his lips, he flipped open the Zippo lighter engraved with the Squad's motto. Squinting in anticipation of his second hit of nicotine, he lit the tip of his cigarette.

One drag, then another. Kingdom followed the smoke drifting off the end of the butt. Half a cigarette later, Cutter spoke up. "When I met her, I had my doubts about Sage," he began, "she not being from our world. I figured a smart and educated woman like her wouldn't put up with you for long, but when it looked like she'd stay with your ass, I worried that she wouldn't survive the club." Cutter took another drag. "She did, proving to me that she was rock solid. You're a cold motherfucker. Ya know before Chopper died, he took me aside and made me swear to take care of you. I didn't think much at the time 'cause, like I said, you're a leader. And a leader doesn't need taking care of." Eyes bleeding with remorse, Cutter said, "I'm damned sorry, Kingdom."

"Nothin' to be sorry for. If I had taken care of her right, she'd be by my side instead of alone somewhere."

Cutter grabbed Kingdom's sleeve and tugged until Kingdom angled his head toward him. "Since she came into your life, you've chilled out. You get what I mean?"

Only a brother could decipher Cutter's circuitous statement. He meant Kingdom was behaving more human.

"When shit changes in the club, you'll be the man. You weren't before her."

Kingdom speared Cutter with a sharp look. "If you've got something to say to me, then fuckin' say it."

Cutter nonchalantly took a hit from his nail as if he wasn't treading knee-deep in a minefield. Cutter was a cool mother-fucker. Kingdom admired that about him, but that didn't mean he'd tolerate a challenge to Prez's leadership. Or a discussion about Prez's health since his first round of chemo had ended. Cutter's comment that he was "the man" wasn't new, but that didn't make it comfortable to hear. He was not only respected by the brothers; he was revered.

"When the time comes, and it will come," Cutter empha-sized, "you're the brother to lead the club. Those assholes will walk through fire for you, and I can't say that about another man here."

"I don't like where you're goin' with this," Kingdom warned.

"So far, so good with his cancer in remission, but Sage fixed you up to be the leader if it ever becomes necessary. Not just any woman, not even a good woman, automatically makes a man a leader. Could be that her lawyering makes her sharp. Shit, sometimes I see steam coming outta her ears, but she has the sense to shut her mouth when brothers are talking shit. She has more sense than to challenge you in front of the brothers, but she'd bust your balls in private if needed. She'll be a good old lady," he voiced.

"True that. She may come off quiet sometimes, but when we're alone, a wildcat comes out to play." A slashing of pain seared across his skin at the thought of her. "Makes for some good fucking."

He smiled to himself. Sage might not understand the many nuances of the MC, but she was a quick learner. A natural. And she was attuned to him, reading his subtle cues with exacting precision. Sage recognized changes in his moods, catching onto the slightest tension in his muscles. He was a stone-cold killer with a talent at shutting down his emotions and putting on a guise of impassivity. Few men could see beyond his death mask. But Sage did.

"All these bitches circling around you like sharks, wanting to suck you off because of your rank, and you find the one woman who won't take any shit from you."

"Sage is honest and loyal," Kingdom conceded.

"You gotta make it right with her. You gotta prove yourself worthy 'cause claiming her once won't cut it. You can't own a woman like her."

"You doubtin' my skills, brother?"

"Nah." Cutter grinned. "The boys and I are lookin' forward to watching you crawl on your hands and knees like a bitch in heat." Cutter put his hands together in prayer, the short cigarette butt crushed between the nicotine-stained fingers. "I'm gunnin' for you." His face turned serious. "I got two hundred bucks ridin' on you, motherfucker. Don't make me fuckin' regret it."

Kingdom snorted, unsurprised that they were turning his agony into a circus. "You assholes are worse than the bitches."

Cutter flicked the butt on the ground to die a slow death, and left Kingdom to his thoughts.

Sage was unlike any other woman he knew. She didn't care about his power. She didn't care about being an old lady. Didn't try to change him. The one thing she wanted from him was respect and loyalty. He didn't deliver and look at what happened. Although, she'd still want his dick. At this point, it was the strongest card he held. He'd have to find a way back into her life, and a way to get to her first.

36

SAGE

The weather was clear and sunny as Sage and Marianne, Greta's mother, took an easy hike through the forest of old-growth hardwood trees in the Green Mountains.

Sage's hand grazed the rough bark of a majestic sugar maple as she trudged up the trail. She'd arrived over a week before and had been met at the small train station by Marianne and her old man, Trucker, who were members of the Green Mountain Boys MC.

After moping around their cabin for a few days, Marianne took her out to see a quaint ski resort town nearby, and now they were hiking through the tall American beeches, yellow birches, and sugar maples of a state park. It was relatively empty despite being the peak of summer tourist season, and the women trailed through the various paths at their leisure.

Arriving a higher elevation, they reached a break in the

trees. Sage inhaled sharply at the vista spread out below her of a small river twining between the bends of rolling green mountains spotted with wildflowers. "This is a beautiful sight. Stunning. Really stunning." She breathed out with a touch of awe.

"Yes, this is one of my favorite spots in the entire world. Whenever I missed Camden, after running away a decade ago, I'd come here and meditate," admitted Marianne. "It might seem funny to miss a city in paradise, but I'm a Jersey girl, born and bred."

"Is that where Greta's dad still lives?"

"Yes, the poor, deluded bastard. He was the epitome of everything that could go wrong in a biker. Cheating. Abuse. Violence. I'm lucky to be alive," the other woman replied softly.

"I know a little bit about the cheating part. Although," Sage quickly added, "it doesn't compare with what you went through." Marianne had told her the story of her life with Greta's dad, and that had been a doozy of a tale to listen to. Afterwards, she'd decided to help survivors of domestic violence when she got back home.

"Betrayal and violation of trust hurts, even if there wasn't physical violence involved," Marianne replied. "May I ask what happened, Sage? I don't want to pry, but it might help me help you."

Sage turned her back to the beautiful panorama and rejoined the hiking path. "You're not prying," she replied quickly, then recounted the incident at the clubhouse and the full extent of Trixie's vitriol.

"You didn't catch Kingdom in the act," Marianne noted.

"No, I'd heard more than enough and ran out of there as fast as I could."

"You haven't spoken to him to hear his explanation?"

"What explanation could he possibly have to offer?" she scoffed.

"Hmm ... I don't know, but something about this seems a little off to me. I've lived and breathed the biker lifestyle since I was nineteen years old, and I know bitches inside and out. I'd take anything Trixie said with a grain of salt. She's obviously possessive of Kingdom. If he were only having sex with you, that in itself could trigger jealousy. Especially since you're an outsider."

Sage's mouth dropped open. She stopped in her tracks and spun around to face Marianne, who was walking behind her. "Are you serious? You don't believe me."

"I didn't say I don't believe you. I'm not sure I believe *her*."

"His best friend, who heard what she'd said, didn't deny any of it."

"Did he confirm it?"

"No," she grunted. "He was furious with her."

"A biker isn't going to discuss a brother's business in public. It's common for brothers to be promiscuous, but just because he didn't deny what Trixie said, doesn't mean she wasn't lying."

"He did try to convince me to wait for Kingdom," Sage mused aloud.

"If there was a misunderstanding, then he believed that Kingdom would clear it up."

Sage pivoted on her heels and trudged up the slope as she reflected about what Marianne had said. "Even if he didn't cheat on me, I miss him too much to take him back."

A laugh burst out of Marianne behind her. "That makes no sense."

"I'm in too deep with a man who lives the kind of life where women are falling all over him. Eventually, he'll break. If Trixie went to such lengths to try to break us up, where does that leave us? Sooner or later, a woman will come between us."

"Now you're just making stuff up and projecting into the future. Did you have a reason to doubt him before?"

"No, but I'm too hurt, Marianne. My heart is in shambles. At this point, it almost doesn't matter whether it happened or not because I'm in so much pain that I can't risk getting hurt ever again. Perhaps if this had been the first time, I'd handle it better, but it's the second time. It was tough getting over Stanton. Now, again? No, no, and a big, fat no."

"Are you never going to allow yourself to get close to a man again? You can't blame it on the fact that he's a biker because Stanton was from your world and he betrayed you."

"I don't know." Sage blew out a long breath. "I really don't know. As it is, I can barely stop crying. I miss him so badly. I miss his presence and his laugh, and the way he takes care of me by buying me lunch, going to prison visits with me, and installing a security alarm system in my house. I miss riding behind him on his bike." Her voice dropped low. "I really miss that. And talking with him. Laughing in bed, cuddling after sex. Oh boy, I'm so screwed."

Marianne grabbed Sage's arm and stopped her. Tears had begun running down her cheeks as she described the things she'd missed about that man. The older woman wrapped her arms around Sage. It gave her the permission to let loose the inundation of feelings—betrayal mixed with bone-deep longing—that had dogged her since the day she'd left Poughkeepsie.

"I fell for that asshole," she cried into Marianne's shoulder.

37

KINGDOM

Sage was back.

In one piece, thank fuck.

One of the prospects on watch called him when Greta dropped her off at home. Hope unfurled within his soul, even though she wouldn't pick up his calls or return his texts or voice messages. Even though Sage had shut him out, Kingdom felt a mind-blowing wave of relief.

He had lived for weeks with a jagged stake of fear lodged in his soul despite Greta's assurances that she was safe. Never mind. She was back, and he had a slew of dirty tricks up his sleeve. Setting out his plan, he gave her a few days to readjust and catch up on work before he charged his way back into her life.

His lips quirked as he threw open the door of the clubhouse and shoved Whistle inside. The prospect had gotten into a bar fight and didn't have the sense to get the fuck out before the cops showed up. Which meant that he had gotten arrested for a simple beat-down. Kingdom shook his head. *What a fuck up.* The kid wasn't even drunk.

Kingdom had to go down to the courthouse and twiddled his thumbs while every damned man, woman, and kid picked up the night before Whistle got arraigned. Once they dragged Whistle in front of Judge Korman, he had to sit through the old man's droning lecture to Whistle. Korman liked to give bikers extra special attention. Fucking finally, the old man ended his rambling and slapped Whistle with a small bullshit charge, and Kingdom bailed him out.

Kingdom planned to use Whistle to get to Sage. First though, the wayward prospect needed to get the beating he deserved. The club didn't need extra heat on them. Ever. Much less now, with tensions escalating with the Province-town Hellions MC. Not from an asshat of a prospect.

Leaning over the bar, Kingdom called out for a beer. Bottle in hand, he waved in Whistle's direction and egged on the brothers. "Give him a good kick in the ass."

A semicircle of rough-hewn men surrounded Whistle and went at him until he curled over, holding onto his ribs. The brothers weren't hurting him much, just enough to make a point. A bruised rib or two was easy to bind up. Might not be able to ride fast for a while, but it was his own damn fault.

"Wrap it up," Kingdom called out. The brothers backed off after giving Whistle a few wayward slaps on his head. Strolling over to the kid, he reached out a hand to help him up. Whistle braced himself on his arm and held onto Kingdom until he was on his feet and stumbled to the nearest stool. Kingdom sat next to him and called out, "Two shots."

Shots in hand, Kingdom toasted, "To fucking shit up." Tossing it to the back of his throat, he warned, "Don't pull that shit again."

Two more shots materialized. After two more, Kingdom told Whistle to get the fuck out of his sight and went back to his beer. Cutter came up behind Whistle and shoved him in the back, causing him to grunt in pain.

"None of you motherfuckers waited for me? I leave for half an hour. Thirty fuckin' minutes and I miss all the fun."

"It's never too late. No one's choked him out yet," Kingdom replied blandly.

"Man, it's too fuckin' late now."

Gesturing toward Whistle, Kingdom spoke to Cutter, "He'll be needing a lawyer. We're gonna go see Sage."

Eyes popping out of his head, Whistle choked on his saliva until Kingdom threw him a dark glance.

"Sage won't see you," Cutter commented.

"She won't see me, but"—Kingdom waved his beer in the prospect's direction—"she'll see *him*. We'll give it a day to let his bruises turn into the colors of the fucking rainbow. She's too soft to turn his ass away."

"That's why you had brothers beat him up."

"One of many reasons, bro."

Turning toward Whistle, Kingdom intoned, "The beating was a lesson. If you patch in, the brothers will protect you with their lives. The least you can do is not get arrested for bullshit."

Directing his words back to Cutter, Kingdom explained, "I'm taking advantage of an opportunity that he set up for me. It's the least he can do for makin' me sit in the same court-room as Judge fuckin' Korman for two hours. Hate that asshole."

38

KINGDOM

Kingdom waited impatiently for Whistle's bruises and cuts to blossom.

Finally, on a Friday, they rode over to her office. He hadn't gotten more than a few bites of food down his gullet that morning and, while the day hadn't heated up yet, sweat gathered around his hairline.

He wasn't nervous when it came to committing a good, honest-to-God crime, but going to battle with a woman that he outweighed by at least a hundred pounds had him sweating. Going to the office was like jumping into shark-infested waters. He might be Special Ops, but he was no SEAL.

Braced over the handlebars of his bike, he accelerated. As they came down the street, he gave a chin up to the brother who was stationed out of sight to watch over Sage. Surveying the surrounding area, he noticed that there were no strange cars parked. Good, no clients to get in his way.

Kingdom opened the office door and roughly shoved Whistle through. He pointed at a seat. Whistle followed his mute command. Judging by her expression, Greta must have heard the bikes. Hers eyes were narrowed and zeroed in on him.

"Greta," he acknowledged her.

"Fancy seeing you here. What do you want?" she asked in a cool tone. Kingdom angled his head toward Whistle. Her gaze slid over to Whistle, and her eyes widened.

Oh my Go" she gasped.

Finally. His hard work was paying off because that bitch was the guard dog to Sage's inner sanctum. Being around Greta was like being in a Matrix movie. Stressful as hell. "Looking good, isn't he?"

Greta was momentarily speechless. Kingdom rolled his eyes. She was getting distracted by more than his bruises. She took her sweet time giving Whistle a nice look over. Jesus, he did not have the time for this. Almost as if she'd heard him, her focus snapped back to Kingdom. He watched nonchalantly as her eyes flicked between Kingdom and Sage's closed door.

"She doesn't want to see you." Her gaze swept away from Kingdom's scrutiny. "I thought it might be good for her if you apologized and she could have closure with you, but she doesn't want to. She made herself clear on that point."

Kingdom leaned against the desk languidly and cocked an eyebrow. His heart rate was kicking up a panic, but he'd be damned if he showed weakness. "I'm here on business," he explained, motioning toward Whistle.

"She doesn't want your business."

Strung up tight from the knowledge that Sage was a few feet away from him, Kingdom loomed over her. "Unless you accommodate me, I'll fuck with the next client who walks through the door."

Greta stiffened. "Don't you dare threaten Sage's business."

Kingdom couldn't afford to lose his temper when Sage was so close that he could almost smell her. Greta was furtively checking out Whistle during their tug-of-war. Women couldn't stay away from Whistle, even though the kid was a dumb little shit. *Makes no sense, but hey, whatever floats her boat.*

Clamping a hand on Whistle's shoulder, he gave Greta an indulging smile. "My brother needs a lawyer. Sage is the only one the club trusts with this fucker. Take a good look at him, Greta. You gonna leave his ass with an ambulance chaser?"

He cast a look down at Whistle. There were deep discolorations around his eyes and a large stitched cut across one eyebrow. Even he had to admit, the boy looked pathetic. Whistle winked at her. She giggled, then shot Kingdom a warning look. She could lob him as many dirty looks as she wanted but the fact was that her libido and pity had won out.

"I'll see what I can do," she huffed. "I wouldn't put it past you to have beaten him up yourself."

"Never," he said in an offended tone. *Pfft. Of course he did.*

❋❋❋

Greta squeezed through the door she'd opened, her hand hanging onto the inside knob, and thumped her back against it.

Sage laughed. "What happened? You look like someone died."

Lifting her hair off the back of her neck, she forced out, "Kingdom's outside."

She paled. "Kingdom?" Dammit. She couldn't believe she

was flustered, but her heart was knocking against her breastbone like a jack-in-the-box.

"Yeah, he's with Whistle."

Pressure squeezed her chest, and oxygen rattled in her lungs like she was an asthmatic. Thank goodness he was okay. For a moment there, she was worried that he'd been picked up for something, but her relief was swiftly supplanted by fury. Rationally, she should be grateful that he'd stopped pursuing her after she had refused to open her door to him, but disappointment multiplied like cancer cells inside her gut. A week? Seriously? A week and he'd moved on. He was over her so quickly that he thought it was perfectly okay to come by her office with Whistle. The man was a heartless opportunist.

Over the weeks she'd spent with Greta's mom, she'd concluded that she'd dodged a bullet with only a graze to her heart. It was a complete lie, but, hey, that was the story she was going with. She did her best to patch up the gushing wound he'd left on her soul, scraped herself off the floor, and got on with life.

Hoisting up from her chair, Sage began to pace. Her shoulders slumped forward, and she braced her arms against the window casement. *I'm not ready to see him.* Another lie. A hum of anticipation wracked her treacherous body. She was greedy to lay eyes on him and watch him move like the lithe panther he was. She hated him, but damn her, she also missed him desperately. Her life was a hot mess.

Sage closed her eyes as she gathered every ounce of self-control and donned her mask of impenetrability. She hadn't become a trial attorney without learning a few tricks to keep her wits about her. Spinning around, she prepared herself to face him like the front line in a battle. *He's going down.*

Seeing the look on Sage's face, Greta warned, "Whistle's pretty beaten up."

Speaking more to herself than to Greta, she said, "After three weeks of absence, we don't have a choice what idiots we take on as clients. Don't worry about me, Greta. I'll meet Kingdom once and make my position with respect to our past relationship crystal clear. If I decide to take Whistle's case, there will be no reason for Kingdom to accompany him in the future."

Greta tilted her head to the side, wearing a dubious look, but Sage nodded resolutely. "You may set up a consultation with them."

Greta shifted her weight. "He insists on seeing you today. Now, in fact."

Piqued, Sage queried, "Is that right? He has the audacity to give orders?"

"He said that he'd dissuade any clients that arrive for an appointment from seeing you until you see him."

"He's unbelievable!" Despite her roiling stomach, she ground out, "Bring them in. I'll get rid of him once and for all."

Greta didn't move. "You feel for him still."

Raising her chin, she replied, "Whether I do or not is not an issue. It's categorically over between us. There obviously wasn't much there to begin with or he wouldn't have fucked another woman."

Greta turned the handle behind her. Swinging it open, she almost slammed into Kingdom, who was standing right outside Sage's office. As she stalked past him, she sneered, "You better leave her alone after today."

39

KINGDOM

Kingdom halted in his tracks, the wind knocked out of him.

Standing stock-still, just inside her office, he took a moment to drink her in. She looked gorgeous. Her glossy dark hair, creamy skin stained with emotion on her cheeks and throat, and her flaming eyes... *Fuck.* He'd stalked her from afar, but nothing compared to being near her.

He barely restrained himself from mauling her. The urge pounded in his blood to hike her over his shoulder and administer a hard slap to her bouncy ass. For her impertinence. For shunning him. He'd take her to his warehouse and tie her to his bed until she learned that he was her owner, her lover, her protector ... her everything.

Like a leashed beast, Kingdom prowled toward her, eating the distance between them in a few strides. Palms down on the desk, he leaned over until there was only an inch separating them. Her skin flushed deeper, and her tongue darted out and bit down on the side of her plump bottom lip. Fucking hell, so sexy. God help him, he'd bite her if she didn't let go of that lip of hers.

Between clenched teeth, he commanded, "When I call, you pick up. When I text, you text back. What you don't do is ignore me. Try it again, and you won't be able to sit down for a week from the paddling you'll get." Domineering? Yeah, and he gave zero fucks about it.

Sage surged up from her chair. "You!" She took a whack at his chest. "You abdicated the right to order me around."

Towering over her, Kingdom grabbed her thick locks of hair and hauled her close. Her chest expanded and collapsed in rapid succession. Fisting her hair, he tugged her head back and exposed her neck. His eyes flicked down to her parted lips, noting each pant slipping past. Her pupils dilated, darkening her eyes to midnight blue. Oh, he recognized the telltale signs of her arousal. She attempted to twist her head away, but Kingdom tightened his hold. They were locked in a battle until, finally, she shifted her gaze down. He released her hair, rewarding her with a caress and collaring the delicate tendons at the base of her neck.

"It'd be a pleasure to teach you how to show me respect. My advice to you is not to push me 'cause I'm at my breaking point." He gave her a forbidding look. "You fuckin' left me without a word. Not. One. Word. I didn't know if you were alright. You didn't give me a chance to explain—"

Rage flashed in her eyes like lightning bolts. Flinging his hand off her, she cut him off, "What the hell were you going to explain? Were you going to explain why you fucked Trixie? Or were you going to give me a blow-by-blow of how you did it? Did you fuck her with your head between her thighs, like you did me? Was her mouth on you where mine had been?" Her voice slipped as she swung around, giving him her back.

"Calm the fuck down," he growled, his fingertips touching the line of her back.

She attempted to shrug off his touch. Kingdom backed off when he felt her shivering—in anger or despair, he couldn't tell. Aching to comfort her, he moved around the desk and turned her to face him. Smoothing a thumb over her collarbone, he brushed over the curve of her breast. Her pulse was going fast. Sage's eyes darted away, trying to hide from him.

"Where were you, baby? I was worried every minute of every day you were gone."

"Greta's mom. In Vermont," she replied.

Coaxing her closer to him, he bent down and licked the seam of her lips. Sage parted her lips in a small gasp, and he swooped in to feast on her mouth. They both moaned at the contact of their tongues. Sage drove in deeper, and their tongues wound around each other, twined like fibers of a rope. Clutching his head roughly, she unleashed her anger into the kiss. *Bring it, baby.*

She caught the vulnerable flesh of his lower lip and clipped him. He drew in a sharp breath. Blood mixed with her taste. Black spots swam before his eyes, and he had to push her against the wall to brace himself from falling. Regaining his vision, he took satisfaction in looking into her glazed eyes and hearing her moan.

"Lick the blood off," he said gruffly.

She sucked his bruised lip, licked it dry, then drew it into her mouth. His cock stiffened, and a grunt erupted before he had a chance to clamp down on it. Sage's attack brought him to the raw edge of his breaking point. Feeling savage, he slid a hand under the hem of her skirt and palmed her mound.

"I said it before, and I'm saying it again. This is *mine.*"

His declaration of ownership snapped his control. Adrenaline coursed through him. A primal urge to dominate his female gripped him by the throat. He twisted her around and bent her over her desk. Coasting over Sage's curved back, he grabbed hold of her ass. Christ, he missed this. He couldn't believe how desperate he was to get at every inch of her smooth, silky skin.

Sage's cheek lay flat on the surface of her desk. As she succumbed to his sensual assault, her eyes drifted closed.

"Open your eyes," he demanded roughly. She opened them, blinked slowly, and lifted them up to him. "Never hide from me, Sage. Never leave me again. I died when you left. It was like Chop all over again."

He lifted her skirt until her ass was exposed in her thong. His fingers splayed over one cheek. "Fucking Christ. Were you wearing this thong when you were away?"

Blood rushed to his head at the thought. Those were for him alone. Whenever he saw her, his first instinct was to unveil her and discover what kind of sexy lingerie she hid underneath her civilian clothes. His woman had a wicked sense of retribution. It was another lesson in refuting his assumption that she was an average woman. His throat cinched closed, but he forced himself to croak out, "Dirty, dirty girl."

Following the edge of the lace, his hand reached the crux between her thighs. Underneath the fabric, his thick digit went and dragged along her wet slit. He spread her slickness over her lips without penetrating. She clamped her thighs tightly and squirmed. Oh, she wanted it bad. "Christ, baby, you're primed for me. My fingers are gonna bang your tight pussy."

Attempting to slow down before he came in his pants, he resolved to mark the unblemished flesh of her neck. First, he suckled one specific spot with brutal determination, working to leave an imprint as dark as ink. Sage struggled, jerking her neck this way and that, but he followed with his teeth. Her fight fueled his determination to brand her.

"I have court tomorrow," she protested.

Kingdom gripped her hair to control her movements. "Wear a fuckin' scarf."

"Please, Kingdom," she begged.

He licked her bruised flesh. Just as she sighed in relief, he bit down again. Teeth clenched on her skin, he thrust two fingers into her weeping pussy. She bucked, grinding back against his crotch. His mouth watered. Swallowing the saliva did nothing for his parched throat.

"This is a reminder of who you belong to. If you knew your place," he chastised, "I wouldn't have to mark you."

She scoffed. "Oh, please. You'd mark me anyway."

He nuzzled her hair. Yeah, he had no intention of stopping. One day soon, she'd wear a permanent mark of his possession. She have to come up with a tat she liked, otherwise it'd be "Property of Kingdom." Although, he could see the appeal of sucking on her neck. It could quickly become his new addiction. The point was that no man would doubt who she belonged to. He doubted he could stop men from lusting after her. Afterall, it wasn't realistic to gouge out the eyes of every man who ogled her, but he'd make damned sure they didn't get too close.

He pumped his fingers impatiently and chuckled when her pussy sucked down on his fingers each time he withdrew them. Sage hefted herself upright on locked arms, but he pressed his chest against her, his thumb working her clit.

Between her pants and huffs, she snapped, "We are not having sex in my office."

Kingdom withdrew from her throbbing sheathe and

brought his fingers to his mouth. Smacking his lips around his dripping fingertips, he closed his eyes. "Tastes better than I remember. Love feasting on your juices. My favorite flavor." Eyes open, he plucked his fingers out of his mouth and gave her an unyielding stare. "My cock. Inside your pussy. Now."

※※※

Sage glanced over her shoulder at the lethal male. Damn, it turned her on when he got bossy. She was mad at herself, madder than mad, because she didn't have the willpower to stop him *at all*. He released her clit, and she almost wept. She'd been so close, and the bastard knew it.

Kingdom pulled her satin blouse up her chest and dragged the cups of her bra down until her heavy breasts fell out. From behind, he nestled them in both hands, squeezing them lightly. "It's a crime what you do to me. Your tits should be fucking outlawed."

Cursing inwardly, she was powerless to do anything but thrust her breasts into his hands. The rough texture of his calluses strummed her sensitized nipples. Kingdom yanked her skirt over her ass and left it bunched around her waist. Exposed and vulnerable, her inhalations accelerated. Sensing her nervousness, Kingdom licked the edge of her ear and shushed her, "I got you, baby girl."

"Greta can walk in any minute," Sage stammered.

He chortled. "Doubt it. She knows I'm fucking you in here. Anyway, a SWAT team could bust in here, and I'd protect you. You're mine alone."

Kingdom unbuckled his belt, tugged down his zipper, and dragged his jeans over his narrow hips. Curse the man, she was trained to react when she heard that sequence of unique sounds, knowing his heavy cock would spring out. *Smack*. And there it went, slapping his taut abdomen. A shiver shuddered through her. She didn't need to look to know that his massive cock was proudly jutting out. Her pulse skittered as he ordered, "Spread wide for me, gorgeous."

Too slow to comply, he kicked her legs out. Her gaze flew back and locked in on the reverent expression on his face as his eyes coasted the curves of her ass, her legs, and then rested on her heels.

"Fuck me, those heels," he rasped out, shaking his head. In response to his praise, her ass thrust out, begging for more. Her gaze dipped, and she was unable to tear herself away from his beautiful thick cock. Her pussy flexed in anticipation, because no matter how many times they'd had sex, his shaft stretched her muscles with a bite that she craved.

"You deserve a reward"—he bent down and flicked her engorged clit—"for those heels."

She jerked against his chest. He flicked again. Apparently deciding not to waste any more time, Kingdom nocked his cock at her opening and gave her short, shallow thrusts meant to drive her insane. He entered in one hard thrust, and her walls contracted around his invading cock. He bottomed out. She heard the sucking sound as his cock withdrew from her grasping pussy.

Wet slaps of flesh against flesh filled the air as he drilled into her, his heavy balls spanking her clit. He looped her hair around his fist and using it as leverage to begin fucking her for real. A rumble rose from his chest, reverberating on her back. He muffled her with the palm of his hand. Thrashing her head to dislodge his grip, her mind suddenly blanked. Shots of soul-ripping pleasure whipped through her. Pounding back onto his shaft, she released her screams between his fingers.

"My baby's a screamer."

Sucking in air through her nostrils as her climax

whipped through her, Sage crumbled. Kingdom wrapped around her waist and powered into her with vigor. She clawed at the papers of her desk, shoving neat piles of files off her desk. Kingdom slapped her ass cheek with a loud crack.

"You need to fuck my big cock, don't you, girlie? Say it."

Stifling a moan, Sage struggled to remain mute, but she didn't give in. He clamped down on her ass cheek while freeing her mouth. "You love my hand on your ass. Say it," he warned, "or I'll swat that ripe ass of yours until you don't sit right for days. You haven't had it nearly rough enough. Test me because I'd love to show you."

"Yes, damn you. I love your hand on my ass, okay? Satisfied?" she huffed out.

"I love it when your mouth gets filthy. It's almost as good as when I dirty it up with my come."

Her muscles clamped down on his cock like a vise. She was helpless when he talked to her like that. Covering her mouth again, he plunged his fingers into her curls, giving them a good yank. Sage cried out and tried biting him, but a hard smack on her ass had her spitting fury between the digits wrapped around her mouth. Pulling out, he taunted, "You sassin' back at me makes me harder for you." Driving back in her core, he said, "Feel it. Feel my steel cock in that wet pussy of yours."

He rode her with a steady pace punctuated by furious thrusting. A second orgasm roiled like a tempest and left her mouth in a high-pitched shriek caught by his clamped hand. When it tapered off, her head lolled to one side. Kingdom took her hips with such force that he'd leave bruises to match the ones on her ass cheeks. She could feel when his restraint snapped. Like the loose ends of live wires, his thrusts became increasingly erratic. Stiffening behind her, his seed shot out in jets, and Sage came over his cock. His forehead dropped against Sage's nape.

"Swear to God, I've hit pussy gold, and I won't ever take that privilege lightly."

Fucking her will never be enough. Kingdom wanted his seed to mean something. He wanted his cock to paint the inside of her pussy with come until she was fat with his child. Her ass was tilted high up in the air, his cock buried deep inside. He angled his head to get a nice long look at her glossy pussy, dripping with their come. *Hot as fuck.* One reason he loved fucking her from behind was that he could cup his hand and catch their juices like he was doing right now.

Kingdom's chest expanded in satisfaction. Not able to let her go just yet, he grabbed hold of the crown of his shaft to spread the last drops of his seed on her buttocks, and then dipped between the wet crack of her ass. The creases he'd carried on his brow for weeks finally softened.

Carefully raising her up against him, her sweat coated his chest. He savored the docile softness that entrapped her during her afterglow. Usually, Sage cuddled into him afterwards, taking her time to return to reality. Running his hands down her flanks, he burrowed into her neck and breathed her in. He couldn't get enough of her scent.

Sage's body hardened against him. "Are you satisfied?" she asked.

Her fire never failed to get his cock hard again. Placing a scattering of kisses along her shoulder, he replied, "Yup. We're good."

40

SAGE

Sage was livid.

"One bout of intense sex does not make us *good*," she thundered.

Elbowing him off her, she whipped around and glared bullets at him. Her skin was still wet. The thing she was proud of when they were intimate turned sticky and itchy. Scratching like she had a rash, she cast around frantically for the closest piece of clothing to rub their come off her.

Kingdom tucked in his semi-erect cock and pulled a bandana from his back pocket. Swatting her hands away, he bent down to clean her. Huffing, she folded her arms over her chest. *How dare he?!* Kingdom tugged her panties over her hips and straightened out the rest of her clothes, which was a good thing because her hands were shaking with rage.

"Yeah? Good to know you think our fucking was 'intense.'

Intense sounds good to me," he replied, leaning back against the wall.

"You didn't even have the intention of talking about what happened between us when you came here? All you wanted was sex. You're unbelievable."

His face hardened. "No," he said slowly. "I couldn't keep my hands off you. That's what this was," he said, flicking his forefinger between the two of them. "I have every intention to talk, but not with Greta and Whistle outside. We'll talk about it when I come over tonight."

"You're not coming over tonight. Seriously, the gall of you to assume that I'd want anything from you. Anyway, I have plans tonight."

He angled his body to cage her between himself and the desk. His expression was filled with suspicion when he asked, "What *plans*?"

A shiver of fear ran down her spine at his tone. Wait a minute! Why was she jumpy? She was the wronged party here, not him. Noticing her papers and folders strewn across the floor, Sage fell to her knees and hurried to pick them up. This mess pretty much summed up what was left between them. Narrowing her eyes at him, she retorted, "It's none of your business. You have no rights over me. You barge in here with a pathetically transparent excuse about Whistle getting arrested. You got what you wanted, so now you can get out." She flung her hand out and pointed at the door. "God even knows why you felt the need to come here, considering the stash of women at your beck and call."

Flailing her arms around, taking in the disarray of her office, she accused, "You don't respect me, Kingdom, and you obviously never will. You came here to prove what? That you can still use my body? You fuck me and then assume that we're good. You need to leave because I must clean this mess and organize my work. My work. Because my work is my life."

She clenched papers in her fists. "This"—she waved the ruined papers in her hands—"is what keeps me sane. I'm warning you, stay away from me. I don't want to see your face again, and if you come near me, I'll get a restraining order against you."

Kingdom joined her on his knees and cupped her cheek, but Sage jerked away from him. "I deserve that. I saw you and couldn't help myself. I've missed you so bad, and I ache for you, baby girl. I want you to know that I never hooked up with Trixie."

"Are you kidding me? What does it matter if you technically had some form of sex or not? Whatever you did was bad enough for her to throw it in my face. The brothers didn't blink an eye, as if they'd seen it happen. God!" She shuddered. "To think I thought I was different from the others."

"Babe, you are different. I'll never be worthy of you. You're beautiful. Sexy and smart. The sweetest piece of ass I've had the privilege to touch. I didn't know women like you existed."

One slim coat encasing the ball of despair in her heart melted away.

"I couldn't keep my hands off you when I walked in here. It wasn't disrespect. My cock needed inside you. Bad. Since you were gone, I couldn't concentrate. Didn't know where you were." He swallowed audibly. "Had nightmares of finding you in a hospital or morgue. Give us a chance to talk tonight," he pushed.

Lifting to her feet, she declared, "I have a date tonight."

His eyes narrowed into two slits, reminding her of a panther with its ears flat and tail twitching. Kingdom surged upward and gripped her by the shoulders. He blasted out, "Hell fucking no!"

Sage struggled, but she couldn't budge him. Fine, then. She'd counter with words. "Don't you dare get upset with me. I didn't fuck around with another man. I trusted you!" Her gaze cut into him. "You say you care, but you didn't care enough to keep your dick in your pants. You told me that I owned you. Remember that? Infidelity, Kingdom. That's what it was, and I won't tolerate it. I had a fiancé who cheated on me."

"I know."

Sage did a double take, then resumed, "If you knew, then why did you do the one thing I couldn't tolerate? I can deal with a lot, like the fact that some of the brothers are misogynistic assholes or that the club has dubious dealings. I could have dealt with those things, but not unfaithfulness. You touched on the one sore spot that I won't abide."

"I'm sorry, babe—"

Holding up a hand, she said in a voice that shook. "Not good enough, Kingdom. I don't want your apology. I want you to respect my boundaries and leave me alone."

The tic of his jaw pulsed away. His grip on her arms tightened, but she twisted out of his hold. This time, he released her. Wiping tears with the back of her hand, she said, "Would you trust me if I had fucked another man?"

Kingdom scowled, but she didn't have any patience for his anger.

"You've made your point," he ground out.

"Have I?" she answered, her voice dropping to a whisper. "I'll represent Whistle, but if he needs babysitting, then make sure he gets it. Anyone but you. I don't want to set eyes on you ever again."

"I agree to meeting with Whistle without me, but we have an urgent matter that you need to deal with. Either you break your date, or I break his legs."

Aghast, she intoned, "You wouldn't!"

"In a fucking heartbeat, Sage. Break the fuckin' date," he ordered, dead serious. He loomed in close to her, his posture unyielding and his features forbidding, displaying what made him a high-ranking officer of his club. He'd never exhibited this side to her before. She was too exhausted for this standoff.

Unfortunately, he was the epitome of unwavering determination. "We're not over, Sage. Not by a fuckin' long shot."

He hauled her up and drove his tongue between her lips. An instant later, his mouth was gone, leaving her breathless and aroused. God, she was such a slut when it came to him.

Planting a hand on the wall to steady herself, her brows dipped as Kingdom dropped down on his haunches. He made quick work of collecting each file and slips of paper from the floor and organizing them on her desk. The man was beyond frustrating. He hurt her, threatened to beat up her date and then cleaned up the mess she'd made. Seriously, in her state, she was beyond making sense of him. Once done, he threw open the door, popped out his head, and bellowed, "Whistle, get your lazy ass in here!"

From her vantage point, she saw Whistle jump out of his seat. As the young biker passed him, Kingdom cuffed him upside his head. "She says jump, and your only question should be 'how fuckin' high.'"

"We're over," Sage called over Whistle's shoulders blocking her view of Kingdom.

"We'll see about that," he countered and shut the door.

41

KINGDOM

ombre, this ain't the time to get inked up. If you were any other man, I'd kick you out and tell you to come back when you're sober."

Men outside the Squad didn't speak to a brother in any tone other than respect, but Kingdom didn't have the energy to feel disrespected. After seeing him come back numerous times, searching for any info on Sage, Angel had stopped throwing him out. Finally, Angel let him into the work room, where they had hung out a few times. After the debacle with Sage, he found himself at Angel's.

"If you don't do it, some other man will, and it'll be on your conscience when I come in with jacked-up ink on me."

Angel glowered at him, cursing as he prepped for a session. "Men who are drunk, high, or in pain are my worst nightmares."

After Kingdom described what he wanted done, Angel released a breath of relief. "Not gonna ask you why you want me to ink half a fuckin' tat when I can do the whole thing in one session."

Kingdom exposed the skin he'd chosen and leaned back. With a forearm covering his eyes, he remained still for Angel. Silence reigned for a few minutes until Angel cleared his throat. "Heard you stopped by the shop last week and Camilla wouldn't make an appointment for you."

Kingdom grunted.

"One good thing came out of this shitshow. My woman turned RoboCop on my ass in bed. I appreciate the extra fucking. Not so much the attitude when Sage didn't answer my woman's call. Thank fuck she's back and Camilla can settle down."

Kingdom hissed when the needle hit a sensitive spot.

"Sorry, bro."

"Fuck you, Angel. Do the fuckin' tat and shut up."

Another deep press. Kingdom flinched and lifted his arm, scowling. Angel smirked. "Sensitive spot you chose. Real close to your junk."

"I've killed men for much less than an asshole like you threatenin' my dick."

"It's the least you owe me for makin' my life hell."

"Alright, I get it. You want the story. Anything to shut your mouth and get you to stop mutilating me." Kingdom paused for a long moment. "I almost hooked up with Trixie, a biker bitch, a while back. Trixie opened her big bitch mouth and pushed some real pain on my woman."

The needle lifted, and Angel shot a look of shock at Kingdom. "You ain't claimed?"

"No, motherfucker, I didn't claim her. If I had, no bitch would pull that Hannibal Lecter shit on her, no matter what

I'd done." Kingdom peered down at Angel. "You better wipe that look off your face."

"Shit, how was I supposed to know you were that stupid? So what are you gonna do?"

"She's not takin' me back. She's hooked to my dick, but she's not letting me back in," Kingdom said.

"She's in pain."

"No fuckin' shit, Einstein."

"She'll pull out of it." Angel nodded sagely. "I watched what that bastard fiancé did to her, and she bounced back." His gaze found Kingdom's. "You know about him, right?"

Kingdom shrugged; he'd play ignorant to get additional info.

"Big shot dude," Angel began. "Comes from money. They were gonna get married."

Jealousy lodged an egg-sized rock in his throat, and he struggled to quash a beastly roar.

Angel's hand tightened around the iron in his hand. "They were together for years, and he had a string of women on the down low. A couple months before their big-ass wedding, she caught him in the act. *Hijo de puta.* Camilla had to drag her out of her depression. Hit her confidence bad."

"Asshole. His ghost could fuck up my chances."

"Nah, those scars of hers are your blessing, man. She's sufferin', yeah, but she ain't dead. What you did doesn't compare to what that *puta* did. You fucked up, but you didn't fuck ten or twenty women. You two weren't getting married. Whole world of difference. Believe you me, when a woman starts hearing wedding bells, shit gets hectic."

Kingdom grunted in pain, and it wasn't from the needle. "I don't deserve her."

"True that," Angel piped in.

"You're not helping."

"Yeah, I'm helping. You're good for her. Don't get me wrong, when you came in here lookin' for her after she left, I was mad pissed. But I've seen her since she came back, and it's not the same as with that *hijo de puta*. I'm thinkin' you're crazy for her. I pulled the same type of shit on Camilla once. Biggest mistake of my life. My mama kicked my ass from here to Mexico and back. Had to stay low profile 'cause every one of my sisters was out on the streets, looking to kick my ass too."

"Camilla took your ass back in the end," Kingdom stated.

"Yep. See, you're one step ahead of me. You've recognized your mistake. It took me a long time to admit that I lost somethin' good, and it took me longer to lick my wounded pride for fucking up. By the time I came back, she was with another dawg." Angel chuckled to himself. "I thought I was a badass for showing up at her doorstep. Shows how ignorant I was, thinking she was waiting on me. Fine *chica* like her."

The buzzing from the coil reverberated in the enclosed room. Kingdom gave an impatient sigh, waiting on Angel to finish his story. But he knew better than to prod a man into revealing his life with his woman. It was as elusive as a sasquatch.

"I groveled, my friend. I begged for months while having to watch Camilla go through three fucking men. I couldn't do anything about it. I was the one to cut her loose, so I had no leverage. All I could do was beg and wait, beg and wait. Taught me a lesson. Deal with my shit before it deals with me. My mama and sisters pleaded my case, and honest to God, I think that's what tipped her over."

Angel's brow furrowed as he concentrated on a fine detail. "Welcome to hell. Beg and wait, son, beg and wait."

"Is this your way of helping me out?" Kingdom asked skeptically.

"Nah, bro. Me pleading your case with Camilla is my way of helping you out."

42

KINGDOM

A week had passed, and Kingdom found himself at her door, ringing the bell.

He'd tried, really he had, but he couldn't stay away. Hunger racked his system, leaving havoc behind. Sage opened the door, and his eyes roved over her curves, memorizing every detail. She looked fucking amazing, wearing only a pair of short shorts and tank top with a cute pair of glasses settled on her nose.

"Can I come in?"

Moving back a couple steps, she pulled the door open enough to allow him in. "Sure, let's get this over with once and for all," she muttered.

Kingdom knew he had to put in the time to break through her armor, but impatience ripped through his chest like a grenade. Twitching like an addict in the throes of withdrawal, he was plagued by jealousy. Usually there was a prospect on her, but there were times when the Squad needed all hands on deck, giving Sage the leeway to do what she wanted without his knowledge.

The tracking app on her phone showed that she had dined at *La Traviata* one night. Fancy joint, and not the kind Sage would spend money on. He guessed that she went on a date with one of her attorney friends, which made him see red. The thought that she had chosen an attorney, the opposite of Kingdom in every way, near killed him. He'd cornered Greta, who'd admitted that she was out with "colleagues." Some shindig a bunch of attorneys did every three months. But he still harbored suspicions.

Gesturing toward the living room, she sat down on the armchair across from the couch. Her laptop and folders were spread out on the low coffee table between them. Bending over, she closed the folders and the lid of the laptop as she asked, "What can I do for you, Kingdom?"

"How have you been doing?" he asked as he sat across from her.

"I'm busy," she replied, gesturing to the files. "Greta held down the fort and I did some work up in Vermont, but I've been rushing to catch up." There was a long silence. Eventually, Sage queried, "And you? How are you?"

Always so polite. He was banking on her being unable to slam the door in his face.

"There's stress coming from an outside club."

"Is that why you have a prospect watching my place constantly?" she asked wryly.

"One of several reasons, yes," he answered honestly.

Sage's arched brows bunched together. "What other reason could you have?"

"To make sure you're being good."

"Good?" She huffed out a laugh.

"Yeah, to make sure you don't fuck another man."

Quivering with rage, she shot to her feet. "Unlike your man-whoring ways, I do not randomly hook up with anyone."

"Date anyone since you left?"

Her gaze slid away from his.

"Oh, fuck no, you didn't," he snarled.

She squirmed under his scrutiny. "I don't know why I should feel guilty about it," she countered in a haughty tone.

"I warned you about dating any-fucking-man. You disobeyed me," he growled.

"I don't much care whether I disobeyed you or not. Newsflash, Kingdom, I'm no longer following the dictates of a man who *crossed* me."

Flooded with vicious possessiveness, Kingdom ripped the cushions off her couch and threw them across the room. It tipped over a table lamp. In the echo of the crash, Kingdom rounded the coffee table, seized her by the waist, and scraped the tender lobe of her ear with his teeth.

"Baby, you're my good girl. Truth is you don't wanna be with anyone but me."

Kingdom took her by the nape and licked the throbbing pulse below the graceful curve of her jaw. Catching the tender skin between his teeth, he gave her a sharp nip. Sage's breath hitched, but she rallied with a series of smacks to his chest.

"Being a good girl hasn't worked out for me. I'm turning over a new leaf," she shouted, eyes squeezed shut.

Kingdom's eyes flashed at her persistent stubbornness. Enclosing her neck in the restraint of his hand, he fixed her with an unblinking stare. "Open your eyes."

She blinked up at him.

"You fuck him?" he persisted. After cutting off his balls, he was gonna murder the man. Unwittingly, his hand tightened as he prayed that she'd reassure him. She swallowed around his fingers.

※※※

Kingdom's hand went slack and turned into a caress. God, his touch felt good. It was so unfair that he had that kind of power over her. The telltale burnished amber of his eyes told her that he was aroused. Gauging by the spreading darkness of his eyes, aroused but also desperate. Sighing in frustration, she closed her eyes. It wasn't in her nature to be spiteful. She fully intended on turning a new leaf, but she wasn't going to kill off her genuine desire to comfort people. Gliding his hand off her collarbone, she strode away from him to the mantle of her fireplace. In a muffled tone, she admitted, "I wasn't interested in being physically close to another man, but I wanted to feel appreciated. To feel wanted."

His labored breaths blasted against her spine as she heard his strangled voice. "Were you *appreciated*?"

Over her shoulder, she nodded affirmatively but confessed softly, "I wasn't into it. It wasn't you."

"Who was he? Stanton?"

She whipped around and planted her fists on her hips. "Are you insane?"

"Russian roulette would be easier than having this fucking conversation," he grumbled. A worried expression popped up on his face. "How many dates, Sage? And how many men hit on you?"

"Jealousy doesn't feel good, does it?"

Lunging at her, he spun her around. Her breath whipped out of her as she held onto the sleek, sinewy muscles of his shoulders. Kingdom towered over her with a dangerous air.

"I only went on one date." She replied evasively, "As for being hit on, it happens. Not that often."

Kingdom's nostrils flared at the dismissal in her tone. She was downplaying that shit. "Bullshit. It happens all the fuckin' time."

She placed a hand over the center of his chest. "Kingdom, I interact with macho men every day. Not only my clients, but most of my colleagues are men. Then there are guards, policemen, prosecutors, and other attorneys."

"Attorneys like Stanton."

Her temperature shot up, her blood pounding in her veins. She was quick to make her position clear. "There's no chance in hell that I would take him back. Stanton's like a shark. He smells weakness and goes in for the kill."

Nothing seemed to penetrate his fog because next thing she knew, he had her corralled into the fireplace, her back scraping the bricks. She gave him a pointed look. "I can take care of myself. After two disasters," her tone turned brittle, "I refuse to depend on anyone but myself. Period."

"I never doubted you could," he muttered. "Problem with you is that you don't understand that I should be taking care of you. My woman shouldn't worry about anything. Your job is to work, go out to lunch or brunch or whatever the fuck women do, and buy sexy lingerie for me to rip off you before I bury my cock into that candy-coated pussy of yours. What you don't do is get stressed out. What you don't do is have to fight off men."

"Okay, I don't fight off men, but let me repeat myself for the hundredth time. I don't need protection. I'm. Not. Your. Woman."

"You *are* my woman, and the sooner you get that shit through *your* stubborn head, the easier our lives will be."

"And you need to get it through your head that you tore us apart and killed any rights over me."

Shoulders bunched up and chests heaving, they stared each other down like gunslingers. Kingdom backed off and raked his fingers through his hair. Damn, he looked sexy, all hot and bothered, his hair sticking up in all directions.

"Your lifestyle includes women hitting on you all the time. Seriously, there's no way you can possibly convince me that it's a temptation you can fight," Sage blurted out. It was one of the thoughts that had plagued her the most in the conversations she'd had with Greta's mom.

Horizontal creases grooved his forehead, and his eyebrows cinched over his hazel eyes. The color surrounding his pupils darkened to a burnished hue. The shudder of his pained exhalation rattled down her own spine. Ugh. She was such an empath, but this time she would not be moved. Dammit, her head ached from being this close to him without touching him.

"I'm not going to touch another woman," he vowed. She rolled her eyes. "Truth is, I was hard for you when I brought Trixie to my room. I closed my eyes and fantasized that you were the one underneath me. This was before you and I had sex, but I was already feeling things for you, and I panicked. That's why I took her into an empty room, but I recognized that I couldn't fuck this up between us. It took me going to the edge of the cliff to get my head on straight."

He hung his head as he finished, "Hurting you gutted me. But the worst part is that it destroyed the trust between us. I failed you like I failed Chop, and I won't forgive myself for that."

Recounting the particulars of his dalliance ripped through her heart like a cleaver, but hearing that he didn't actually have sex with Trixie was a tremendous relief.

"I haven't touched another woman since that one time. Fuck, Sage, I haven't gone without fucking for a week since I was a kid. Four weeks walking around with a hard on and jacking off with my right hand. I wake up with come on the sheets from dreams of your pussy creamin' my dick. One thought of those tits of yours, and I get hard as a fuckin' rock. Get it through your head, woman, you're the one I want."

Undeterred by his frustration, she raised her voice, "Whatever happened, happened, but it's over. I can't afford to trust you."

"I'm not a damned animal who can't control my dick. Fuck, you know how much I get off on being in control." The cadence of his voice dropped low and seductive. "You have firsthand knowledge that I'm a demanding motherfucker. When I tell you that I won't touch another woman"—his jaw locked up—"I won't." He cupped her jaw and brushed his lips over hers.

Oh, God, being so close to him and knowing he hadn't actually gone through with fucking Trixie, along with the days of her body yearning for him cumulated into a crescendo of longing that she couldn't fight. She opened for him, and he obliged her with thorough sweeps of his tongue inside her mouth. Breaking their kiss, he bent down and grasped the back of her thighs. Sage looped her legs around his waist, and he strode toward her bedroom.

43

KINGDOM

This could be their last time.

Even with her pliant beneath him, he was plagued with the fear that she'd disappear. He was a lost soul, and fuck if the devil didn't know it and was working overtime to speed up his demise. Although he had eyes on her almost every minute of every day, her heart was as distant from him as when she was away in Vermont, but no way was he standing down.

Kingdom stripped her of her clothes in under a minute. Poised near her entrance, he yanked at his jeans. His cock burst free from its confines, slapped again her pussy, and caused them both to moan. He needed this.

"Hands and knees. Cheek on the mattress, babe."

Rolling onto her stomach, she said, "No calling me 'babe.' I have a name, so use it. We're fucking, but that's all this is, Kingdom. I'm going to lay out a list of rules."

He let out a grunt. Fucking hell, he had no choice but to play by her rules for now, but he was closer than he'd been twenty minutes before, and that was small but definite victory. Gripping the root of his cock, he stepped back. "No other men, Sage. Only me."

Whipping her head over her shoulder, her eyes glazed over with lust, she nodded once. Thank fuck. Taking hold of her hips, he propped her onto her knees. He loved the visual of her perfect ass. A breath of relief escaped from his parted lips. At least he'd learned that it was displayed for him alone. She'd agreed to his one rule: no other men. Better fucking be for him alone or he'd go on a shooting spree.

His fingers skimmed over her spine to her tailbone. With a sharp grip on her tresses, he dragged her back until her back arched and her throat was exposed. Satisfied, he positioned himself behind her, his cockhead finding her wet heat, and he drove inside.

The bites on her neck had faded long before, which pissed him off to no end. Frustrated, he took his hand to her ass cheek, giving it a smarting smack. His throat tightened as her pussy swallowed him whole, sucking down the length of his shaft until he was buried. The position of her body allowed his cock to go deeper than normal. He loved gazing down at her entrance, her pussy lips stretched around his thickness, knowing the fullness undid her. She felt so full it held a tinge of pain for her. Her slick heat put him in a trance. Words didn't do justice to the experience. The scent of cunt wafted up to him, clouding his vision. "Fuck, girlie, you're suckin' me in."

Twisting her head to scowl at him, she dictated, "Faster, dammit."

Stroke by stroke, he accelerated his pace, his abs contracting with each flick of his hips. "Gonna fuck you all night," he swore. He'd make sure she was so exhausted she'd end up falling asleep and he'd stay the night. Between her shoulder blades, he rested his forehead. Driving in with bruising force, he pulled out until only the rim of his cock touched her glistening flesh. She began to protest but swallowed back her complaint when he slammed into her, filling her up.

"Give me what I want, and I'll give you what you need," he gritted out between clenched teeth.

She began to climb toward her climax. Molten heat invaded his veins and arteries, thickening, drowning him into a vortex of unrequited longing. In tune with her body, Kingdom slipped two fingers around her peaking clit, toggling it the way she liked.

"More," she implored. The more strength he pummeled into her, the harder she came. He knew what she liked, but he decided to deny her. His hips propelled forward in a hard snap as he released her clit. *Smack!* A love tap on her clit, cutting off her breath.

"You come when I say," he commanded.

Her pussy pulsed tight around his cock, and she was coming. A series of screams ripped out of her throat, loud enough to pierce eardrums, prompting him to increase his pace to match her cries. Crushing her clit again, she cried out his name as her orgasm thundered through her. Her arms gave way, and she collapsed below him, grinding her ass against him while her pussy quivered around his dick.

Tension burned in his balls as his pace became brutal, and seconds later, he pumped out his come, streaking her ass with streams and pulses before slowing down to drip on her pussy. One thing she couldn't deny was his cock. Reinforcing his thoughts, she breathed out, "I'm wrecked."

That was an understatement, and it wasn't just about the sex, although that had crippled him even further. He padded into the bathroom to get something to wipe her off, then came back and cleaned her skin with soft, gentle swipes. After dropping the hand towel in the laundry hamper in her closet, he returned to her bed. She was lying on her side, head on top of her folded hands, watching him. Stretching out beside her, he said, "I want us back together, Sage. I'm not giving up on us. Not happening. We can do this your way for as long as you need, but there's no way I'm letting you think that I'm going to settle for anything less than having you as my old lady."

She closed her eyes, and he noticed the bags under them. It seemed like she wasn't sleeping any better than he was. "I can't do this right now."

He tucked her under his arm and replied, "Then don't. Just let me hold you tonight. Okay?"

Eyes still shut, she settled into his side and nodded. Besides her soft body hugged against his torso, the scent of her shampoo, her unique fragrance, and the smell of their coupling in the air wrapped around him like a comfortable blanket, and he fell instantly asleep.

44

SAGE

"You're killing yourself with work. How's that working out for you? Because you look like shit?"

Camilla took a quiet sip of her tea. They were sitting on the worn sofa in the tiny lounge area at the back of the shop. One of her feet jangled in the air over her crossed legs.

"If you're trying to be sly with that question of yours, you're doing a sad job of it," replied Sage.

Camilla dunked the tea bag with a calm hand, but Sage felt Camilla's sharp assessment. *Avoid her eyes.* Camilla didn't know what was going on, and it was best to keep it that way. Combing her fingers through her hair, she attempted to restore order to the bird's nest of tresses streaming from her scalp. Aww man, she'd forgotten to brush her hair. Or brush her teeth. Gross.

"If you go on like this, your hair will turn prematurely gray, and then how are you going to find a man?"

Sage stabbed a spoon at the bowl of sugar and threw a huge lump into her tea. "Perhaps you haven't noticed, but 'finding a man' is not at the top of my priorities at this point in time."

"Testy. I get that white girls like to be skinny, but I can't stand by and watch you lose *more* weight. It's unnatural."

Taking a big slurp of tea, she grimaced. She wasn't aware she had dumped so much sugar into the mug. She wasn't in the mood for an intervention. Of course, she was aware of Camilla's concern, but she didn't have the willingness to care. The house was a wreck, her plants needed watering, and Phantom was still with Greta. Driving herself hard, she worked late into the night and woke up at dawn to pick up where she'd left off. The tactic was straightforward: work till you drop. Unfortunately, exhaustion didn't guarantee restful sleep. Last night, she had jack-knifed off her bed and clutched her chest, the nightmare image of Kingdom and Trixie entwined in each other burning the back of her eyeballs.

She slept seldom and ate even less. Camilla was right about her weight, but her appetite had vanished. Cooking was no longer therapeutic, so it only followed that she stopped buying groceries. She'd sit down and attempt to get through a plate of food haphazardly put together with whatever happened to be in the fridge. But when she went to eat, her throat closed up and she couldn't swallow. The range of emotions that she'd stuffed down came rearing back to choke her when she tried to feed herself.

Sage shrugged to herself. Insomnia, undereating, and overworking seemed like a reasonable strategy under the circumstances.

Evidently, Camilla disagreed. "You can't go on like this. At the end of the day, you're still going to have to deal with your feelings."

"Thank you, my very own self-help guru," Sage replied with a dismissive wave of her hand.

Camilla shot her a scary, witchy glare.

After a staring-glaring contest, Sage broke and blew out a sigh. "Okay, okay. I never could deny you anything."

Camilla grumbled, "Oh, you've been denying me a whole bunch of shit. The least you can do is redeem yourself; go out and get drunk with me."

"You can't drink, Camilla."

"No, but I can drink vicariously through you. Believe me, it would give me great pleasure in seeing you get drunk. Anything to get you to loosen up. You've *got* to let go of your pent-up craziness. I'm not interested in bailing your ass out of jail on a manslaughter charge."

"Who said anything about manslaughter? It would be first-degree murder. Premeditated. Planned. You know how anal I am when I set my mind to something."

"Who would be your first victim? It seems like you've got yourself at the top of the list," she said pointedly. "Just sayin'."

"Alright, back off already. My stomach is constantly in knots."

"Not a problem," Camilla responded matter-of-factly. "What you need is a drink for the anxiety and a spliff for the appetite problem."

"What are you, a drug dealer?"

"There is no way a neurotic woman like you can become a drunk or an addict."

"I am not neurotic!" Sage snapped.

Baiting her, Camilla retorted, "Correction. You *weren't* a crazy-ass neurotic. Past tense."

"You can't fool me, Camilla, I know what you're doing."

Camilla rubbed her large belly and said casually, "I'll do whatever it takes to break this spell. There's black juju up in your aura, and since I don't dabble in Santeria or Voodoo, that narrows down our options. Alcohol and weed. You're not the psychotherapy type. Oh"—Camilla held up a finger—"that brings me to solution number three. Sex."

"You're out of your mind. Sex is what got me into this mess in the first place. I knew it was too good to be real. His domineering *you're my woman* nonsense made me weak. Made me think he loves me. Pfft."

"Sometimes you have to fight poison with poison. It's time to use a different strategy than you used after Stanton. You totally underestimated the power of a good fuck and did the celibacy thing, so by the time you met broody, moody Kingdom, you were so hard up that you fell under his spell. The starvation diet put you at risk to his Miracle Grow cock."

Sage spurted the sickly sweet tea out of her mouth. "Jesus, Camilla, where are you getting this stuff?"

"I didn't need to see his dick to tell that he's packing some serious ammo."

"The surge of estrogen is melting your brain. You know, I've heard that in the second trimester, pregnant women are hyperactive in the sex department."

Her eyes danced with amusement. "My sex life is not the issue because I'm getting it on a regular basis."

Sage cheeks flamed, and she took to fanning herself with one hand.

Oh no, Camilla was giving her one of those looks of hers. "Holy shit! You're fucking him, aren't you?"

"Will you keep out of my brain for just one minute?"

"Aha! Don't you deny it! I had a feeling that you were holding out on me, and there's only one thing you would keep back."

"I'm ashamed!" Sage wailed. "I should've flushed him out my system long ago. Kingdom was beating on my door the same way Stanton did, but I couldn't help myself. I can't deny him anything."

"Honey"—Camilla reached out and clasped her knee—"there's nothing wrong with you. If I seem upset, it's because you should've turned to me instead of hiding it from me. It doesn't make you weak, and you know I wouldn't say that if I didn't believe it."

Sage stirred the black tea vigorously and argued, "Yes, it does. Kingdom violated my trust. It may not have been as bad as Stanton's insane feeding frenzy, but it was a violation. My best recourse is to cut him off, but I can't do it. Not yet, anyway. At least, that's what I'm telling myself."

Camilla suggested, "Cutting him off might not be the best solution."

Her head shot up. "There is no way, absolutely no way, I can take him back. There's no room for forgiveness in my heart."

Camilla pressed her lips together.

Sage cried out, "What? You're serious? You think I should take him back."

"It's not my decision. It's yours. I'm not going to try to sway you one way or another, but I will tell you what I see. I see you trying to shut down your feelings. At the same time, you can't cut him off. You've let him in. Sweetie, you've got hope. You didn't give Stanton the slightest chance in hell. You've got your feelings on lockdown right now. Fair enough. But when you're ready to let those feelings come up, it will include the love you hold for him."

Sage reared back and scooted away from her. "Oh my God, you're on his side."

"I might not get easily insulted, but it doesn't mean that I *don't* get insulted. I'm on your side, always. I don't care about Kingdom outside of what he means to you and how he treats you. The thing is, Kingdom isn't Stanton. Yeah, he fucked up, and he deserves to be punished. You better keep on punishing him because we can't let men get away with stupid shit. But he deserves a shot at being forgiven, as my *abuela* said to me about Angel. Give him the chance to do right by you."

Camilla dragged Sage across the sofa with a firm grip. She pushed Sage's head down on her shoulder and went on, "A man like that doesn't love easily. He's fallen in love with you, and he's fallen hard. After getting over the urge to cut off his dick with a sharp knife and nailing it to the wall out front, I thought about him and you. Maybe because his stupidity reminds me so much of Angel, but I think that loving you scared the hell out of him. He was wrong to fuck around, and he was wrong not to come clean about it."

She smushed Sage's head into her bosom when Sage tried wiggling out from under her. "Ow! You're so aggressive!"

Camilla carried on, "Lick your wounds, but promise me to think about giving him a second chance. If he can't do it, then fuck him. But if he can do it, then you need to work through your shit and decide whether he'll make the cut."

Sage stopped struggling and slumped against Camilla. Gliding the palm of her hand over Camilla's bulging belly, her breath stopped when she felt a strong kick.

"Whoa. You don't want to know the baby's gender, but I can tell you it will take after your side of the family." Voice soft, Sage lamented, "Can't I just keep having meaningless sex with him? It sounds so much easier. And safer for my heart."

"You don't do meaningless sex. Consider yourself warned. He's the One."

Sage glared up at Camilla. "Soulmates do not exist."

"Angel's mine."

"Only you and rom-coms."

"It's not as rare as you think, and he might be the closest you get to one."

Sage smoothed her palm along Camilla's belly again, waiting for another movement from the baby. "Enough," she groused. "You're beginning to repeat yourself."

Camilla raised her hands and wiped them clean. "I'm done." Gently, she shooed Sage off her and pointed to the table. "Now drink your tea before it gets cold."

45

SAGE

Sage dropped her briefcase and files on her desk with a dull thud.

Ugh.

She had to deal with Stanton in court earlier that morning, which always put her in a foul mood. Dejected, she slumped in her chair. She hadn't had much success in shutting off her feelings from Kingdom lately, and Camilla's talk only aggravated the situation. Bending down to take off her heels, she propped her foot on her knee and massaged it. She closed her eyes and groaned loudly in relief.

She was all about redemption and second chances. When it came to her clients, that is. People were imperfect. People made mistakes. Sometimes they were life-changing mistakes, but everyone deserved the benefit of the doubt. At times, her clients found themselves in trouble from a combination of an unhealthy environment and bad habits.

Habits. She paused mid-thought. *Huh.* Before her, Kingdom had the habit of empty, meaningless sex. His environment encouraged that behavior. He was part of an MC where women were sexually available, and even aggressively pursued the brothers.

Despite her belief in second chances, she hadn't given him one. She hadn't allowed herself to trust his actions. She rebuffed his advances. Camilla's words came floating back to her. Kingdom was nothing like Stanton. His breach in fidelity didn't compare with the magnitude of Stanton's betrayal. Outside of that one incident, Kingdom was ruthlessly honest and straight-shooting.

Taking her other foot, she kneaded into the arch with her knuckles. The problem was his environment. One of the leading causes of recidivism for people was when they returned to environments that were negative to their progress. The Demon Squad was Kingdom's life.

To be fair, so much about the brotherhood was amazing. It was the women that concerned her. But that was on him. If he wanted to be with her, then she would have to trust that he would remain loyal to her regardless of how many women threw themselves at him. Club or no club, Kingdom was hot as hell. Women would always hit on him.

Can I do it? Can I trust him again? Her hands paused their work. *Yes, I can.* Although startled by her quick about-face, she was ready. Before she lost her nerve, she picked up her cellphone and shot off a text.

SAGE: Are u free later?

She clipped her lower lip with her teeth as she waited. Not even a minute later, her phone vibrated with an incoming text.

KINGDOM: Be at ur place tonight. Regular time

SAGE: I'll pick up steaks.

KINGDOM: Fuck yeah. Food sucks at clubhouse

She let out a breath of relief, and a small, scared laugh escaped. She shouldn't be surprised by his attentiveness. He was alert from day one and had ramped up his focus tenfold since her return. Only now, she wasn't going to fight him, and that felt more than a little scary.

Determined to give him a chance, she decided to wrap up early, hit the grocery store, and prepare him a nice meal. Biscuits, green beans, roasted potatoes. She checked her phone for the time. Yup, she had enough time to bake a cake.

※※※

Sage was in the kitchen, taking out two icy beers from the fridge as Kingdom walked through the door she'd left open for him. She plunged a slice of lime into the bottom. Warmth suffused his chest. She knew how he liked his beer best, even though he routinely grunted in protest.

Seven fucking weeks. Three weeks when Sage went missing, which was pure, unadulterated hell. The last month, he'd been bumped up to purgatory. He'd stalked her like a madman and coerced her into spending time with him, which inevitably led to fighting or sex, and sometimes a mixture of both. After her text, he took a real breath for the first time in weeks. *Finally, the fever's broken.*

"Hey," she greeted him and handed him a Corona. His eyes roamed over her in greedy appraisal. Shrugging off his cut, he threw it over the couch. He hated her bright blue couch. The thing was an eyesore, but he grudgingly admitted that it was comfortable as shit. He knew he was pussy whipped even before admitting that the thing was growing on him. He took a seat among the overstuffed cushions. Traces of her scent and subtle perfume settled around him. He expelled an audible sigh of contentment, the first time in the past seven soul-crushing weeks. Last time he was here, she'd stripped her fridge bare of food. Tonight, she had a cold beer with lime ready for him.

Her sexy glasses were perched on her nose. Resuming his greedy intake of her body, he paused at the swells of her breasts peeking out from her plunging neckline. Her body language and soft gaze tipped him over into a pool of lust. She was out to seduce him. *About fuckin' time.* After dinner, he'd punish her with his dick for torturing him these endless weeks. Once they were lying, sweaty and sated, in her bed, he'd find out the reason for her change of heart.

Kingdom sniffed the air. She'd cooked for him. If there was a God, he'd finally shown him mercy. Without Sage fully back in his life, he'd lost his appetite, skipping meals until his hunger forced him to get takeout or eat the food the club women cooked. Nothing compared to Sage's cooking. Not only was she gifted, but she spoiled him. And there was always extra for the brothers in case they stopped by.

Sage lounged next to him. "I marinated the steaks. They're outside anytime you're ready." She cast her head down in quiet shyness. His cock twitched at her deference. Fuck, he missed her little submissive gestures. Her defiance got him hot too. Hell, everything about Sage got him hot, but it had been a long time since she had shown her gentle side.

"I missed your food," he confessed. Pink colored her cheeks. He stood up, helped her to her feet, and pressed her flush against him from head to hip bone. Sage's pulse beat wildly at the base of her throat.

The feminine touch of her home bled into her backyard with an added punch of color. August brimmed with life in the bursts of flowers scattered in pots on her deck and planted throughout the yard. Of course, she cultivated vegetables and had a compost pile. He found her hippie side adorable.

Sage moved to the sidebar of the grill and added a few last touches to the steaks. Kingdom came up behind her and palmed her belly, pressing her back against his broad, firm chest. Thirty days, she'd rebuffed any intimacy. Sure, they'd fucked, but she pushed him away when he attempted to snuggle or if he showed tenderness toward her.

Kingdom dropped his head, savoring the moment. Cradling her, he enjoyed the simple sounds of her soft gasps. His nostrils flared as her enticing scent wafted up to him. The growing dusk was punctuated by the rhythmic buzzing of cicadas. The simple domestic act of grilling steaks at her house humbled him. He couldn't think of anywhere he'd rather be. Nuzzling her neck, he asked, "You done in the kitchen?"

She hummed an assent. Not wanting to push his luck, he reluctantly released her from his embrace. Sage stood still for an extra beat before stepping away from him and toward the house. She returned with covered dishes, plates, and cutlery. One eye on the steaks, he tracked her with a smoldering burn as she wandered around, gracefully bending to light citronella stalks and votive candles on the table. After flitting around the garden, she took a seat and sipped on her beer.

Kingdom flipped the steaks and looked up to find Sage craning her neck to get a better view of him. He cocked one eyebrow. "See something you like?"

Her eyes slid away from his. He frowned. She was hesitant, and he didn't like it. Unwilling to ignore her discomfort, he scooted a chair out and sat down, stretching his long legs. He smiled smugly against the glass rim of his beer bottle when she eye-fucked his mouth. He purposely took a long draught and watched her expression of unbridled lust as she fixated on the muscles of his throat as they worked to swallow. He felt the caress of her eyes as they dragged over the hollow of his throat, over his defined torso, and ended at the prominent bulge in his jeans. Her eyes shot up to his face in alarm. Her eyelids were weighed down with arousal. His ego gleamed in satisfaction.

He asked her something inane, but she was entranced by his cock, growing harder by the second under her perusal. She snapped out of her reverie and stammered, "Did you say something? I missed it."

"You missed it 'cause your eyes are stuck on my cock. Cut it out if you want to eat dinner because I'm this close"—he held up his index finger and thumb with an inch of distance between them—"to throwing you over my shoulder and taking you to bed." He gave her a wicked smile. "Unless you want me to bend you over and fuck my cock into you."

Heat spread to her face. "Sorry, I didn't mean to objectify you."

"Objectify me all you want, baby, but I'm not a patient man on a good day. If you wanna eat tonight, don't toy with me."

"I wasn't toying with you," Sage denied.

"Don't get me wrong, sweetheart, I like it when you toy with my dick, but I've been waiting a long time to eat your food. Not losing the chance, no matter how bad I wanna fuck you."

Abruptly, he stood up and went to the grill. He saw her suppress a grin. She loved that he appreciated her cooking. Teasing him, she pointed to the various dishes. "Roasted potatoes." "Green beans." Then she swept her hand over the remaining dishes. "Biscuits, salad. You will try the salad," she urged. "Oh, and a cake."

"Thank fuck," he said gruffly.

Sage cocked her head and noted, "You've lost weight. Have you been running?"

He threw her an accusing look. "Been eating at the club-house or takeout."

Sage was right about running. The nights without her, he was awake at the ass-crack break of dawn. He took bruising runs in a useless attempt to pound out his raging lust. It helped to keep him calm enough to deal with her. But his torment was ending tonight.

Carefully moving the steaks onto a big plate, he brought them to the table. Kingdom dug into the food with relish as he asked for details about her day. Sage shifted in her seat, and her fork clattered against the ceramic of her plate. His gaze flicked up at her. She smiled tentatively, picked up her fork, and stuffed food into her mouth. Observing her closely, Kingdom had something kick him in the gut. "Seen Stanton lately?"

Swallowing, Sage fidgeted with her fork again. "This morning. In court. You know Stanton. He's insufferable." Faking a shrug of dismissal, she continued, "I don't let his behavior bother me."

That answer did not placate him in the least. "What behavior?"

Her gaze darted away. Too quickly. "The usual."

Kingdom carefully put his knife and fork down and focused his complete attention on her. "Sage, don't hide from me," he warned.

"My nerves have been on edge lately," she began tentatively. "I haven't been sleeping well, and I might have snapped at him when he came up to me in court. He got angry. For once, he was in the right because he was just being civil. He's been taking every opportunity to talk to me. In the past couple years, we've rarely communicated, and if we did, it was entirely by email. Perhaps once or twice by phone. Recently, he hasn't responded to my emails or calls and waits until we see each other to converse. He's begun to compliment me. Small things, like my clothes or hair. Or about the quality of my work." She added, testily, "I'm not interested in his approval."

"Oh, yeah?" he asked nonchalantly, but his possessive inner beast stirred awake. She'd revealed several interesting tidbits of information. Like him, she didn't sleep well on the nights they slept apart. Selfish bastard that he was, he relished the affirmation that she missed him. But his inner beast was snarling low in his chest. Stanton was sniffing around his property. Prompting her to say more, he asked, "You said you provoked him..."

With a heavy sigh, she confessed, "I may have told him to fuck off. It was reckless on my part."

"How did he react?"

"He may have made a not-so-subtle threat to be nice to him or he would make it difficult for my client's case."

Feigning calmness on the outside, his blood boiled. He was already suspicious of Stanton's intentions toward Sage and suspected that fucker was keeping tabs on her. Kingdom couldn't blame him since he did the same thing. There was a strong possibility that the asshole had heard about their breakup and was trying to move back in on Sage. He was mad pissed, but he was also grateful that she trusted him enough to tell him the truth.

Struggling to rein in his temper, he accused, "Why didn't you mention this before?" On hyper-alert, every one of his nerves thrummed with tension.

"I don't like to talk about him. I don't like to even think about him. It brings up the ugliness of the past, and I don't want to dwell there. He was such a narcissist. He was taken by surprise when I dumped him. He thought I would forgive him because we were so close to the wedding." She huffed. "As if I cared about creating a scandal. He tried everything to convince me to go back to him, but I cut him off completely. After we broke up, it was agonizing to see him in court, but I learned to become immune to his presence. It helped when he got engaged and moved on," she said.

"Not by a long shot," Kingdom grumbled. "No man with a pulse moves on from a woman like you."

Sage giggled and swatted his arm. "You're biased."

"I'm not," he retorted. "I don't know what you see when you look in the mirror, but I know what men see when they look at you."

Sage dismissed his compliment with a dainty wave of her hand. "He's been making overtures lately." She grimaced in disgust. "He had the audacity to invite me for coffee a few weeks ago. It was super awkward."

"Babe, I'm the first man you've hooked up with since him. He's obviously territorial, and I'm a threat. Fucker has no clout with me."

A notch creased the smooth skin between Sage's brows. "He's dead to me," she said in the coldest tone he'd heard come out her mouth. She smiled ruefully. "You're rubbing off on me, you with your MC terms."

Kingdom pointed out, "You're not dead to him. He wants back in, but he's in for a fuckload of pain if he touches what's mine." His eyes dipped down. "You do know this pussy is mine, right?"

Sage's color heightened. Reaching for him, she covered his hand. "Kingdom, you can't hurt him."

"What? You care what happens to him?"

"Not one bit," Sage said emphatically, "but I care about you. Stanton has influence in this city, everyone from judges to the police. He's not a man to be trifled with."

"Nor am I. My job is to take care of you." Leaning back in

his chair, hands behind his head, he said, "Don't underestimate me, woman. Stanton Prescott. Twenty-seven years old. 6'2". 190 lbs." Kingdom snorted at that. "Prosecutor since 2017. Father is a state senator. Bigwig in a small pond. Drives a silver Maserati."

Sage reared back in surprise. "You've researched him. That's a little ... creepy."

"No, it's real. I already told you it's my job to protect you." With a chin lift, he directed Sage's attention to her abandoned plate of food. "Better finish up. You're in for a workout tonight."

Leaving Sage flushed with embarrassment, Kingdom gathered up the dishes and carefully balanced them on his arms.

"There's still cake," she reminded him.

The corner of his lips quirked up. "What kind is it?"

"A chocolate flourless cake with chocolate icing. It's a new recipe, but I think it turned out well."

"Flourless, huh?" He shook his head. "I won't pretend to know how a cake can taste good without flour, but if you baked it, then it's gonna be good."

She gave a nonchalant half-shrug. "I had a slow day at work."

Kingdom chuckled, letting the lie slide. Sage never had a slow day. She'd taken precious time out of her crazy day to cook a whole meal and make a cake. After finishing up her food, Sage joined him in the kitchen, and they took care of the dishes. Once the kitchen was clean and the dishwasher was running, Sage placed the promised cake on the counter with a container of ice cream.

Fuck yeah, she'd forgiven him. She cut two large slices and scooped out vanilla ice cream, his favorite. Kingdom followed her to the living room, his gaze fixed on her swaying ass the entire walk to the couch. She set the plates down on the coffee table. Settling down beside him, she clicked on the TV.

He took a bite and moaned. "Fuckin' hell, I missed your cooking."

"It's nothing."

"It ain't nothin'."

He went back for a second slice. Sated, he lay back as she removed the dishes. He moved to help her, but she placed a hand on his shoulder and shook her head. Lying back, he savored the comforting sounds of clattering dishes and running water. Relief swept through him like a cleansing rainfall.

SAGE

Kingdom pulled her onto his lap and pressed her cheek against his chest. Her body instantly relaxed.

"We've got to clear up everything between us once and for all," Kingdom murmured against her temple.

Sage pushed up from his chest and held his soft gaze. She fell into the spell of his hazel eyes. Her gaze dipped to his supple lips and loose jaw. His mouth was usually bracketed in a frown. He was gorgeous to her, no matter expression he wore.

Nodding, she began, "I'd like you to hear me out, and then you can make your decision."

"Yeah, okay," he said cautiously.

"I haven't been fair to you. I reacted strongly to Trixie's aggressive confrontation."

"That's normal," he replied instantly.

She knew he felt guilty. She knew he finally understood what he'd put her through.

"I was wrong to put you in the same category as Stanton. We were in the beginning of our relationship when whatever happened between you and Trixie. We hadn't declared exclusivity at that point, but I felt like we were together and I was too hurt to listen to your explanation that you were adjusting to a different type of relationship."

All the above was true. Although, she wouldn't admit it out loud, it was learning that Kingdom didn't have intercourse with Trixie that had tipped the scale.

"You're nothing like Stanton," she continued. "You're honest. You're loyal to your brothers. I should have accepted your apology earlier. You made one mistake, and you owned up to it."

Suddenly needing assurance, she inquired, "It was one-time mistake, wasn't it?"

"Yeah. It was," he replied fervently. He deftly brought her face close to his. "I belong to you. Brothers call their bitches their property, but it goes both ways, Sage, because you own my fucking heart. You won it and *you own it.*"

He lifted her up and draped her legs on either side of his hips. Tugging her down, he went in for a deep kiss. His tongue pushed past her lips in punishing stabs as he cupped her full breasts, bringing her nipples into hard tips. His hands glided down her sides, tightened around her waist for a moment, then shoved her skirt up to access her smooth thighs. He palmed her lush ass, spreading her cheeks.

Sage broke their kiss. Breathless, she entwined her fingers in his hair and stared down into his darkened eyes. His hands were rough against her ass. Staring into his eyes, she confessed, "I'm scared."

"I get that, baby, but it's my mission in life to prove to you how much I love you."

✳✳✳

He breached her pussy with measured, short thrusts.

"Fuck, babe, I buried my cock into your heat three times already. It made no dent in that tight puss of yours." He kept up his unrelenting pace. "That's right. Take it. Take my biker cock."

He powered in with one hard lunge until he was fully sheathed. Breathing out, He gave her the chance to adjust to his size.

"Fuck yeah," he crowed. "I love watching your lips stretch around my monster cock when I hit bottom."

His skin crackled like gasoline-laced kindling thrown into a blazing fire. "Gonna give me that orgasm, yeah. Then I'm flippin' you on your hands and knees. My filthy girl loves when I mount her from behind."

Kingdom manipulated her clit, and she gushed around his shaft. "Tell me. Tell me how you like it," he grunted.

She opened and closed her mouth, but it was clear that she couldn't string two thoughts together, much less a complete sentence. Kingdom slowed down, driving her crazy with light, teasing pulses. Crying out in frustration, Sage's eyes snapped fire.

"Answer me," he ground out.

"I love it when you ... fuck me doggy-style."

Kingdom pistoned into her, fast and furious. He growled with each stroke, thrusting roughly into her pussy. "My cock is the only cock for you. I'm not wetting my dick in any other pussy."

"Stop talking and fuck me," Sage griped. She expressed

her irritation by gripping her inner walls around his shaft. Kingdom gave her a wicked chuckle, but he finally relented. He lifted her by the ass, changing the angle of his cock. Butting against her sensitive spot, her walls contracted, and her thighs quivered around his waist.

A smack on her butt cheek, and she flew over. Riding out her climax, Kingdom alternately pinched and massaged her clit until she was a trembling mess. The sensitivity was too much to bear, and she shoved his hand away.

Kingdom's world narrowed to the point where her swollen pussy was milking his cock. Braced above her on his arms, he lost all connection with the world. His cock emptied into her pussy without a single twitch. Seven weeks of torment convulsed out of his cock.

Breathing harshly, he fell back on his haunches. Sage dipped her finger into the come and rubbed it into her curls. She circled her clit with it and plunged one finger inside. *Holy fuck.*

Sweat from his brow dripped onto the ropes of come marking her tits. Kingdom closed his eyes as he shuddered. "What you do to me. I came before I got to flip you over."

She caressed the ripples of his six pack and followed his happy trail bracketed by the V of his belly. Stumbling off her bed, he went to the bathroom and came back with a warm washcloth. Reluctantly, he cleaned his brand off. After each swipe of the washcloth, he lavished kisses along her damp skin. He returned by her side, and Sage resumed her post-coital cuddling.

❋❋❋

It was after midnight and they were lying in her bed, sated. On the smooth dip between the sloped ridge of Kingdom's belly and the sharp rise of his hip bone, Sage noticed the new tat. A card of the Queen of Hearts. Huh. Seemed a bit random, but okay. She traced the intricate design. Another one of Angel's. The upper half of the card was filled in with the portrait of a royal female. The background was surprisingly masculine, swirling flames entwined around curved horns. The lower half of the card was empty. The tender muscle danced under her repeated caress.

"Interesting," Sage observed, "but it's not finished. It seems simple enough to finish in one session. Why didn't Angel finish it?"

"Angel will ink in the king when you take me back for good," Kingdom said. Sage's gaze flicked up to his face. He returned it with a steady, somber one of his own.

Kingdom touched the inked heart cradled in the queen's upturned hands. "My queen holds my heart in the palm of her hand. She holds the power to sustain me or crush me. The choice is hers alone. In the deck, the king trumps the queen, but not for me. The king will hold a sword to cherish and protect his queen above all else. You're my other half, Sage. I'll be whole the day you return to my side."

His admission left her speechless. She averted her eyes away from his face, which was lined with grim determination.

"I'm not a patient man, but I'm waiting on you."

Gaze fixed to a spot on the wall, she warned him, "What if I'm never ready?"

Kingdom tilted her chin his way, prompting her to meet his eyes. "I get that I cut you deep, but I'll earn your forgiveness. You love me, Sage."

He dropped his hand away to wrap it around his cock. Pumping it provocatively, he said, "You pushed me away, but when you fucked me, you gave a part of yourself. Each and every time. You keep coming back for more, and though you swore up and down it means nothing, you let me in a fraction at a time. Wanna know why?"

Focused on caressing his tat, she shrugged.

"Because you still love me. You're too good to kill what's between us. Sex stopped being just sex weeks ago. You've long been making love to me."

Fixated on the sight of his hand gripping his shaft, she burned for him. Sage scooted back on her bed for a better view. She loved watching him pleasure himself. "If you want to make it up to me, then shut up and show me what you can do with your hand."

Kingdom smeared the beads of pre-come bubbling from the slit of his cockhead and sped up his strokes. "My cock is at your service, ma'am."

47

KINGDOM

Kingdom woke to the morning sun striking him in the face.

Christ, whatever happened to blinds?

He didn't feel the warmth of another body in the bed, and panic rushed him like a punch to the throat. Sitting up straight, his breath stalled until he heard the clattering pots and pans from the kitchen. Dropping his chin to his chest, his breath steadied.

Usually, he was a light sleeper, but he'd blacked out after their sex marathon. Which was close to a miracle because the nights they didn't share a bed were laced with insomnia. It was time for one of them to move in with the other. With a little bit of luck, he'd rope her in for good.

Swinging his legs over his side of the bed, he winced. His legs felt like lead. She'd hung him out to dry from their sex spree, but from the humming he heard out there, she was perky as fuck. Didn't stop him from calculating how he'd get her on her back, his cock buried in her tight heat. He had a sneaking suspicion he wouldn't get enough of her.

He rotated his shoulders and stretched his head from side to side until he heard a satisfying crack. There was a change in the air. Sage was propped up against the door jamb, dressed only in his t-shirt.

"Nice show." She lifted her chin toward his nudity.

Eyes coasting over her, his cock stirred. "Back at you, babe."

Sage sauntered over, her gaze sliding over his shoulder and down to the cut of his abs. Following his happy trail, her breath hitched when her gaze landed on the thickening shaft prodding his belly. Kingdom hauled her to his lap and grazed her arms, leaving a trail of goosebumps behind. He lowered his mouth to the junction between neck and shoulder and sucked her sweet-tasting flesh between his teeth. His hand reached for his shaft while he licked the red mark all better.

Sage took over and teased his cock with tight pumps, stopping every now and then to rub the pre-come percolating at the slit of his crown. Sighing, she released him and lifted herself off him. He allowed it because he'd make sure the little vixen got her comeuppance for leaving him hard.

"I have pancakes on, and they're about to burn." She turned her back and escaped, laughter echoing behind her.

His eyes followed her long, bare legs as he called out, "Cocktease."

Not bothering to cover himself, Kingdom followed her out, slipped behind her, and pressed his cock against her lower back. He resumed sucking the same spot when there was a rapping on the front door.

He dropped his head into her shoulder and groaned. "For fuck's sake."

Sage bowed the curve of her spine to rub the top of her ass against him. "Better get the door."

"Leave it. You need some lovin'"

"Whoever it is knows we're here."

"They can go to hell."

Another short series of rapping, only louder and more insistent this time. Grasping the base of his shaft, he lifted the hem of the shirt she was wearing and covered her ass with a streak of pre-come. She arched further to get to his cock, and he notched the crown between her lower lips. Once he had her moaning, lost to the world, he pulled away and yanked the shirt down.

"That wasn't nice," she griped.

Patting her ass cheek, he bellowed out, "Alright, alright, I'm coming."

"Kingdom, you can't answer the door naked!"

"Watch me."

Pissed off, he yanked the door open. "Fuck you. I was about to bend my woman over the counter when you come barging in."

Cutter's eyes dropped down. "Fuckin' shit, man. Put your junk away. I'm getting PTSD seeing your dick hang out."

"*Humph*, you wish you had my size."

"I don't know what you've heard, brother, but I'd beat your ass if there was a contest. What-fucking-ever." Cutter peeked over Kingdom's shoulder. "Sage naked back there too?"

Over my dead body. Blocking Cutter, he jammed the door closed.

Cutter put his hands up. "I'm joking. It's club biz, brother."

"This better be good, or your ass is getting a whipping. Why didn't you call first?"

"*Brau*, I texted *and* called. I sure as fuck didn't drag my ass out of bed to see your junk."

"I must've turned it off. What can I say? I was busy," he said with a smirk.

Cutter snorted. "Yeah, I'll say. Is that pancakes I smell?"

He walked in with a swagger. "Fuck yeah."

Kingdom gave him a glare, thick with warning. Shoving him in the chest, he said, "Hold up," then bellowed out, "Babe, put clothes on. Cutter's comin' in."

Sage automatically got on her tiptoes to wave at Cutter. Kingdom checked over his shoulder and groaned. Unconscious of how good she looked in his shirt, she leisurely sauntered toward the bedroom.

Cutter's head slanted, his gaze riveted on Sage's long, slim legs. "Damn, King, you've got yourself one fine woman there."

His blood pressure shot up.

Cutter wagged his finger at Kingdom as he pushed his way in. "Temper, temper."

With an amused look on his face, his brother strolled to the kitchen as if he owned the place, lifting the covers off the plates of food and serving himself.

Sage came back wearing a pair of sweats. Kingdom mumbled, "Thank Christ."

Staking his claim, he grabbed Sage by the nape and thrust his tongue inside her mouth. Satisfied, he let her go and went to dress.

He donned on a pair of jeans but didn't bother to zip them up, so they hung low on his hips.

Shirtless and barefoot, he returned to the kitchen, where he found Sage stopped cold, taking in every inch of his body. *Good.*

"Stop eye-fuckin' me, baby girl, or you'll be spending the

day with my cock between those pouty lips," he murmured into her ear as he passed beside her.

Sage's cheeks suffused with color as she set a prepared plate of pancakes, eggs, and sausages in front of Kingdom. After they were done eating, Cutter tilted his head toward the backyard. They stepped outside to talk business.

The Canadians they were dealing with had recently been busted for running drugs across the border, and that was going to negatively impact their income. Prez decided it was worth a try at negotiating another deal with the Hellions to tide them over and help as they phased out of their territory and solidified their situation up north.

"That's a good plan," he told Cutter. "Sage and I just made up for good, so I'm going to spend some time with her, and I'll meet up with you at the clubhouse later to figure out how to twist the Hellions into knots and bleed the most out of them."

Cutter chuckled. "This bloodthirsty edge to you is why Kane hates working with us, you know that, right?"

"Too fucking bad for him. I'm already irritated as hell with that mofo. Prez has known him for years and has more tolerance for his bullshit than any other president in the Northern Corridor."

Coming back into the house, he must have looked tense because, although Sage knew better than to query him about club business, she walked into his open arms and smoothed her hands over his back and shoulders until the tension drained from his muscles. Another reason he needed this woman in his life.

Cutter commented, "Damn glad you're taking care of him. Kingdom may be my brother, but he's a fuckin' menace, yo."

"Why Cutter, did you just compliment me?" Kingdom lifted his head half an inch off Sage's shoulder and belted out,

"Get the fuck out of here and do what you gotta do. I'll meet up with you after I'm done fuckin' my woman."

Sage gasped. Taking that as his cue, Cutter left it to Sage. As he opened the front door, he tossed over his shoulder, "It's gonna take a whole lot of fucking before Kingdom calms down. Good luck with that, Sage."

48

SAGE

Sage and Kingdom attacked each other in bouts of lovemaking, exploring each other's bodies with brutal desperation.

In the aftermath of a particularly rough coupling, Sage lay bare against him. Nervously, her fingers played with his coarse chest hair.

Kingdom covered her hand, his thumb soothing her agitation. "Babe, what is it?"

Sage buried her face into his chest and moaned.

He heard the thread of embarrassment. "I can't help if you don't talk to me."

She spoke muffled words into his skin. "I should be over it, I really should, but there's one thing Trixie said that plays over and over in my mind."

Venomous bitch. Kingdom worked to calm his heart rate and not tense up. He was a violent motherfucker, but he had learned in Afghanistan that he didn't have the luxury of losing his cool. It was a sure way of getting himself or his brothers killed. Not once did he think he'd have to use that kind of self-restraint with his woman, but there it was. "Tell me," he ordered gently.

"She predicted that you'd tire of me. She said that you'd go back to the pussy you love. Biker pussy."

"Bullshit," he fired back. "She doesn't know who I am." Kingdom dragged Sage up until they were eye-to-eye. With hands that were trembling slightly, he shook her bare shoulders. "Do you believe me?"

Sage cast her eyes down. Fuck, he wanted to grab her by the neck and fuck her until all the pain was gone. Shrugging his hands off her, her voice cracked. "Never mind." Clearing her throat, Sage choked out, "It doesn't matter."

Kingdom pushed strands of loose hair behind her ear. *How long until this ordeal is finally over?* Tracing the outline of her lips, he intoned, "You have your doubts, but time will show you the truth. And the truth is that no other woman will do."

Searching his face, Sage warned, "You'll break up with me because I won't be able to keep you satisfied. You're used to women with a lot of experience. I've only been with one man before you, and that sex wasn't even particularly good. It's only a matter of time before you move on to other women. I can't beat them in this game."

"Babe, I fucked Trixie for years, but she meant nothing to me. I stopped cold once Chop died. It was empty fucking. And yeah, some women are more experienced than others, but that doesn't automatically make the sex good. In all my years of fucking, I've never found a pussy like yours. I'm not dumb enough to choose empty pussy over your honey-tastin' snatch. Swear to God, you've got me by the balls, babe. Trixie's talking out of her ass because she wanted to be my old lady for years, but I chose you. The bitches ain't got shit on you."

Kingdom's voice dropped to a rich bass. "You're the whole fucking package. Not only are you the kind of sweet that makes my teeth hurt, but you're passionate with a spine of steel. You've got a smart mouth on you that pisses me off and gets me hard at the same time. You've got a lush body with an ass like a peach, tits that make me hungry to suck, and long legs that wrap around me like a vise when I'm buried in you."

Shifting her above him, he let her settle on his lap. Scooting her back a couple of inches, his cock was cushioned between the cheeks of her ass, just where he liked it.

"Woman, we walk down the street, and I gotta hold back from bashing the face of every man checking you out. You're walking next to an ugly motherfucking biker like me, and those pansy-ass boys still can't keep their eyes to themselves."

Taking hold of her hips, he ground her down on his cock. "One look at you, and they're hooked, their tongues hangin' out like dogs. I wanna rip the eyeballs out of their sockets. Can't blame them because the day I laid eyes on you, my world tilted on its axle and toppled over."

"Stop exaggerating," she huffed.

"Claiming you, gorgeous, is like winning the lottery." Grabbing her ass with both hands, he teased, "This is prime meat, baby."

Sage rolled her eyes, muttering drily, "I love it when you compare me to meat. Really. So sexy."

"The last thing is to brand your plump ass with my name."

Wrinkling her nose in distaste, she said, "I am not getting a tramp stamp with your name on it."

His hands roamed over her ass, spreading the cheeks before one swept across to softly rim the tight hole. Her head jerked up.

"Been waiting to take this," he mused. His gaze snapped back to her. "Soon, babe. I want my hands over my name when I fuck you from behind."

Sage struggled against him, but the motion of her hips inadvertently ground her clit against his groin. She moaned as he trapped her between his arms.

"Settle down," he rumbled. "It's cool if you're not ready, but I'm telling you that a time will come when you'll beg me for it."

"I seriously doubt it," she retorted.

Grinning, Kingdom flipped them over and rotated her legs in an angle that opened her hip joints to give him more access to her core. He was going to give her another lesson about how much she meant to him. Despite his assurances, he sensed a slight hesitation before she melted against him, as if doubt still clung to her.

49

S AGE

SAGE ENTERED the clubhouse and surveyed the scene.

Like cattle at a watering trough, the men sat along a bar lined with beer bottles and shots of liquor. Gunner sprinted here and there, attempting to serve the rowdy crew. A few other clubs were visiting for a big meeting, so there were several new faces.

Sage smiled as she spotted Tank and Loki. Although there were a few holdouts, most of the brothers had come to terms with Sage's presence. Recently, even Loki seemed more relaxed around her despite his issues with Kingdom. He acknowledged her, if one counted a head nod and grunt as a greeting, and last week, he had even struck up a conversation with her. She wasn't quite certain what put her in his good graces, but, hey, she wasn't going to look a gift horse in the mouth.

Loki rivaled Kingdom as one of the toughest men in their crew. A lethal energy tightly wound around his body. Ink covered most of his chest, with two large military tats running down his flanks. She'd seen him shirtless. Even clothed, a few crawled up from underneath the collar of the black t-shirts he wore. Then there were his eyes. *Yikes.* It was cataclysmic to have Loki's laser vision bore into you. Sage wasn't easily daunted, especially now that she was an old lady.

The day after they officially got back together, Kingdom took care of that. Whew. She was as safe as she'd ever be among the denizens of the Squad. A light giggle escaped her. Kingdom was sparse on the details when he talked about the problem between him and Loki, but they had Chop in common, so they were bound to work it out eventually.

Sage pulled up a barstool and plunked herself down between Tank and Loki. Loki was talking guns with the man next to him. Turning toward her, Loki's eyes flashed with an emotion she couldn't recognize. He wasn't a man easy to read. His eyelids drooped as he took her in slowly. Sage squirmed under his scrutiny, and her body went limp. Even though she wasn't attracted to him, Loki had that effect on women. Like a hypnotist or snake-charmer.

Beside him sat a man from one of the visiting MCs. He didn't attempt to hide his appreciation for her. Sage laughed at him, and one eyebrow raised up.

Leaning toward her, Loki dipped his head. "You okay over there?"

Sage purposely widened her eyes with an innocent expression. "Of course, why wouldn't I be?"

Loki's lips quirked. "Mm-hmm," he responded noncommittally, then stood up and walked away.

The strange biker slid into his spot beside Sage.

Sage pivoted around to Tank and started a conversation, "How's it going?"

Tank grunted. Undeterred, she pressed on, "Is there a special occasion, or have you decided to start your own personal collection of bottles and shot glasses?"

Tank grunted a second time.

"Words, Tank, use your words."

The stranger barked out a short laugh. "The woman's got sass."

Tank replied, "That she does. At the clubhouse, there's always a reason to party, but our Rhode Island chapter is here, along with another MC, the Provincetown Hellions." Waving to the man, he said, "This here is Kane, President of the Hellions. They're our guests. Kane, this is Sage, Kingdom's old lady."

Tank waved Gunner down and placed his order. Scanning the room, his eyes settled on Sadie, a new hanger-on, and beckoned to her. Smiling wide, she sauntered over to him and giggled when Tank jerked her onto his lap. Then he bent his head and thrust his tongue into her open mouth.

Okay, then. She'd talk to Kane instead. Wracking her brain for a subject of conversation, she blurted out, "So, how many weapons are you packing tonight?" Her pulse picked up pace, and heat burned her cheeks. God, she hated her skin's reaction when she got embarrassed.

Kane broke into a slow smile.

"One." He raised his shirt to show his Magnum in the holder concealed in his waistband.

Flashing a wicked smile, he exposed a sharp knife flush against his right leg. "Two." The man didn't joke around when it came to protection. Sage hummed her appreciation. Kane's head snapped up. Grim eyes held Sage's gaze. He shook his head and warned her, "If you weren't Kingdom's property, you'd be face down on my bed."

Sage reared back. Her heart pounded hard, smacking against her breastbone. *What the...?* None of the brothers dared flirt with her, much less make outrageous declarations like that. A sliver of fear mixed with a pang of intrigue snaked up her spine and lodged in the primitive part of her brain. She stammered, "Umm ... I'm with Kingdom."

He smirked. "Yeah, I got that." He bent his head toward her and cautioned her in a conspiratorial whisper, "Make sure you stick close to him 'cause I ain't the only brother who would fight for you." He pulled back and gave her a sensual once-over. "I *know* you'd be worth the trouble."

Interrupting them, Gunner popped over and asked, "You need a drink, Sage?"

Sage tore her attention away from Kane, but she felt his continued intense perusal. She opened her mouth, but he beat her to the punch and ordered, "Two shots." He turned his attention back to Sage. "You good with taking a shot with me?"

He was the president of a club close to the Squad. She couldn't afford to disrespect him, so she did what she felt she had to do. A few shots, and then she could subtly move away from him. "Sure," she replied.

Gunner shuffled behind the bar, concern creased between his brows. Leaning over the bar, he said, "You don't usually drink the hard stuff."

Kane scowled at him. It was audacious of a prospect to comment on an officer's actions.

She flashed him a brilliant smile to alleviate his worries and said, "Thanks, Gunner. I could use a shot."

That part's true, at least.

He produced two shot glasses and poured. With a flick of his wrist, a perfect dome of liquid quivered above the rim of the shot glass. Sage brought it to her lip, and her tongue darted out to sip at the fiery liquid.

Kane groaned. Good, that'll teach him to mess with her. With one swift move, she downed the whiskey. Her eyes fluttered closed as she took in the fine burn down her throat, enjoying the warmth in her belly. She opened her eyes to find them staring at her.

"Oh, I see. You assumed a woman like me doesn't do shots." She wagged her forefinger at them. "It's not nice to stereotype."

Kane downed his shot and commanded, "Another."

Gunner refilled their glasses.

Sage winked at him. "This will be my last."

Kane braced his legs on the stool and widened them. Settling in, he laced his arms across his chest and sat back to watch at her.

"Being a civilian, I figured you'd be a weak little thing, but it seems like you've got a backbone. Knowing Kingdom like I do, he would've cut you off if you couldn't handle his brand of fucking."

Sage's mouth gaped, but she quickly snapped it shut.

Kane threw his drink to the back of his throat and nodded to Gunner to pour him another. Looking past her, he laughed derisively, "Kingdom." His name came out like a curse.

The back of her neck prickled. Twisting around, she froze.

Kingdom had a woman's legs wrapped around his hips and arms clinging to his neck. Her head was thrown back, and she was laughing. Blood drained from her face like blood gushing from the sliced throat of cattle in a slaughterhouse.

Not again.

She fought to hold back tears. Here she was, waiting for Kingdom to be done with whatever he was busy doing, tolerating another man's advances, and he had a woman wrapped around him like a python. She watched as he laughed and squeezed the unknown woman closer. She stifled a gag. He *swore* never to touch another woman. She shook her head. There must be a simple explanation, surely there must.

Breaking though her racing thoughts, Kane chuckled. "Up to his old tricks again." Tearing her gaze away from Kingdom, she attempted to focus on Kane, but her head began to spin. She swayed and caught herself by grabbing his arm. Through her blurred vision, Sage saw him track the movement and clasp his hand over hers.

"They have history, him and Suzie," Kane explained. "She's Wolf's old lady, the President of the Rhode Island chapter of the Squad, but she steps out on him for Kingdom. Always has."

Tears shoved through her defenses and tracked down her cheeks. Kane's visage took on an expression of pity. Yanking up his shirt to his sternum, he went to draw his gun. Sucking in air, she gripped his hand and used all her strength to dislodge his hold on his Magnum. He swatted her hands away, but she kept struggling with him. He captured her hands in one of his and raised them above her head. She was on the verge of hysteria, a tempest of conflicting desires—to kill Kingdom, to save him, to hate him, to love him—raging through her. She was beyond speech, but her eyes begged him for mercy.

Huffing out his exasperation, he relinquished his grip on her and his Magnum at the same time. His shirt dropped down over his gun, and it was concealed once again. It was a sign of how bad things were if Kane showed her more respect than Kingdom did.

Kane took her face in his palms, and her gaze instinctively lifted to his. The tender care he was showing her anchored her. She fought to hold herself together. He talked over the white noise droning in her ears. She followed snippets of his speech.

"— babe, you don't deserve any bullshit from him. You've got class, but Kingdom likes trash." He snorted with disgust. "I bet they got in a quickie while you were waiting here for him." He dipped his head until his eyes were level with hers. "Give 'em a taste of his own medicine, then cut him loose."

She peered into his face, rough and intent, hovering near hers. Numbly, she tilted her head toward him and pressed her lips to his. He traced the seam of her lips with his tongue and moaned. Taking hold of her nape, he smashed his mouth on hers, catching the edge of her lip with his teeth and drawing blood. The unwanted tangy taste of blood and the aggressive, foreign tongue jolted her out of her trance. Shoving against his chest, she inched herself away and begged, "Let me go. I can't do this."

His fingers clawed into the base of her skull to prevent her escape. "We ain't doin' anything."

"I'm hurting," she whimpered.

His eyes were as dark as a set of cold, black coals. He clasped her arm in a bruising hold. Sage yelped and yanked her arm away, but it was like jelly in his brutal grip. Like a tourniquet, his grip stopped the flow of blood, and her hand was turning numb.

"Don't play shy with me," he warned.

"I'm not!"

Palpitations throbbed in her chest, and she was struggling to breathe. A plaintive sound tore out of her clenched vocal cords.

✲✲✲

Kingdom stood at the end of the hall facing the clubhouse,

waiting for Sage. His arm was slung over one of his favorite people. Suzie was like an adopted sister; she'd given him succor in the days after Chop's death. She'd shown him tenderness, even when he was at his worst. No matter how much he swore at her, Suzie had the kind of stubbornness no man could defeat. She was Wolf's old lady, but somehow got him to accept her decision to take care of another brother, and from another MC, no less.

Kingdom checked his phone again. Sage was late. The hair on the back of his skull prickled. Something was off. His gaze tracked his surroundings carefully and halted on Kane. He was grappling with a woman. In the dim lights and the haze of smoke, he couldn't make out who it was, but the Hellion's jerky movements held his attention. He stiffened, and pressure compressed his chest like a car crusher in a wrecking yard. Kane turned toward him, and the figure of woman came into view. His eyes burned.

Standing beside him, Suzie asked, alarmed, "What is it?"

He heard a pained sound and let out the roar. He propelled through the air, thrashing through a crowd of brothers, and pounced on Kane. He wrenched him off Sage. Caught in a jumble of legs, her arms flailed and she flew backwards, arching over the rim of the bar top. Kingdom caught her before the back of her head struck something. Glimpsing blood dripping from her lip, he lost his mind.

Guarding Sage with his body, he bellowed, "Cutter!" Her expression of terror caused him to modulate his tone. "Get to safety, baby."

Cutter appeared, pried her out of his hold, and whisked her away. A flash of relief washed over him. He was free to focus on killing her aggressor. He rammed his head into Kane's chest, throwing him off balance and going down with him. Rolling around on the ground, Kingdom straddled on his back and ground his face into the cigarette butts on the floor. He put down his knee and twisted it in Kane's back. Kane grunted but otherwise didn't fight back. Kingdom shot to his feet and threw a couple of kicks to his ribs, roaring, "You motherfucker!"

Hellions men swarmed around their president, but they were outnumbered by the Squad brothers from two chapters. There would be hell to pay for beating up their president, but he didn't give two fucks. An explosion of fists rained down onto Kane. Blood flew from his nose. Kane was twice Kingdom's age and not half as enraged. Scanning the room and seeing his corralled men, he raised his arms in protection and took his beating.

50

SAGE

S age saw blood spray everywhere and screamed.

She threw herself around Cutter to try to stop Kingdom, but Cutter caught her by the waist and snapped, "Leave them."

Tears tore down her cheeks into the cut on her lip. "They're going to kill each other!" Sage strained her head but could see nothing past the tight circle of brothers enclosing the two men. She tried twisting out of his grasp, but he hauled her over his shoulder and dragged her off.

Pushing against the crush of bodies, he managed to get to the outskirts of the room. He strode down an empty hallway and veered into an office. The door closed behind them, he firmly removed her heaving body off his shoulder and set her away from him. He crossed his arms and stood guard against the door.

"What the fuck were you thinking?" Cutter clipped out. "Kane might die out there because you let him touch you!"

Sage got in his face and screeched, "Kingdom was all up on her. After all we've been through, he swore to me he'd never touch another woman. I turn my head, and what do I see? Huh? Him all over another woman. His hands all over her. How could he do this again?" Her surge of adrenaline was crashing, but she persisted on. "He flaunted one of his floozies in my face—"

"Shut. The. Fuck. Up." Cutter's sharp voice cut through her ravings. Tugging his beard, his voice turned calm, although it didn't lose its curtness. "Kingdom's not fucking her. Her name is Suzie. They're close friends, but she's another president's old lady, for Christ's sake."

"Yes, Kane explained to me how close they are. Suzie and Kingdom had a thing in the past, and Suzie cheated on her old man for Kingdom, and now they're cheating on two people at once!" she wailed.

"Sage!" Cutter snapped, "Kingdom and Suzie never had a thing. They're like siblings. Suzie helped Kingdom after Chop died. She took care of the funeral arrangements and accompanied him when he had to deal with the police during their investigation. She'd lost her little sister a few months before, and, *out of the goodness of her heart*, she stepped in and took care of Kingdom. Her old man was privy to every damned moment they spent together. Believe me, that fucker is protective as hell. He only allowed it because helping Kingdom helped Suzie pull out of her depression. That's all there ever was between them. Understand?" He raised his hand. "If the Trixie incident made you insecure, then that's on you. Kingdom was waiting on you to show you off to Suzie and Wolf. Instead, he and Kane are killing each other out there."

Aghast, Sage's face burned. Kane had played her, although

she was at fault for so quickly doubting Kingdom. She'd had a moment of clarity when she'd reminded herself that there was a simple explanation, but then she got wooed by Kane's terrible words. Scratch that. Not words. Blatant lies. Large shakes rattled her frame as shame drenched her in a cold sweat. Sage stepped back and faltered. *Thump.* Her shoulder hit the wall by her side.

"Steady," he rumbled. Cutter raked his fingers through his hair and muttered, "Christ, Sage, thought you were smarter than this."

Her legs trembled, and she slid down the wall. Bent over, she wept into arms folded over her knees. Her chest rose and fell. It felt like she was sucking air through a muffle of wet wool. The harder she tried to breathe, the less air she seemed to get into her lungs. She just wanted to lie down and pretend none of it had happened. Closing her eyes, a jarring pain slammed against her right side. A beat later, she was out.

❋❋❋

Kingdom blasted through the door like a madman, his expression bleak and knuckles bleeding. Swaying in the doorway, he hung onto the door jamb. Sage was sprawled out on the floor, her head cradled in Cutter's lap. Dread stabbed through the rushing roar of bloodlust in his veins, and he fell to his knees. "What happened?" he rasped as his thumb and fingers wrapped around her slim wrist to feel her pulse.

"She thought you were cheating with Suzie. Kane fucked with her head. He's got an evil streak, but he's gone too far this time. It was revenge because he's unhappy with the way our latest talks panned out. Hell, it's not your fault you're a better negotiator than him."

"Hold up. She thought I was cheating on her?"

"Yeah, she saw you and Suzie hugging. Kane told her you were cheating on her. I told her the fucking truth"—he motioned to Sage's prone body—"and she fainted."

Kingdom crawled over to her and gently lifted her onto his lap. His heart quivered as he caressed the wet locks of hair off her forehead. "I did this."

"She was wrong to let Kane touch her."

"She was provoked. She's out, so we can safely assume that she was in shock. It comes back to me. She wouldn't have jumped to the wrong conclusion if I hadn't fucked with Trixie."

"Kingdom," Cutter warned, "shit happens. It doesn't mean it's your fault."

"I gave her cause to doubt me."

Sage's head lolled back and forth.

"She's coming to. Cutter, get a cold wet cloth, water, and whiskey."

Cutter snorted. "*Um*, I don't think she needs whiskey."

"It's for me, dumbass." Stroking her back, Kingdom murmured soothingly, "It's over, baby girl. Come on back to me, baby."

Her hand covered his, and then her fingers ran up and down his arm as if to make sure he was there. Kingdom exhaled and whispered, "I love you more than my next breath."

Sage's eyes fluttered open, and she cupped his cheek in her warm palm.

✳✳✳

Sage stared out the window of the car at the cracked sidewalk as Kingdom drove them to the warehouse. When she'd regained consciousness, she found him sweeping strands of hair from her forehead as she lay across his lap. He helped her sit up and sip water until color came back to her face. He did it quietly and shushed her when she tried to explain herself, telling her they would talk when they got to his place. As if she could justify her gross misinterpretation of his hug with Suzie. Her head ached as if her brain was one big, throbbing mush of oatmeal.

Sage suppressed a sigh. Kingdom had been nothing but understanding, but she was scared as hell. She was his newly minted old lady when she'd turned to Kane, the man who hated Kingdom above anyone else. It was like taking a match to a fuse doused in kerosene. Kane had manipulated her, for sure, but the onus was on her *not* to go insane each time Kingdom touched another woman. She wouldn't blame him for dumping her for leading the club into a train wreck.

Kingdom took one hand off the steering wheel and squeezed her thigh. "You have the right to be upset."

Her eyebrows raised up to her hairline. "W-what?"

His gaze left the road and cut to her. "Your reaction was normal. I didn't take you seriously when you told me that you were scared about me going back to biker bitches. Christ, you're one strong, gorgeous woman. I want you bad every fucking minute of every day. It's hard to remember that you might get insecure." Taking the back of her neck, he guided her toward him on the truck bench and kissed the crown of her head. "Fact is, there's work to be done, but we'll do it together."

She nearly keeled over in relief. Her shoulders drooped as she strained to hold back the waterworks threatening to spill from her eyes. God, she felt like dirt.

Kingdom must have sensed her dismay because when they arrived, he dragged her through his home and tossed her on the bed. Crawling on top of her, he attacked her with open-mouthed kisses. Her split lip burned her, but she craved to have him inside her. Her nerve endings were singed with desperation. She wanted him to take her and take her rough.

Instead, he swept her into his embrace, intertwining himself around her until they were melded together. Her heart jumped to her throat, cutting off her demands to just fuck her. Breaths sawed in and out of her lungs until the beating of his heart and the rhythm of his breathing banked her manic energy. Relaxing into him, her pulse took on the same tempo as his. He was taking the time to reinforce their bond. Sage's headache eased, and a heaviness overtook her limbs. She wondered aloud, "Why did he do it?"

She heard his labored sigh, and then a kiss was pressed to the crown of her head.

"You already know that no one touches an old lady. Especially a brother. He knew the deal when he moved in on you. It was a direct attack on me. You were a pawn, baby girl, so don't be too hard on yourself. All ties are cut with the Hellions."

"Is this going to lead to trouble or something?"

"Not yet. Kane paid for his actions, and there will be some serious negotiations going on in the future to prevent an all-out war, which neither club wants at this moment."

Rubbing the cracked blood etched on Kingdom's knuckles, she inquired carefully, "What happened after Cutter took me away?"

"I fucked him up, then we allowed his brothers to drag him out of there alive." Kingdom shrugged nonchalantly. Although she didn't condone violence, she'd tied herself to Kingdom, and it was her responsibility to come to terms with his life. It was a life intricately woven in bloodshed. Kingdom turned to shut off the lamp, swamping them in a dusky light. Turning her to the side, he spooned her. Petting her thigh, his hand glided over and rubbed circles along her ass. "Loki is in trouble for leaving you alone."

"Why? Tank was on the other side of me."

"Yeah, but Tank was occupied. Loki should've stayed, but I suspect he left you alone with that conniving asshole as a little fuck you to me as well. He's been wanting to get to me for some time." Kingdom stilled his hand as he confessed, "I've caught the way he looks at you. He's crushing on you."

If she hadn't glimpsed over her shoulder and seen the somber expression on his face, Sage would have laughed at his statement. Perhaps it wasn't preposterous enough to ridicule, but still. "I assure you"—she rubbed the spot on her lower lip—"Loki doesn't have feelings for me."

Kingdom's expression darkened. "Any man with a cock wants a piece of you."

"You're completely exaggerating. You just fought a brother for me, so of course you'd think that."

As he hoisted himself above her, she rolled over, and his palms instantly landed on either side of her head, caging her in. "I'm not a fool. I see what I see, and I know what I know. Especially when it comes to a brother and how he thinks. If anything, you're the one who's naïve. I make no bones of the fact that no man gets you but me. Say it, Sage."

Sage snorted. As if she'd allow a repeat of what had happened today.

"Sage ..." he warned. The hard planes of his torso brushed over her chest.

Looping her arms around his nape and bringing him down to her, she whispered against his lips, "No man. Only you."

51

KINGDOM

Loki sauntered into Prez's office and stood at attention with a wide stance and his hands clasped behind him.

The cords of Kingdom's neck bulged, his jaw clenched, and his eyes burned with the fury boiling inside him. Their eyes locked in a battle of wills. This was a smackdown. People would pay good money to see this fight.

Slam! A slap on the hard surface of the desk echoed through the tension rippling through the air. Prez. He warned, "Calm the fuck down, you two."

Loki broke their stare-down and trained his gaze on Prez, who leaned back in his chair like a king on his throne. His hands were braced behind his head, and his feet were up on his desk. Kingdom almost bust out laughing. Not one of the brothers in the room was fooled by his easy pose.

"I ain't in the motherfuckin' mood to put up with your

bullshit anymore, so we're gonna end this dispute to-fuckin'-day."

Loki nodded and limped to the leather sofa, easing himself down with a wince. Kingdom curled his lip. His lungs expanded in satisfaction at the discoloration around Loki's eye. When he found out that Loki had left Sage alone to be preyed upon, he didn't hesitate to throw a punch in his face. Loki leaned his arms on the back of the couch and spoke a false apology. "My bad for leaving Sage."

Kingdom's jaw slammed together with an audible crunch. "Man the fuck up and give a real apology. Why don't you admit you set her up? As Prez is my witness, if you fuck with me and mine again, I will murder you with my bare hands."

Any other man would be pissing on himself by now, but Loki wasn't just any other man. "You can try. You fucked around on her once. You're bound to fuck her over again." He leaned forward. "Because that's what you do. You fuck people over. But I'm warning you, if you mess with her, I'll make her my bitch."

Prez grabbed Kingdom a second before he launched himself at Loki. Digging into Kingdom's shoulder with a painful grip, he growled, "Stop with your games, will ya. Christ, Loki, I can't have brothers catfighting over women like we ain't got enough pussy to go around. Rules are rules, and you purposely left an old lady hanging out to dry." He released Kingdom, who shook with repressed rage. "Not only did you break the peace of my club, but you broke my trust."

Loki struggled to rise in indignation.

"Sit the fuck down before I personally backhand you," Prez threatened. "Instead of begging for Kingdom's mercy or mine, you dig a deeper hole for yourself like you don't know better. If you need someone to teach you how to act right, then you've come to the right man. You've left me no choice. You're Kingdom's bitch. You're his prospect until I say otherwise."

Loki sat dead still. Speechless. Even Kingdom was shocked. Sure, he'd expected a punishment, but a demotion to prospect was a cut above getting thrown out of the club. Prez's gaze bore into Loki with dangerous condemnation until the younger man dropped his eyes.

"Kingdom was loyal to you. You blame him for Chopper, but the time has come to face your wrongs. Chopper was gonna die. He wasn't playin', or else he would've made a call to save himself. He *wanted* to die, feel me? Get that through your thick head and stop condemning Kingdom or yourself, because the truth is that you blame yourself. To be clear, this punishment is about all the bullshit you've thrown Kingdom's way these past months. Letting Kane get to Sage was the stick that broke the camel's back, is all."

Kingdom's heart hurt. Fucked up memories looped around his heart like titanium link chains, crushing it to the point of bursting. It hurt so bad to go back there, but he wasn't running away. He felt Sage as if she were standing behind his shoulder, placing a cool hand over his heart and whispering gentle encouragements. Her devotion was like a cool breeze on his scorched, sweating skin.

Facing Loki, he said, "I didn't blame you when you left. We made a pact, and I was proud that you chose me to watch over Chop. Except for the time you dressed me down for wastin' my life, you didn't do much of anything for him. Shit, you were gone so long between tours that Chop stopped counting the days for the end of your deployments."

Loki paled. Kingdom studied him with tired eyes. "You chose yourself over Chop. I'm not judging you, but I faced my truth. It's time you face yours, and your truth ain't got shit to do with me."

Prez bent down and clapped a steady hand on Loki's shoulder. "Son, Kingdom's your brother. Take a couple of bottles of tequila and go out to the gorges. Either you jump off a cliff or you don't, but if you come back through the front door of this club, that means you buried your grudge out there. Then you'll take your punishment. It's gonna hurt, but when it's over, it'll be done for good."

Prez stood up and gave Loki a chin lift toward the door. "You're dismissed."

※※※

Kingdom eyed Loki as he headed for the storage room. Moving to a window with a view over the front yard of the clubhouse, he watched as Loki came out with buckets of cleaning supplies and soapy water swinging in his fists. Kingdom bust out laughing when Whistle stopped soaping up the bike he was working on to follow Loki as he stood before Kingdom's bike. Eyes bulging out of their sockets, he stared as Loki dropped to his haunches and prepped Kingdom's bike to wash down.

Loki had returned from the gorges or wherever he'd gone drunk as a fucking skunk in the back of Cutter's truck last night. Kingdom still itched to aim his gun at Loki's skull. He needed a fuckin' drink. Moving toward the bar, he ordered three shots and downed two in succession. Loki's betrayal was like a needle in his claw. Even though Chop's death and Sage's rejection had hurt him, neither had been disloyal. Loki was a good brother and a soldier, part of the Squad's inner circle, but trust took time to rebuild. Didn't he have firsthand experience with that considering what he'd had to do to earn Sage's forgiveness?

Sage. His lodestone. His hand lifted the last shot to his lips, then placed it back down. The stiff tension of his neck muscles relaxed, and he rolled his shoulders. He was done with Loki's punishments for good. Loki was on his own without Kingdom as a crutch.

A slap on his back interrupted his musings. He grunted, pretending to be pissed off, but he appreciated Cutter's support.

"Shit happens, my brother. Turns out Loki's made of blood and flesh like the rest of us. Fucker fell off his high horse."

"I still wanna kill him," he muttered before tipping the last shot of whiskey down his throat. Hissing from the burn, he berated himself, "I wasn't thinking when I touched Suzie."

"You done pissin' on yourself? Yeah, you found out the hard way that Sage hadn't recovered as well as you thought. Yeah, it was the wrong move at the wrong time. But Loki had dropped her in the lap of a sociopath. End of fuckin' discussion." Cutter shook his head in disgust. "Christ, it's pathetic to see a man go crazy over a bitch."

"No offense taken," Kingdom commented dryly, "but your turn to fall will come. I'm gonna kick you when you're down on your knees and laugh in your fucking face."

"Ha, I'll die before that shit happens to me. For real, though, Sage has the respect of the club. She's got markers from half the brothers, and with the life we lead, the rest of us will owe her by the time the year is out. She'll be rakin' in markers like a card shark in Vegas."

"Stop singing her praises, already. One brother almost got killed crushin' over her. After Loki, I don't trust any man."

Cutter chortled. "Sure ain't gonna be me because I'm not looking for a good girl. You know I like them *nasty*." Rubbing his hands in anticipation, Cutter wondered, "What's his punishment?"

"Damn, you're as bad as an old woman, the way you gossip."

"There's no shame in my game, bro. Brothers are gonna have a field day with an officer getting toppled."

"He's cut out of runs, and he's my prospect till Prez says otherwise."

Cutter guffawed until he was clutching his belly. Then he shouted out to the room, "Let the games begin! Loki's fresh meat, brothers. We have a duty to welcome our new prospect in style. Puck, you owe me ten Franklins! I told ya Loki's toast."

"Fuck no!" Puck yelled out.

"Fuck yes!" Cutter hit back.

"Loki's been working his way toward a whippin' for a long while," Tank said, grinning from ear to ear.

Several brothers rushed Kingdom, yanked him off his seat, and cuffed him left and right. Gunner raised a bottle of Jack with a mischievous glint in his eyes. "This calls for a toast."

Cutter nodded. "Line up, boys. Loki's gonna be everybody's bitch around here." He glanced around the clubhouse. "Where's he at?"

"Out front. Cleaning my bike," Kingdom answered. Several brothers rushed out to torture Loki while the rest reached for their shots and raised their glasses in unison.

"To the bitch," Tank intoned.

Cutter cackled, "Christmas came early this year."

"Shut the hell up out there. I'm tryin' to get work done." Prez's voice boomed from his office.

The brothers laughed and whooped. He didn't join in, but his gruff response was his seal of approval.

52

SAGE

Sage's arms were wrapped around Kingdom's waist as they rode up to the clubhouse.

Her eyes landed on Loki, and her stomach bottomed out. Manning the entrance was a prospect's job.

She didn't comment, but a blade of guilt speared her.

In his office, Kingdom finished draping her legs over his lap and shouted out Loki's name. The door swung open, and Loki entered, face carefully blank. Standing at attention, his eyes fixated solely on Kingdom. "Sir."

"Get me two beers."

"Yes, sir."

Sage's gaze swerved back and forth between the two men, her mouth hanging ajar. After the office door shut behind Loki, she stared at Kingdom with an unspoken question in her wide eyes. He remained silent, so she prodded him with an elbow to his side.

"He has to take the consequences," Kingdom explained, "and it's my job to dish them out."

"Is he like your personal servant or something?"

"Prospect," Kingdom corrected.

"He was standing guard outside." Yes, she knew she was stating the obvious, but she was struggling to wrap her mind around the callousness of the Squad's code.

"Yep."

"He must have been standing outside the door to get in here so quickly after you called his name."

"That's the point. He's at my beck and call, and he's gonna hear you screaming my name when I fuck you in this chair."

"No," she breathed out, shaking her head in denial.

Kingdom took her chin and held her gaze with a hard expression. "You care?"

"I thought you guys worked it out, and, well, I'm not exactly an exhibitionist," she squeaked out. Her eyes dropped to her fingers, fidgeting with the front of his cut. There went her conscience eating at her again.

"Yeah, this is what you call working shit out. I'm the judge of what the penalties are, and they include hearing me fuck my woman. *My woman,*" he emphasized. "As for my woman telling me she's not an exhibitionist, she's fucked me loud enough in public before. I have faith in your abilities."

She froze in place, leather crushed between her fingers. He was right, of course. There was that one time in the bar restroom. "You can't compare the two situations. Yes, we were in public, but there was only the risk of strangers overhearing us, and the music was loud in that place. Here, it's so quiet, you can hear a pin drop. Not only that, but I'm going see Loki around like... forever."

"Don't worry, when I'm balls deep inside you," Kingdom

promised, "you'll forget your own name, much less his presence."

She groaned, and her eyelids dropped to half-mast. Like magic, his dirty talk vanquished her nerves, and he'd become the center of her focus. She squirmed on his lap; wetness seeped her panties. God, she was halfway gone already.

Scraping her clit against the damp silk, her voice dropped to a sultry, teasing tone, "How dare you use me for your nefarious purposes."

He threw his head back, and a rumble shook his chest. "Keep talking to me with that sexy vocab of yours, and Loki will walk in with my face buried between your thighs."

"You'll have to work hard to convince me," she warned.

"Lucky for you, I'm up for the challenge."

Her nervousness dimmed further when he twined her hair around his fist. Goosebumps peppered up and down her arms. Tugging her head sideways, Kingdom guided his mouth to her throat. She jumped when he latched on to her skin.

A loud rap on the door jerked her out of her trance. Forgetting that Kingdom still held onto her tresses, she yanked her head away and yelped at the pain.

Carefully drawing her back to her original position, he admonished, "Easy, babe. He'll be gone soon."

Casually returning to his task, he sucked on her tender skin. Loki was outside, waiting, listening closely for Kingdom's permission to enter. Her breath accelerated as she imagined the sounds he heard.

Kingdom examined his ministrations. Seemingly satisfied with the mark on her skin, he finally responded to Loki's second set of knocks.

Eyes flashing, Loki walked up to them and plunked two bottles of beer on the desk. The bottles clattered precariously against the wooden surface.

His eyes flicked over Sage.

Heat crept up her neck.

Fighting Kingdom's hold on her hair, she buried her face into his broad shoulder.

Kingdom ordered, "Get out and stay outside until I say otherwise."

The instant Loki closed the door, Kingdom wasted no time and lifted Sage's skirt. He palmed her mound while his other hand pressed against her inner thigh. She acquiesced to his silent demand and opened her legs for him. His fingers delved into her panties, dove into sheath, and curled upward. Sage's inner core immediately gushed. She hadn't forgotten Loki.

On the contrary, she was hyperaware of their audience.

Kingdom drew her tank top down, and her breasts spilled out of her demi-cup bra.

Her hands fluttered nervously around his head as he placed hot open-mouthed kisses across each breast. She buried her hands in his thick hair as he suckled on a nipple. He sucked harder, and then he bit down on her pink tip. A jolt of pleasure-pain scorched through her veins.

Ravenous, she attacked him, her mouth and teeth seeking contact with his silky skin. She targeted his neck with the precision of a vampire and returned his bite with a much sharper one.

His breath whooshed around her nipple as he took the hit of pain.

Appeased, Sage laved the teeth marks with her tongue. Licking down to the crux of his neck, she clenched down on a sensitive tendon. Kingdom broke into moan around her slick breast.

She shifted off Kingdom and shuddered when she heard the suctioning sound her pussy made as she pulled off his thick fingers.

Kingdom raised his head, eyes narrowed in disapproval.

Sage shoved hard at the chair, heavy with Kingdom's weight.

Understanding dawned on him and he scooted the chair back. In the tiny sliver of space offered, she went down on her knees. Trapped between the desk and his lap, she gazed up at him. She relished the unbridled expression of lust she found on his face. He was such a whore when it came to her mouth on his cock.

"Fuck, babe," he exhaled as she grazed her teeth against the crown of his cock. He liked that little bite of pain. Splaying his legs as wide as possible, his cock quivered in readiness for her mouth. Sage's tongue darted out and flicked at the pearl of pre-come on the shallow slit of his tip. Tilting his cock to expose the underside, she ran the tip of her tongue along the bulging vein snaking up his shaft.

Kingdom hissed. "Teasing my cock ain't a good idea, Sage. You wanna suck, then suck it in your mouth like it's a big-ass lollipop. Otherwise, you're ridin' it."

He stood up sharply. The back of his knees hit the chair with an echoing scrape. He braced his hands on the desk, effectively caging her in.

Against the backdrop of his large, sculpted thighs, his cockhead bumped against her lips.

"Open up," he commanded, his voice hoarse with need.

He scraped up his pre-come and popped it into her mouth. She sucked it dry and pulled back with one lazy, teasing lap of her little kitten tongue. Then she tilted her head back, opened wide, and swallowed him deep until it hit the back of her throat.

Fondling her breasts, he swore, "You're the fucking sexiest woman I've been with. Look at your fat tits hanging out, nipples tight and pretty like raspberries." He pinched and pulled hard. "Sexy mouth wrapped around my cock, deep throatin' me. Fuck, you're a damn fantasy come true."

She hollowed out her cheeks and relaxed her throat further.

Taking hold of her head, he thrust into her stretched mouth, expertly pulling back to spare her gag reflex.

"Yeah, babe, take that cock deeper. Come on, suck it like you own it. It's yours, baby girl," he growled.

Commands and grunts reverberated loudly off the walls and out into the hall. Sage sucked in his potent musk through her nostrils. His fingers collared her throat, and she moaned against his shaft. The vibrations shot down to his balls, pulling them high and tight. One of her hands found them and rolled them like a pair of dice.

"I don't want to come," he voiced with a tinge of desperation.

A surge of empowerment rippled through her because Kingdom was losing that iron-clad control he was famous for. This was a rare occurrence and she was the cause of it.

Her fingers darted down to rub herself, but he cut her off. "No touching what's mine. It's my fucking job to satisfy you. You'll come when I'm tongue-fucking you after you're done feeding on my cock."

Sage shot him a look filled with desperation.

"Don't give me that look, girl. The sooner you're done, the sooner I take care of you."

He pulled out, stroked his wet shaft, and ordered, "Now suck harder."

Oh, and did she oblige, bobbing and sucking and licking until Kingdom let loose and gushed down her throat. Eyes unfocused, he shouted her name as she swallowed everything he gave her. Then, she leisurely tongued him clean.

His thumb rubbed her bruised, lush bottom lip.

"Pouty lips. Cherry red and wet with my come. Tell me you love it," he demanded roughly.

"I love doing that. I love seeing you lose control," she breathed out.

His cock twitched.

Oh, dear God, she was beyond aroused. "If you don't touch me soon, I swear I'm going to kill you."

"My woman wants to come, yeah?"

Hauling her to her feet, he hoisted her onto the desk.

"Alright, I'm gonna show her mercy."

"Tease," she complained.

With a smirk, he tore her panties off. A ripping sound echoed in the office.

"Seriously, another pair?" she huffed. "I don't have an endless supply, you know."

Unfazed, Kingdom slipped off her shoes and placed her feet on the desk. Her toes instinctively curled over the edge for purchase. She spread wide open for him, her skirt slipping down and bunching at her hips.

"Look at that hard little clit popping out. Fucking beautiful."

He smacked it lightly, and Sage clamped her thighs, trapping his hand between them.

Kingdom chucked. "Spread them open."

She shook her head, a rebellious glint in her eyes. His trapped hand pushed against one thigh while his free hand grasped her other knee. Her thighs trembled as he forced them open. Before she could slap them closed again, he jammed his broad shoulders between them, bent down, and took a long taste with the flat of his tongue.

Tracing her swollen lips, he took his time lapping up her juices like a cat with a plate of sweet cream. Sage's head lolled backwards on her shoulders, and she gave him a low groan.

He grabbed hold of her hips and invaded her pussy with his jackhammer tongue. He worked her over until her thighs trembled from the onslaught of pleasure.

Plunging three fingers into her pussy, he latched onto her clit. Sage unleashed a series of screams. Her climax pounced on her abruptly. She was barely aware of her nails scoring the sides of his head as she exploded like a supernova and gave out on the desk.

Kingdom cupped her ass and buried his face, smearing her juices over his mouth and chin. Shaking his head like a dog, his cheeks and mouth were shiny with her taste.

Sitting back on his heels, his gaze perused her, clearly enjoying the fact that she was spread out before him.

With unabashed gloating, he taunted, "Christ, baby girl, you're loud."

Eyes glazed, Sage blinked down at him. She was feeling too good, floating in her afterglow, to get mad at him.

Kingdom got to his feet, scooped her up, and adjusted her on his lap with his cock nestled between her ass cheeks.

Once he'd fixed her clothes, he bellowed out, "Prospect."

Loki slowly opened the door and entered, his face rigid with fury. His eyes went to the wall behind them as he waited, legs spread apart, hands clasped at the small of his back.

"Beer taste like shit. Get me two shots," Kingdom ordered.

Loki's eyes dropped to the untouched beers. He grumbled under his breath.

Kingdom inclined his head. "You got something to say? Speak up."

"No, sir," Loki gritted out.

Sage nervously averted her eyes. She knew what Kingdom was doing. She knew that he had to do, like an alpha dog staking his territory. But that didn't make the situation any less awkward.

Stroking her hair, his hand coasted down her throat and encircled the base gently. He dismissed Loki with a flick of his hand as his other palm massaged her clenched belly.

Minutes later, Loki knocked again and walked in.

Kingdom gestured to the desk. "Place them in front of me."

Loki slammed them hard on the desktop.

"Closer," Kingdom snapped in a deadly tone. He inspected the shots critically, as if to make sure that Loki hadn't spit in them. Satisfied, he lifted one to Sage's lips. The tension was so thick that no knife was sharp enough to cut through it.

Boy, did she need a drink. She took the shot and closed her eyes when the harsh burn raced down her throat. Kingdom handed her his shot. Without pausing, she downed his as well. Eyes closed, she waited for the alcohol to settle her rattled nerves.

He dismissed Loki again. Once they were alone again, Kingdom said, "Next time I fuck you, I want you off the pill."

Sage's head snapped up. "What?"

53

KINGDOM

Next time they fucked, Kingdom wanted it to be for life.

He pulled back, giving Sage the space she'd naturally seek as she inevitably reacted to his statement.

Sage spread her hands over his chest, shirt damp from their exertions.

"You did not just say what I thought you said," she said.

"I'm sure I did. Fuck, babe, you're the only one for me. Why can't we make this permanent. Nothing's more permanent than a kid."

"You don't get to tell me what to do. It's my decision if I want to get pregnant," she snapped.

Kingdom fought back a smile. Of course, his angel would fight him. How many women begged him to fuck them raw or tried to trick him so they could be his baby mama? Not his Sage.

Reading himself for a fight, he decided to play dirty by stripping off the drenched shirt clinging to his torso. At least it momentarily distracted Sage, who fixated on his bulging biceps before shaking her head and returning to their conversation.

"I hope you're happy," she griped. "You killed my afterglow."

"Babe, you're my woman. I'm only gonna to fuck you. This shit between us is going to last forever. *Forever*," he insisted. "I don't get what the problem is." A disturbing thought hit him abruptly, and he narrowed his eyes. "Unless you're ashamed to have my kid."

"God, no. I can't even bear to hear such a thing come out of your mouth, Kingdom. It's just that normally couples *discuss* life-changing decisions. Some couples even plan years in advance, whereas you pounce this on me—and you somehow manage to make it sound like a command."

Expression stern, he demanded, "Do you want my kid?"

Sage huffed out, "Of course, I've thought about having children... with you."

"Then what's the problem? Let's fuck and make a kid."

"Jeez, Kingdom, it's not as simple as that. Honestly, until now, I wasn't sure you wanted kids," she ventured cautiously.

"I wasn't until I met you," he replied simply.

It was the God honest truth, but now that he'd said it out loud, it was all he could think of doing with her. He wanted to see her round with his baby—their baby.

"What if it's not the right time?" she rattled on. "What if you're making a rash decision because you just had an orgasm? It's not a decision you can come back from. I don't want you to regret anything."

"Told you enough times not to worry about me. I know what I'm about, and if I made this decision, I'm not going back on it." His hand dropped to her breast, and the image of his kid's mouth suckling her nipple, feeding on her for survival, clenched his gut with an inexplicable yearning.

Gruff, he said, "I want you to have my kid. More than one. Two, three, maybe four. The last number is up for discussion."

Sage's eyes widened. Her breast slipped out of his hold as she slid off his lap. She planted her fists on her hips and said, "Four. Four! Have you lost your mind? No way am I pushing four kids out of this body. Labor hurts, I'll have you know."

Kingdom suppressed a grin. Playing with her was too much damn fun. "Don't they give you a shot? For the pain," he inquired mock-innocently with a shrug. "Can't be that bad if there's a shot for it."

Her chest heaved. "Oh. My. God. Oh my God, you know *nothing*," she practically shrieked, waving her hands around manically. "I was there during Kira's birth. I've never heard Camilla—or *any* woman—scream so loudly." She shuddered.

Kingdom took her hand and placed it over his heart. Her lids dipped low over her eyes as his heartbeat beneath her palm infused her with his steady calm. "I'll be with you every step of the way. During pregnancy, I'll hold your hair while you hurl into the toilet. I'll listen to you scream at me about how I'm the fuckin' asshole who did this to you when you're pushing our baby out. Sage, when are you gonna get it? I will take care of every fucking thing for you. Stay the fuck out of my way and let me do my job."

"I'll probably kill you along the way," she blurted out, her eyes suddenly flaring wide. "You'll be dead, and I'll be a single mom with your kid, which, with my luck, will be a boy that takes after you. Stubborn, pigheaded, and too smart for his own good. It'll be a disaster."

"Gorgeous, no boy can be as much of a badass as me," he snarked.

"Yes, he can, because you'll be dead!" she screeched, half-hysterical.

"You're afraid," he stated calmly.

Crossing her arms over her chest, she flat-out denied it. "Am not."

He took her hand and scooped her into his embrace. "Yes, you are. Babe, give me your fears. I'm strong enough to carry them for you."

Sage's eyes fluttered closed and snuggled closer to him. Turning her face into his chest, she in haled deeply a few times, opened her eyes, and met his steady gaze.

"You really want to do this?" she asked softly. "Like, really?"

He nodded silently.

"So ... I guess we're having a baby."

Kingdom cupped the sides of her face and brushed his lips over hers. "Yeah, we are. I'm going to do right by you, Sage. You don't have to worry. We're going to get fucking married and go on a honeymoon. Then we make a baby. Not to worry, woman, he'll be a mama's boy."

"That, I seriously doubt," she huffed.

EPILOGUE

KINGDOM

Kingdom walked into Sage's office and surveyed the scene before him.

His woman was on her knees and hands, ass up in the air, her swelling belly swaying beneath her. Damn, but she looked hotter than ever with that big belly. He loved keeping her in bed late into the morning, rubbing her belly and cooing at their son or daughter growing in there.

Grubby, sticky hands grabbed hold of Sage's hair and yanked hard. Kira, the devil child. Swear to God, for a cute as fuck kid, she was the devil's playmate on earth. Sage was attempting to extract strands of hair from Kira's death grip when the she-devil child screeched like a banshee, at the top of her lungs.

Kingdom chuckled, but stifled it and growled low, "What the hell is going on here?"

Both woman and child's heads snapped up from the floor,

eyes flared wide in surprise. They were so involved in their scrimmage that they hadn't heard him come in through the door.

Kira broke into a huge grin, lowered her gaze coquettishly, and giggled.

Sage rolled her eyes at him and snapped, "What does it look like? I'm trying to get my hair back before she rips it out of my scalp. She's going to leave me bald."

"Kira. Let go," Kingdom rumbled deeply.

Kira's smile slipped a little at his scowl. She whimpered and reluctantly released her grip on Sage's hair.

His woman exhaled in relief and rubbed the spot where Kira had attacked her hair.

Kingdom walked up close and towered over them both. He crossed his arms over his broad chest and spoke sternly to Kira. "Kira, no pulling hair."

"How do you get her to do whatever you want?" Sage grumbled.

Kira's eyes watered, but Kingdom stymied her imminent hysteria by swooping her up and bouncing her in his arms.

"Kingdom! Kingdom! Kingdom!" she repeated in a mantra with each upward bounce.

Bobbing her effortlessly in one arm, he tickled her as he crooned softly, "My girl knows better than to pull hair. You're my good girl, aren't you, Kira?"

Kira gave him doe eyes as she nodded emphatically. "I'm a good gurl!"

"You are a good girl, and good girls don't pull hair," he emphasized. It would go in one ear and out the other, but at least, she'd behave with him around.

Kira nodded maniacally as she focused her strength on hanging onto Kingdom's cut as she jiggled up and down.

Kingdom nuzzled her hair. "I smell strawberries. Did you eat strawberries with *Tia* Sagey?"

"Yes, yes!" Kira resumed her giggling as she clung to him like a spider monkey.

Meanwhile, Sage leaned back on her heels and braced a hand on the ground as she struggled to stand up.

Eyes twinkling, Kingdom teased, "Don't get off your knees for my sake."

"Kingdom!" She glared. "You're corrupting the child."

"Woman, this one"—he bounced Kira high up in the air, eliciting a joyful shriek from her—"is going to be a hellion. Make no mistake about it."

"Don't use that word around her. It will give her ideas. It's bad enough as it is." Sage whispered loud, "She's a little terror."

Once on her feet, Sage bent her knees so she was eye level with Kira. "It was not fun, young lady. You gave Sagey a boo-boo."

Kira's face fell. She reached out to Sage's cheek and touched it lovingly. "No *boo-boo*."

Sage sighed in defeat. "Oh, I give up. You have everyone wrapped around your finger, don't you?"

Kingdom glanced down at Kira with a mock frown. "Not me. Who's the boss, Kira?"

Gleefully, Kira poked his chest and piped up, "You! You boss. Kingdom boss!" She frowned seriously and poked it again for good measure.

He nodded sharply. "Don't you forget it, little lady." Shifting his attention to Sage, he asked, "Did you finish up for the day?"

"Ha, I can't get any work done with her here."

"You got the car seat with you? Grab your work, and let's

go to the club. The brothers and I will watch her so you can finish what you need to do, and not one minute more."

Sage stood up, and her eyes turned into slits. "Exactly which brothers are you referring to? You wouldn't be speaking of *your* brothers. You would be insane to suggest such a thing. You know how it is when I bring her over there."

"What? They'll be putty in her hands. Pathetic suckers." He shook his head sadly. "They're a bunch of puss—"

"Kingdom!" she shouted. "They won't be able to control their mouths. You can barely do it and you're *trying*."

"They'll learn when I slap them up across their heads," he promised.

"By the end of the day, Kira will have learned every curse word in the book. Camilla will kill me. Then," she mused, "Camilla will kill you." She tapped her chin. "Not a bad idea..."

"Not funny. I'm the only man with influence over her daughter. Angel is wrapped around her little pinkie. The girl needs discipline. Who do you think is going to beat the boys away when they come sniffin' around her?"

Sage hissed, "Shush."

Kira's head snapped back and forth between Kingdom and Sage as she tried to follow the conversation. Sage glanced on the floor of her office at the abandoned memo she'd been reviewing when Kira was dropped off.

She prevaricated, "Well...if we went over to the clubhouse, I would be there to watch her while getting work done. I'll text Camilla. If she approves, then we'll go."

Sage bent down to pick up the phone from off the floor where she'd probably dropped it when Kira had gotten hold of her hair.

Staring down at his woman's nice round ass, he noted, "Nice view."

Sage shot right back up. "Kingdom, I'm warning you for the last time. Stop your nonsense," she scolded pertly.

Kingdom smirked. Oh, he liked when she got all persnickety. Hot fucking lawyer boss lady. God, he was a lucky fuck.

He nodded to the phone and reminded her, "The text, Sage."

Sage turned away from them both and quickly shot off a text. A response came an instant later.

"Okay." Sage breathed out. "It's a go."

Kingdom distracted Kira while Sage gathered her files and laptop.

At the front door, he relieved her of her briefcase and laptop case. She gave him a quick smile of appreciation. Kingdom's chest locked up. Christ, one smile had the power to stop him in his tracks.

With the pregnancy, he was extra sensitive to the smallest expression of affection. And the sex, by God, was fuckin' fantastic. He planned on keeping her pregnant for years to come.

With her consent, of course.

Sage turned the hanging sign on the door to "Closed" and locked up. When she finished up, she turned, and her jaw dropped open. Kira was seated demurely in her car seat, batting at Kingdom's cheeks as he buckled her in. He smirked. He knew how it went when Sage buckled her in. With him, there'd been no screeching bloody murder, no hanging onto the car door, no crying, or throwing things.

Sage yanked the driver's door open as she grumbled about how unfair life was and his diabolical ability to charm her favorite niece into doing anything.

"I'm a man," Kingdom called out. "It's in a woman's nature to submit to me."

Sage slammed the door hard and switched her complaints from difficult children to domineering men.

Kingdom shook off Kira's hands and shut the door. Going around the car, he opened the driver's side door, pressed Sage back against her seat, and ravaged her mouth. "Admit it, you love it when I'm in control. I bet you're dripping wet right now. When we get to the clubhouse, you'll drag me to my office, and fuck the living daylights out of me."

"No!" Sage objected. "I will not do that!"

"Gotcha," he teased.

Sage slapped him in the chest.

Kingdom wrapped his hand around her nape and squeezed firmly in response. "I'd never fuck around when I'm taking care of Kira. Gotta say, I didn't think Camilla would let Kira into the clubhouse after she came back saying the word 'fuck.'"

Sage pitched her voice low. "You must be kidding. She loves you."

Kingdom promptly dipped between her lips. He slid his palm down her spine to her plump ass. He squeezed one cheek for good measure, then moved away, leaving Sage aching for more.

Pleased with her reaction, Kingdom sauntered over to his bike, straddled it, and waited patiently for his woman to pull out. Alert, Kingdom smoothly pulled up behind Sage's car like her personal bodyguard, keeping close watch over the ones he loved.

THANK you for reading Kingdom's Reign! I hope you loved meeting Kingdom and Sage. The next book in this series is Cutter's Claim.

· · ·

WHO NEEDS MORE than bikes and willing women?

Not Cutter.

Until he meets Greta, a former biker princess who turned her back on club life.

She challenges him every step of the way, and Cutter doesn't tolerate disobedience.

I APPRECIATE your help in spreading the word, including telling a friend. Reviews help readers find books! Please leave a review on your favorite book site.

Sign up to my newsletter on my website, www.monique moreau.com, to find out when I have new books!

MORE BY MONIQUE

Steamy Biker Romance Series

Kingdom's Reign (Book 1)
Cutter's Claim (Book 2)
Loki's Luck (Book 3)
Stanton's Sins (Book 4)
Puck's Property (Book 5)
Whistle's War (Book 6)
Her Hidden Valentine (Book 7)

Lupu Family Mafia Romance Series

The Chosen Heir (Alex's story)
The Recluse Heir (Luca's story)
The Savage Heir (Nicu's story)
The Perfect Heir (Tatum's story)
The Bastard Heir (Sebastian's story)
The Princess Heir (Emma's story)

Empire Academy Series

A High School Bully Mafia Romance Series

UNFORGIVABLE (Starlene's story)
UNREGRETTABLE (Crina's story)
UNFORGETTABLE (Gabriela's story)
UNDENIABLE (Zoe's story)